HE LOVES ME...KNOT

RC BOLDT

He Loves Me…KNOT

Copyright © 2017 by RC Boldt

All rights reserved.

Editing:

Editing 4 Indies

www.editing4indies.com

Bex Harper

https://www.bexharperdesigns.com

Evident Ink

http://www.evidentink.com

Proofreaders:

Deaton Author Services

http://jdproofs.wixsite.com/jddeaton

Judy's Proofreading Services

http://www.judysproofreading.com

Cover design:

Cover Me Darling

http://www.covermedarling.com

All rights reserved. No part of this book may be reproduced, distributed, or transmitted in any form or by any means, electronic or mechanical, including photocopying, recording, or by any information storage and retrieval system without the prior written permission of the author, except for the use of brief quotations in a review.

This is a work of fiction. Names, characters, places, brands, media and incidents are either products of the author's imagination or are used fictitiously and are not to be construed as real. Any resemblance to actual persons, living or dead, events, or locales is entirely coincidental. The author acknowledges the trademarked status and trademark owners of various products referenced in this work of fiction, which have been used without permission. The publication and use of these trademarks is not authorized, associated with, or sponsored by trademark owners. Any trademarks, service marks, product names, or named features in any media form are assumed to be the property of their respective owners, and are used only for reference. There is no implied endorsement if one of these terms are used in this work of fiction.

Please note: Although the Jacksonville Jaguars are an actual NFL team, liberties were taken in order to accommodate the storyline.

If you upload this work to any site without the author's permission, it indicates piracy which is stealing. Both are ridiculously uncool and if you do so, then you understand that you'll forever be labeled a pirate (and not the super hot Johnny Depp kind) and the Book Loving Gods will be watching you. And when I say that, I mean they'll be watching EVERYTHING you do. Especially when you do *those* kinds of things. Just a heads up.

Visit my website at www.rcboldtbooks.com.

Sign up for my mailing list: http://eepurl.com/cgftw5

Excerpt from *Out of the Ashes* Copyright @ 2017 by RC BOLDT

Dedication

Matty,
I'd been on the verge of giving up on finding true love—the kind everyone dreams of, the kind everyone writes about—when my second chance finally came around.
You.
P.S. I still love you more. It's confirmed since I dedicate ALL of my books to you.

A,
You have no idea how much you are loved, sweet girl. Just remember to <u>never</u> give up on finding your "one".

*Just a quick heads up, though… Your "one" is **not** the guy who still lives with his mother, plays video games all day, and doesn't make you laugh and/or feel like the most beautiful person on earth (even when your hair's a godawful mess and you have no makeup on). Find yourself someone who has a steady job, laughs at your silly jokes, and appreciates sarcasm. Basically, find a cross between your dad and Grandpa M. because, trust me, then you'll be golden.*

About The Book

SOMETIMES LOVE NEEDS A SECOND CHANCE...

I never looked back after skipping out on my own wedding, even if it did leave me estranged from most of my family. Eight years later, I have the life I've always wanted. As an advertising account executive, my world is damn near perfect.

Until I come face-to-face with my past. With the man I once loved. The man who holds my future in his hands. The man who's hell-bent on getting even with me for leaving him at the altar.

Even with all the unfinished business between us, I still love Knox Montgomery. The only problem?

He loves me…KNOT.

Pronunciation Note for the Reader

THE CITY OF MOBILE, Alabama is often mispronounced and I'd be remiss if I didn't clarify this for readers who might be unfamiliar with this lovely, southern location.

Pronunciation: MO-*BEEL* (with emphasis on the second syllable)

Prologue

EMMA JANE

"Bless her heart."

This—the quintessential Southern phrase "bless her heart"—is the ultimate kiss of death.

The irony isn't lost on me since I just avoided my own kiss of death, figuratively speaking. Instead of walking down the aisle, I'm trudging along the Pensacola Beach boardwalk in my wedding dress.

Alone.

With tear-stained cheeks.

Two elderly women peer at me, blatant curiosity etched across their features, and one turns to the other to hiss, "I wonder if the groom left her."

"Would you blame him?" the other woman responds, disdain dripping from her tone. "She's got a"—she utters the next words much like they're absolutely scandalous—"*nose piercing.*"

My sunglasses conceal the dark glare I direct at them,

so with a dismissive huff, I continue plodding along, swiping a hand across my tear-streaked cheeks. Judging by the black smudges on my fingers, my waterproof mascara clearly lied.

Damn jackass mascara.

Damn jackass groom. I'm starting to see a trend here…

The longer I walk, the more stares I get. One little girl in a tutu bathing suit points at the top of my head and squeals with joy, "Look! A princess!"

Damn jackass tiara and veil my mother insisted I wear.

I march over to a large trash bin and—without any finesse whatsoever—begin tugging the pins holding this awful tiara-veil combo in place. As I'm attempting to remove it, agitation takes over due to my sad lack of progress. I bunch the veil in my fists and give it a firm tug from my elaborate updo. Bobby pins shoot and ping in various directions, and I distractedly pray no one gets too close and loses an eye. Shoving the obscene length of fabric in the trash, I feel a bit lighter.

The June sun beats down on me as I stand on the stamped cement of the boardwalk, the heat radiating through the soles of my favorite flip-flops. My eyes flutter closed as I inhale a deep breath of the salty Gulf of Mexico air.

God, I love this beach. It's always been one of my favorites, especially since it takes just under an hour to drive here from Mobile. The water is a gorgeous shade of blue-green, and the sand is perfectly white and free of pesky shells. Any other time, I'd be kicking off my flip-flops and running toward the surf. Now, though, I have different priorities: a stiff drink. Or ten.

Or twenty.

The challenge is finding a place where I might not draw attention—*er*, as much attention. I slowly survey the nearby choices of bars and restaurants lined up along the boardwalk; I scan and dismiss them one by one.

"No…no…no…n—"

Wait a minute.

One particular sign snags my eye. It has an outline of two men standing back to back, their forms filled with a swirl of rainbows and the name Be-Bob's written in script-like font beneath it.

A gay bar.

Perfect.

With my key ring clipped to my small wristlet, I stalk over to the bar, doing my best to ignore the startled looks and gawking from other beachgoers. Tugging open the heavy door, I step over the threshold and into the brisk air conditioning.

Into a place where I might find slightly more acceptance.

I slide my sunglasses to rest atop my head and take a moment to allow my eyes to adjust to the dimmer light. There are only about eight people scattered about, chatting over drinks. When I don't earn more than a brief glance before they return to their own conversations, I breathe my first sigh of relief. Most of the patrons are likely indulging in the great weather and enjoying a Saturday at the beach, not looking for refuge and hiding out like I am.

I scan the framed photos adorning the walls, which feature local drag queens and scantily clad male models before striding over to the bar. I hoist myself up onto a worn leather barstool, and catch the eye of the only bartender behind the counter. He appears to be taking inventory of the liquor, if his clipboard is anything to go by.

When he turns around and gets the full visual of me,

his expression is priceless as his eyebrows nearly hit his hairline. I'd laugh if I had it in me, but I'm emotionally spent.

As he regards what's visible to him from the top of the bar on up to my hair, his light brown eyes soften and the corners of his mouth tip up slightly. Without batting an eye, he reaches below the counter and produces a wet wipe. I gratefully accept it and he rests his forearms upon the lacquered surface, regarding me with interest as I rid my cheeks of the dark mascara streaks.

The bartender waits until I'm finished and then accepts the wipe from me before tossing it into the trash.

"Well, I can't say I've ever served a runaway bride before." My makeup-fail savior appears to gauge me, as if expecting me to burst into a river of tears.

Funny enough, the drive here has expended me of those and I'm firmly entrenched in the anger stage of my fiancé's betrayal.

I prop an elbow on the bar, rest my chin on my palm, and offer what I know is the weakest excuse for a smile. "There's a first time for everything, right?"

He doesn't immediately answer, eyeing me curiously until his lips stretch into an easy smile. His eyes do that little crinkly thing at the corners, and he has what I call "kind eyes."

Then again, I remind myself, *what the hell do I know?*

I'm clearly not the best judge of people. That much has become all too evident.

The bartender reaches out a hand. "Casey."

I grasp his hand, noting his impressive manicure. This guy's cuticles are better than mine, and I love the shade of metallic gray polish on his nails. "Nice to meet you, Casey. I'm Emma Jane."

He Loves Me...Knot

He reaches beneath the bar and I hear a clinking as he scoops ice, before he brings a cup into view. Then he works his magic and pours in a bit of this and that from one bottle to the next. Finally, with flourish—and a maraschino cherry tossed in—he slides the plastic cup across the smooth surface.

"It's my special secret mix. I call it"—he leans in toward me and lowers his voice, his eyes dancing with mischief—"the Panty Dropper."

One of my brows arches as I stare back at him with dismayed skepticism. "I hardly think I'm a prime panty-dropping candidate right now."

Casey lifts a shoulder in a half shrug, his eyes flickering over my shoulder before returning to me. His smile grows wider. "You never can tell."

With a tiny laugh, I shake my head and wrap my lips around the straw to take a sip of this concoction he's made me. Just as I swallow the sweet drink, I both feel and smell a person sidle up next to me at the bar.

Hell. The reason I came here was because I thought for sure my chances of getting hit on would be slim to none. But as I glance at him from the corner of my eye, I observe strong, muscled forearms, tanned and sprinkled with dark hair. The scent of him is appealing and masculine, with a cologne that doesn't overpower. Just the sight of those arms alone, however, makes me incredibly wary to see the rest of him.

Casey doesn't address the newcomer, his focus still on me. "I'm all ears, Emma Jane. Been told I'm a great listener."

Good Lord. Where do I even start?

Before I can answer, the man speaks up, his deep voice booming. "Are you cheating on me, Case?" He makes what sounds like a gasp of exaggerated indignation. "I can't believe you'd betray me like this."

I glance up to see Casey's expression full of mirth, and he rolls his eyes. "You know better. I'm still waiting for you to switch over."

A husky laugh greets my ears, and it sounds far too male—far too appealing—which is why I refuse to turn and look at the man beside me.

"I might switch if you'd agree to root for my team."

"Not gonna happen," Casey scoffs before his gaze meets mine. "Isn't that drink exactly what the doctor ordered?"

I muster up a smile because he seems like a sweet guy. "It is." With a start, I realize I haven't given him my card to pay or to at least start a tab. I reach for my wristlet. "What do I owe you?"

He waves me off. "Honey, that one's on me as long as you promise to dish before we get slammed in a few hours."

A loud exhale spills past my lips. "It's a pathetic story, really."

"Let me guess." Mr. Forearms's husky voice is a deep timbre, amusement threaded in his tone. "You caught him with your maid of honor."

I let out a harsh laugh and fiddle with my straw, using it to move around the ice cubes in my drink. "Nope." *If only it were that simple*, I muse internally.

"Caught him with his best man?"

This time, his suggestion drags a lighter sounding laugh from me. "Not even."

"Well, you know I can't leave here without hearing the story. I'm intrigued."

This guy is something else, that's for sure. His voice is

He Loves Me...Knot

the epitome of sexy, yet, even with all that's transpired, I have zero interest.

Finally, I drag my attention from my drink and my eyes travel up those muscled forearms, over the bulging biceps stretching the short sleeves of a dark-blue polo shirt, and up to the face that—

My breath catches in my throat as recognition floods me, my eyes widening as I take in the man beside me.

Becket Jones, the quarterback for the NFL team in Jacksonville, Florida. He's a two-time Heisman Trophy winner from the University of Florida and was the second overall draft pick by the Jacksonville Jaguars. Adding to that impressive resumé, he's a Lombardi Trophy recipient and was recently voted MVP. His face is in commercials and on billboards everywhere. Living in Mobile, Alabama, and in a state without a pro football team, most of us either gravitate toward the Atlanta Falcons, the New Orleans Saints, or the Jacksonville Jaguars.

I don't follow NFL as closely as college football, but I'd have to live under a rock not to recognize Becket and his pretty-boy face. Even beneath the brim of the ball cap, which curls under at the edges and draws shadows over his eyes, I'd recognize that wide charming smile of his anywhere. He's slouching against the bar but I know he pushes well over six feet.

His features cloud as he observes my response, his large hand reaching up to tug his cap lower. "Please don't tell me you're going to sell some seedy story about seeing me in a gay bar to a stupid gossip rag."

"Of course not. I'm just..." I falter for a moment. "Surprised."

His chin lifts, gesturing to a couple of guys standing nearby a jukebox, laughing and talking. One of them is wearing a shirt with bright pink flamingos printed on it, along with a yellow feather boa draped around his neck.

"I'm with my brother, Brantley—the one who insisted on that crazy getup—and his roommate, Vonn, whose birthday we're celebrating." His eyes flicker to them briefly, obvious affection in his gaze, before returning to me. "I drove in from Jacksonville late last night to join them."

I nod politely, not sure what to say. "Well, I hope you guys have a great night." I turn back to my drink and studiously take another sip of the dangerous concoction, acknowledging Casey and Becket have fixed their attention on me with unfettered curiosity. This drink is deliciously sweet and I know it's masking the copious amount of liquor Casey put in it. And I can't get hammered. I should —and I *really* want to—but I can't. I have bigger fish to fry.

Like figuring out my freaking life.

With a long sigh, I unzip my wristlet and withdraw my cell phone—whose ring had been silenced—to face the "music" I know is about to blare at me.

Let this be noted as mistake number one. Because I'm certain my phone is going to overheat from the number of text messages and missed calls I've received already. Mainly, the ones from my father.

Dad: You'd better get back here now, young lady.

I continue scrolling past all his other messages until I get to the last one, time stamped from about five minutes ago.

Dad: Consider yourself disowned. Don't even think of coming back to this house after the way you've embarrassed everyone.

Huh. Well, thank heavens I'd already thought of that and had made a quick stop at the house before driving here. I'd scooped up the items I'd need most, knowing my father's reaction would be extreme. Maybe I was delusional, but I'd hoped it wouldn't come to this.

Just as I'm about to place my phone back in my wristlet and avoid the remainder of the painful messages sure to come, another one comes in.

Dad: Forget your job at the magazine. It's done. You're done. You did this, Emma Jane.

My chest tightens, and my stomach churns sickly. I knew it was coming but it doesn't make it any less devastating. I'd worked my ass off for *Southern Charm Lifestyle* magazine at their new location in Mobile. I know I have the potential to rise up in the ranks.

But now it's gone. Poof. All because of my father. The one and only Davis Haywood, city councilman, owner of the local newspaper and the city's largest magazine, and commercial developer galore. He has the money and power to make things happen in Mobile.

I just never thought he'd use that money and power against his own daughter one day.

"So." Becket startles me from my own drama-filled thoughts. "You might not know this about me, but I was brought up to be a gentleman."

I regard him warily, unsure where he's going with this. "O-kay," I drag out the word slowly.

"This means I can't leave you sitting at this bar, staring down at your phone, looking like your puppy just died."

I shoot him a hard glare that would normally cause people to rear back…but then I recall that this man faces the risk of being tackled by two-hundred-plus-pound men on any given game day.

So as much as my dangerously narrowed eyes might flare with the "Don't even go there" vibe, my glare does nothing.

He looks around first before slipping his ball cap around on his head, the brim now at the back. And honestly, on any other grown man, it would look juvenile. On Becket Jones, however, it actually looks cute.

Casey slides a bottle of water to him, which Becket uncaps before downing half of it. Resting his arms on the bar, he playfully nudges me with his shoulder.

"Go ahead. Spill."

Exhaling loudly, I peer up at him skeptically. "You really want—"

"To hear all the sordid details?" He grins at me, nearly blinding me with his pearly white teeth. "Absolutely."

Shaking my head at him, I take another sip of my drink and toy with my straw, making the ice cubes clink together in my cup. "Fine. But don't you dare give me a *bless your heart* that's chock-full of pity."

"Deal."

Letting a long sigh loose, I answer, my voice muted and laced with pain. And I hate the way it sounds.

"I'm running from a man who doesn't really love me."

One Hour Later

"WELL, HELL, GIRL...." Brantley looks on with widened eyes at the culmination of my tale of woe. He and Vonn had sidled up to the bar next to me and Becket just as I'd begun to divulge everything.

"I'm still stuck on this dress." Vonn waves his hand, gesturing to my attire. "The organza is breathtaking. So delicate." He lets out a dreamy sigh. "Perfect for a summer wedding."

Brantley promptly shoves him. "Dude! Salt in the wound."

I heave out a breath, blowing some stray strands of hair away from my eyes, and half-heartedly wave him off. "No biggie."

"So what now?" Brantley asks.

"That's the million-dollar question." I slump my shoulders and rest my elbows on the bar—everything I've been lectured *not* to do my entire life. The ladies of The Women's League would have a field day, as would my lead cotillion and debutante instructors. Heck, those women gave Emily Post, the queen of etiquette, a run for her money with their stringent doctrines.

With a weary groan, I fold my arms upon the smooth surface of the bar and lay my head down on them. I close my eyes, wishing this was all just a bad dream.

If this doesn't work, I can always try the whole Dorothy click-my-heels-together thing.

Brilliant. Maybe I should also ask Casey for a side of desperation with my next drink.

"I could help."

I slowly raise my head to stare warily at Becket. He'd kept quiet as I told the guys about the whole ordeal. "How so?"

He shrugs. "I know people."

A tiny laugh bubbles up from me because he doesn't realize who my father is.

"My father is notorious in Mobile. He owns the local newspaper, *The Bay* magazine, and is a major commercial developer for properties all over the area." I break off and avert my gaze wearily, dejected. "He's already ensured that my job's been terminated and that I'll be shunned if I go back."

"Blue."

My head swivels slowly to stare at the famous quarterback who has apparently given me a new nickname. His dark eyes study me with utter seriousness as he reaches out to tuck a strand of hair behind my ear. And it dawns on me why he's calling me Blue.

In yet another act against my father's dominating ways, I dyed a streak of my hair for my "something blue."

"I have a good friend who's VP of marketing and advertising for *Fit & Fashion*—in Jacksonville. I mean, you'd have to prove yourself to her, but I could get you an interview. She's searching for reliable staff."

"You're..." I falter because, well, this guy doesn't even know me. Not really. We've been in each other's company for a little over an hour now. Not to mention, *F&F* is a well-known magazine with a far larger readership than *Southern Charm Lifestyle*. "You're offering to help me find a job? In a different city?"

A smile tugs at the corners of his lips, and he tips his head to the side, those dark eyes shining with kindness. "We all get knocked down. Sometimes, we get knocked down hard enough that we need help back up." He shrugs. "Plus, it sounds like a fresh start, away from everything, would be a good thing."

"But you don't even know—"

Becket interrupts me, and leans in closer. "I know you never once asked me for my autograph, didn't take a chance to snap a photo of me or text anyone about me or my brother and Vonn." He pauses and I notice his eyes have flecks of gold amidst the deep brown. "In my book, that speaks volumes."

He Loves Me...Knot

Leaning back, he holds my gaze. "We're friends, Blue."

"Friends," I repeat slowly, a bit stunned.

Now, it's not like helping others in need is foreign to me. Heck, I was born and raised in the Deep South. We're known to stop alongside the road to help strangers change a tire and offer a cool glass of sweet tea to the mailman when he stops by on one of those "fry an egg on the driveway" kind of days.

But this is different somehow. Bigger.

My lips press thin as I ponder Becket's offer and I cock my head to the side. Finally, I hold up my index finger.

"If we're going to be friends, I want us to be as equal as possible. You're helping me in a huge way. What can I help *you* with?"

"You could be his beard."

Both my head and Becket's snap around to where Casey is mixing up drinks for the new patrons sitting on the far side of the bar.

My eyes dart back and forth between Becket and Casey.

With an eye roll, Becket's attention returns to me. "What he means is that I need a woman, a 'plus one' who would attend functions with me and—"

"Not be a paparazzi whore or an embarrassment."

Becket narrows his eyes at Casey before finishing with, "Not expect a relationship or a proposal."

Amusement spreads across my features. "Honey, I can assure you that's the last thing I'd ever expect or want."

His lips quirk into the grin that's graced magazine covers and billboards, and he holds out his hand. "We have a deal then?"

I reach out, and the instant I place my hand in his, it becomes engulfed. We shake briefly. Then, Becket slings an arm around my shoulders loosely, giving a quick tug-like hug before he backs away and smiles down at me.

"I have the feeling that this is the start of a beautiful friendship."

And I have the feeling that maybe not everyone's fairy godmother is of the female variety.

1

Emma Jane

EIGHT YEARS LATER
JUNE
JACKSONVILLE, FLORIDA

"We're looking forward to working with you." I shake the hands of the four *ESPN* representatives I've managed to dazzle in order to seal a mutual advertising agreement. By far, this is the largest deal I've signed since working at *F&F*.

As the two men and lone woman file out, one man lingers and it takes everything in my power to bite back a weary groan.

Teegan Rodriguez. A former pro-baseball player, he'd slipped right into a position with the well-known sports network, putting his college degree in business and communication to good use.

"Any chance you're free for dinner tonight?" Teegan flashes me a grin that I'm sure drops panties by the dozen.

Not mine, though. Probably because I know he'd lose interest as soon as my panties dropped.

"Sorry, Teegan. I have to attend a benefit this evening." I offer my most apologetic smile as I gather up the thick file with the necessary documents for our legal team to finalize.

"With Jones," he finishes, a slight bite to his tone.

Geez Louise. Jocks and their grudges. Just because he came in second to Becket winning *ESPN*'s Fan Favorite Athlete. You'd think someone just peed in his grits or something.

I narrow my eyes with the slightest warning in my voice. "With my best friend."

"Right."

Okay, I'm done here.

"Good to see you, Teegan." I stride toward the open door of the boardroom with him trailing me. At the last moment, he steps in front of me, drawing me to halt.

"Maybe another time?" He reaches out and dusts his index finger along the back of my hand in what I assume he believes is a seductive caress.

"Perhaps." *Perhaps never.* I offer another polite smile, casually moving my hand out of his reach and sidestepping him. Then, I call over my shoulder, "See you later, Teegan."

It's only once I reach the confines of my office and close the door that I exhale a sigh of relief. As soon as I drop down into my chair at my desk, I notice a text message notification light up on my phone's screen.

This time, my smile is genuine.

Becket: Do I need to lay the smackdown on Rodriguez? I presume he asked you out for the hundredth time.

Me: No need. I did it verbally. I swear that man can't take a hint.

Becket: That's my girl. By the way, I sent over a dress for tonight's shindig.

Me: Beck. You need to stop. I thought we agreed I could wear the blue one I already have.

Becket: I saw this one when I was in Miami and had to get it for you.

I can't restrain a sigh because, although my best friend is simply the sweetest, I really wish he'd get himself a girlfriend. Honestly, attending some of these events as his 'plus one,' being the subject of the continuous "Is she or isn't she his girlfriend?" debate, can be more than a little exhausting at times.

Me: I have a little surprise for you tonight.

Becket: What is it? Two hot Brazilian women who have a thing for American quarterbacks?

I laugh softly, knowing Becket's most particular when it comes to women, especially after his painful past. Everyone automatically assumes he's a ladies' man since he's such a charmer, when, in reality, he's the furthest thing from it. I just wish he'd date more often than he actually does...which is occasional, at best.

Me: I'll give it to you tonight. It's nothing spectacular like a dress but I think it's pretty special.

Becket: Then I know I'll love it. Pick you up at

seven and the dress should be delivered to your office shortly.

Me: See you then.

Picking up the *ESPN* file along with a few other necessary pieces of paperwork, I exit my office and hand them to my assistant.

"Alissa, if you can please scan these and send them to Legal, that'd be great."

"On it." She accepts the files with a smile.

"How much longer, now?"

Her smile grows brighter at the mention of the impending birth of her first child. "Only eight more weeks."

My expression sobers. "You let me know if you're not feeling well or if I'm overloading you with work, okay?"

"Yes, ma'am."

Alissa is lying to me because she's one of the hardest working women I've ever known. She insists on calling me ma'am even though I'm a few years younger than she is. But she's the best assistant I could have ever asked for.

As I turn to head back to my office to tackle some more work, Alissa stops me. She glances around before speaking in a hushed tone. "There've been some rumors about Martin selling the magazine to some media bigwig in the region, but they're trying to keep the details hush-hush."

I cast a curious look at my assistant before lowering my voice. "Do you know if there's any truth to that?"

She shrugs. "Honestly, I don't know. There's been talk in the past that he's not the best with money…" She trails off with a slightly worried expression.

I purse my lips thoughtfully, since I've also heard that

mentioned. "Well, I'll see if I hear anything, but it might just be harmless gossip."

She nods and I return to my office with the niggling thoughts of that rumor clinging to the back of my mind.

"YOU LOOK BEAUTIFUL."

Becket smiles down at me, and for a split second, the joy and affection filling his expression makes me forget that I'm upset with him for purchasing this dress for me.

A dress that cost him well over six grand.

Squinting up at him, I tsk. "Don't think you can sweet talk me out of being sore with you over this dress."

"But, sugar," he drawls, attempting to imitate a Southern accent, "I knew this dress would accentuate the beauty you already possess."

"Smooth talker."

He flashes me a wide, toothy grin. "You know it." Extending me his hand, he dips his head. "Shall we?"

"We shall." I slip my hand in his and we exit the limo. Becket helps me out as carefully as possible to ensure my dress doesn't get snagged.

This strapless evening gown, as heinously expensive as it was, is too gorgeous for words. The deep-red satiny material shimmers as the light hits it, and the Swarovski crystals sewn around the waistline sparkle.

I should be acclimated to the onslaught of flashes from the cameras after all this time, but it still takes a moment for my eyes to adjust. Becket's hand holds firm to mine and he glances down at me.

"Ready, Blue?"

"Ready."

With smiles firmly in place, we pause for photos, not

responding to the shouted questions pertaining to our relationship or rumors of an engagement. The real blessing is the fact that Becket's manager has assisted in preventing anyone from getting wind of my past, what I'd left behind in Mobile. I know that's also very likely due to my father who would do everything in his power to prevent bad press from overshadowing his business.

I swear, there's always a stray rumor about Becket popping the question every other month, but I know that's more wishful thinking on behalf of the local media, hoping their famed quarterback has found love. Although, I must admit I'm extremely grateful the "Is she or isn't she pregnant?" debate has ended.

Finally, we enter the large ballroom designated for the gala tonight to honor the athletes included in *ESPN*'s latest Body Issue. Becket—along with twenty-five other athletes—posed nude in the feature, strategically and creatively covering his crotch.

Once we exchange a few greetings with some acquaintances, I guide Becket to a quieter spot off to the side. His eyes, gleaming with curiosity, meet mine and I merely offer a sly smile before I unclasp my clutch purse and withdraw a small flat item. At an outward glance, it appears to be a trading card of some sort.

Placing the object in his large palm, I watch as the realization hits—the relevance of it and of this date.

The look on Becket's face is one I'll not soon forget. His eyes light up in heartfelt appreciation, and his smile turns more intimate. It serves as even more proof that I have one of the best friends on this earth.

"Blue." He stares down at the small card, his voice husky with emotion, before his dark gaze locks with mine. "You mean the world to me, you know that?"

Tears begin to prick my eyes because I *do* know. I know

it because he means the world to me, too. I firmly believe it was fate that brought us together, stumbling across one another in that bar eight years ago.

"I know."

His lips quirk upward and his eyes sparkle mischievously. "If I could manage to kiss you on the lips without wanting to puke, I'd totally marry you."

Laughter erupts from me and causes a few heads to turn at the sound of it. I grin up at him. "I know."

He looks down at the trading card I'd had made. It was the photo we'd taken immediately after we'd agreed to help one another out that summer night in the Pensacola Beach bar. Me clad in my wedding dress, him with a backward ball cap, you can see the smiles on our faces, although mine looks a tinge hesitant.

This photo marked the very beginning of a friendship unlike any other.

I'd dated it and had a friend in our graphics department show me how to dress it up. Photoshop was still not my friend, but I'd managed to create this for our "friendship-iversary."

Becket withdraws his wallet and carefully slips the card inside before tucking it away in his pocket. "I'll have us with me wherever I go." He frames my face with his large palms and places a soft kiss on my forehead before whispering against my skin, "Love you."

My eyes drift closed, and I murmur, "Love you, too."

The sound of a clearing throat interrupts our moment, and we dutifully turn and greet one of the gala hosts.

"EXCUSE ME, but I have to steal this beautiful woman away for a dance."

Becket's deep voice sounds from behind me, his palm landing at my waist. The ladies I've been speaking with all titter, succumbing to my friend's inherent charm and looks.

As he leads me away to the large dance floor, I notice the instrumental version of Miranda Lambert's "Better Man" being played by the musicians on the stage. In my heels, the top of my head nearly reaches Becket's forehead.

"Superficial conversation?" he murmurs into my ear.

"You have no idea. Not to mention, the rumors have managed to spread even further about *F&F*'s unknown future." My lips twist. "Someone mentioned seeing the new owner here tonight."

Laughter rumbles through his chest. "Dare I say I'm your savior, then? Rescuing you from such distressing talk?"

I lean back slightly and flutter my lashes playfully, allowing my Southern accent to become more prominent. "Why, how can I, a woman as imperfect as myself, ever repay you?"

His grin matches mine. "By giving the gossips something else to talk about. Hold on tight."

With that, Becket spins me out before smoothly tugging me back, flush against his chest. He dips me gaily, holds me nearly parallel to the floor, and whispers to me.

"And you've got to remember, Blue." He deepens his voice slightly to recite a line from my favorite movie, *Good Will Hunting*. "People call those imperfections, but no, that's the good stuff."

He steers us upright again. The musicians finish the song and everyone pauses to offer their applause. That's when something catches my eye. Or rather someone—a man—and an odd sensation falls over me. On the opposite side of the ballroom, he shifts his stance, and I can't quite catch sight of his face, but there's something so familiar about him and the way he holds himself.

"Blue?"

I jerk, finding Becket's concerned expression fixed on me. With a tight smile, I attempt to shake off the feeling of déjà vu.

"Sorry. Just…thought I saw someone I knew."

"You okay?"

"I'm fine." I put more effort into my smile. "Promise."

He studies me for a beat before he tips his head in the direction of the large tables filled with a variety of hors d'oeuvres. "Feel like grabbing some food?"

"Absolutely."

After we partake in some of the delicious catered food, we're soon caught up in conversations with those inquiring about Becket's take on some upcoming free agents or those curious about my job with *F&F*.

And the entire time, I can't shake the unsettling feeling like my past is at the periphery, haunting me.

"EXHAUSTED DOESN'T COVER how I feel right now."

After kicking off my heels in the back of the limo at the end of the night, I let out a soft moan as I wiggle my finally uncramped toes.

Becket leans his head back against the seat of the limo, eyes falling closed. "Same."

With my cheek against the smooth leather, I regard him affectionately. "You'd make a really great boyfriend, you know." My voice is soft, tone hushed as I study his profile.

One corner of his mouth hitches slightly, but his eyes remain closed. "That so?"

I reach out, slip my hand in his, and grasp it tightly. "Beck, you know so," I whisper softly. "I think it's time to get that new game plan ready."

He shifts his head to the side and peers at me within the confines of the dimly lit vehicle. "Using some sports terminology on me now?"

With a half-smile, I answer, "I was told once that a game plan was needed when you decide to execute change…"

"Sounds like a wise person."

"He is." I swallow hard, braving my next words. "But he needs more—*deserves* more—than to continuously dote on his best friend."

He stares at me in heavy silence. And I should know better than to think I can toss this out at him without him being more astute. Becket's often pigeonholed as a dumb jock, but he's the furthest thing from it.

As is proven with his next, hushed words.

"I could say the same for you."

2

Emma Jane
THE FOLLOWING MONDAY

"Oh, and Emma Jane? Gail wanted to see you before you get started for the day." Alissa catches me as I'm entering my office, about to set my briefcase down and unpack my things.

My head snaps up as unease ripples through me. Gail, VP of marketing and advertising, normally has a loose rein when it comes to me doing my job. She's a wonderful mentor but also isn't one to keep constant tabs on me.

"Okay," I answer slowly as I set my briefcase on the floor against my desk. After I open the top drawer, I place my keys in it before tossing my purse in the back of the bottom drawer. Then I grab a legal pad and a pen and make my way down the hall to Gail's corner office.

Her secretary, Margo, calls on the intercom before waving me into her boss's office. Striding in, I'm startled by Gail's quiet request for me to close the door, leaving us ensconced in silence for a moment.

Running a finely manicured hand down her sleek, gray bob hairstyle, Gail's attention settles on me.

"Please have a seat, Emma Jane."

Stepping toward one of the plush chairs, I perch on it, bristling with curiosity.

She steeples her fingers, resting her elbows on the mahogany surface of her desk, and levels a look at me. "I assume you've heard the rumors about Martin."

My brow furrows. "I assumed they were just that: rumors."

"Sadly, no. It's been confirmed that the new owner will be arriving tomorrow."

My stomach flips, but her next words make it feel like the floor drops out from beneath me entirely.

"And word on the street is, our new owner has major plans for restructuring."

The blood leaves my face, and I instantly pale. *Restructuring?* I reach up to pinch the bridge of my nose as I attempt composure. Inhaling what I hope to be a calming breath, I meet Gail's eyes.

Only to see everything I feared written in the depths.

"I've already submitted my resignation to HR and have accepted a position with *Style&Now*."

"But—"

Gail offers me a sympathetic smile. "Emma Jane, I'm far too old to go through the rigmarole of jumping through hoops for some young print media mogul. I need stability."

"Yes, but—"

"And this means great things for you." Flashing me a knowing look, she adds, "Because this way, you'll have the opportunity to slip into my position."

My lips part in surprise. I mean, sure, I've always set my sights on moving up, but I also knew Gail wouldn't be retiring for a while. Now, with this new development and her leaving…

"Oh, wow."

Gail lets out a subdued chuckle. "Yes, dear. Wow,

indeed." Raising her eyebrows, she returns to business. "You'll need to ensure that you make all the right moves with the new owner, get off on the right foot so there won't be any doubt that you should be promoted. I've already written that in my notes to HR."

The fact that Gail thinks so highly of me is an immense compliment, but my excitement begins to ebb at the challenge I face ahead.

I have to do everything in my power to compel this new owner to not only keep me on staff, but to also promote me to VP of marketing and advertising.

Holy hell in a handbasket.

"SO YOU'RE TELLING me she doesn't even know the guy's name?"

I'm FaceTiming with Madison, who is one of my closest girlfriends and *F&F*'s beauty editor, while I finish typing up some proposals in my office.

I immediately called her once I returned to my office after the unsettling talk with Gail, praying Madison would be available since she's down in Miami for some conference.

"Get this. No one seems to know anything about him—not his name or even where he's from—except for the fact that he's hell-bent on restructuring and cutting jobs."

Madison stares back at me, her blue eyes wide with dismay. "That's insane! What the hell happened with Martin?"

I roll my eyes. "Apparently, he did some not-so-savory things with earnings from this place, and it got him into some pretty hot water, financially speaking."

"Wow."

"Tell me about it," I breathe out on a sigh. "Gail's using up her personal leave because she's already accepted a position with *StyleNow*."

"You should have no problem convincing this guy you're the right person for the job. You've got this in the bag. I mean"—Madison waves a hand dismissively—"you've practically been groomed for the job all along."

"From your lips to God's ears."

I hear someone call to her in the background. She nods and offers me an apologetic look. "Sorry, but I have to get going." She crosses her eyes. "More complexion remedies for sweaty breakouts and clogged pores."

"Have fun with that."

She makes a face. "Pray for me. If it's another one of those godforsaken peel-off charcoal masks…"

"Ah, the fad that needs to die a quick death." I wink at her. "At least your pores will be clean and clear."

She sticks out her tongue playfully before we say our goodbyes and disconnect.

Tuesday

"EMMA JANE?" Alissa's voice sounds over my speakerphone the following day. "I just wanted to be sure you received the email about the mandatory meeting in Boardroom G for the marketing and advertising department."

"Sweet sugar," I curse beneath my breath, dragging my attention away from my work. The latest proposal I've been working on had caused me to lose track of time. Now I only have a few minutes to haul my butt down the long hallway to catch an elevator and make it to the designated boardroom on the next floor. With a sigh, I press the intercom button on my phone. "Thanks for the reminder, Alissa."

Scooping up my legal pad and pen, I rush out of my office, mentally preparing to meet the new owner. Once I exit the elevator and make my way to Boardroom G, I manage to snag a seat at the far end of the long oval-shaped table.

Barely a minute passes before the din of light conversation ebbs to complete silence when a man enters the room and heads straight for the opposite end of the table. I can only see the back of him as he takes long, powerful strides, one hand grasping a thick binder. Something seems so familiar about him... My eyes track his movements, and my forehead creases as I try to place him.

His suit is well tailored, and it's evident the man works out, the black pinstriped dress pants failing to mask his powerful, muscled thighs and firm backside. When he sets the binder down, his suit jacket shifts and hints at a firm, flat stomach beneath the button-down shirt. My appraisal continues down to his hands when he draws one hand back from the binder.

An odd sensation overtakes me, and a rousing awareness crackles within the air, causing me to immediately grow still.

Then he turns, fully facing everyone in the room, and it's at this moment my breath is completely robbed from me.

As if in shock, my mind refuses to operate on all cylinders, acting sluggish. I continue to take in the sight before me, cataloguing my observations. The square jawline that used to remain clean-shaven now has a short, neatly trimmed beard of the same dark shade of brown as his hair. My eyes skim over the straight nose that has the faintest bump on the bridge from the time when he was five and fel—

Sweet Lord, *no*.

As the man's identity dawns on me, my eyes flicker over my co-workers seated around the large table before I return my panicked gaze to the individual who's garnering attention with his commanding presence.

He surveys everyone in attendance, and those piercing green eyes, framed by dark lashes, scan each person and slowly travel around the table. My heart skips a beat when his eyes land on me. If I weren't scrutinizing so intently, I wouldn't have caught the slight pause, the faint shift in depth of his gaze, as it grows frigid before he continues his perusal of the remainder of the staff members.

My throat grows dry, and I immediately wish I'd brought my water bottle along. A stick of gum, even. Anything.

I should've known better than to think my past wouldn't catch up to me at some point.

In my case, however, it seems my past is the new owner of my place of employment.

Knox Montgomery. The man I left at the altar.

3

Knox

THE SIGHT of her nearly sends me rearing back. It's such a jolt to my system to be in the same room with her and have her focus centered on me.

It's disturbing how easy it is to recall how much I loved having her attention years ago.

I hate that she's still so beautiful, that she doesn't look like she's aged aside from the way she now carries herself. Her poise—the air of confidence—is evident. I can't deny the nostalgia that washes over me at the sight of that tiny diamond stud in her nose, nor the disappointment when I notice the lack of a wild streak of color in her dark hair.

Her eyes are the same; those pale-blue orbs that always felt like they could see straight through me. Her slim, elegant hands once held mine as if they'd never let go. Those nearly perfect lips, always a light shade of red, had once whispered words of love.

Only to mutilate my heart in the worst way possible.

Sometimes I wonder if it would've been easier to deal with Emma Jane skipping out on me if it hadn't been our wedding day. If I hadn't been standing at the altar, waiting for her to walk down the aisle with that sparkle in her eyes I'd come to adore. If I hadn't been the focus of pity for what seemed like forever afterward.

Throwing myself into work has been a haven for me. I've been living and breathing my career, have achieved success, even going so far as to be featured in *Business Weekly* as an up-and-coming entrepreneur and hailed the "Turnaround King" for bringing businesses and companies back from the "dead."

Now, though, alongside my duty of "trimming the fat" and restoring *Fit & Fashion* magazine to operate in the black, it's my turn to serve up a dish of retribution.

APPARENTLY, the marketing and advertising crew are an emotionally fragile bunch. *Jesus*.

As soon as I finish detailing my plans for the employees assembled around the table, identifying my expectations—ones which are decidedly *not* unreasonable—an employee by the name of Madeline Grove jumps up from her seat, sending the wheeled desk chair rolling. "But you can't give me two weeks to do those tasks! I have plans!" She waves her arms wildly, outraged.

I narrow my eyes in a cold stare. "Perhaps you should rethink your plans." My voice is low with a lethal undertone.

It's evident that she finally comprehends the dire situation when she blurts out, "I quit!", scoops up her things, and flees the room.

Once the room has settled again, I regard everyone seated around the table, and restrain the urge to linger on one particular woman.

I pick up my pen and place a checkmark next to Madeline's name. "Let's move on…"

Twenty minutes later, after conveying my intent to do everything in my power to pull this magazine out of the red, financially, I call an end to the meeting. The marketing and advertising team rises and files out of the boardroom quietly. Emma Jane makes it within two feet of the door, within two feet of freedom, when I stop her.

"Ms. Haywood, I'd like to have a quick word with you, please."

Her spine noticeably stiffens, as if her body recognizes a threat.

As I notice the effect my request has on her, it takes every single ounce of my self-control to restrain the predatory smile itching to break free.

Right now, I reckon Emma Jane Haywood deserves a big, Southern pitying "Bless your heart."

Emma Jane

HIGH SCHOOL
TENTH GRADE

Knox Montgomery is so confident and far too cute for his own good.

"We had advanced algebra together last year, remember? I was the handsome guy sitting two rows over on the left."

His infectious grin should be outlawed. The problem is, he knows it. Especially since it seems to captivate most of the female population.

I steel myself against his charm and studiously ignore him. I know he thinks I'm a snob—most people make that assumption simply because of who my father is—but I'm not. After what happened with Patrick, I can't help but have a wary distaste for guys. Especially guys who are such smooth talkers.

When I reach inside my locker for the book I need for my next class, someone bumps into me and it causes my hand to bang into the edge of the metal.

At the feel of a sharp sting, I jerk back and notice a small cut along the side of my palm. I reach for the packet of tissues I normally keep in my purse but before I get that far, my wrist is caught in a gentle but firm grip.

"You're hurt."

At his touch, my breath lodges in my throat, and I watch in disbelief as Knox withdraws a handkerchief from the back pocket of his khaki pants. The slightly frayed edges indicate it's seen better days, and he proceeds to carefully, tenderly, blot at the small cut.

Knox Montgomery carries a handkerchief?

Green eyes rise and lock with mine, and I realize with dismay that I've spoken aloud. "It used to be my grandfather's." He averts his gaze, inspecting my cut that's no longer bleeding, thankfully. His thumb grazes over the top of my hand in the lightest caress.

Unsettled by his touch, I give a slight tug, silently requesting that he release my hand. Once he does, the absence of contact is tangible, and I'm not sure what to make of it.

"I can pay for your handkerchief to be dry cleaned so the blood stains come out," I blurt out, internally cringing at the nervousness in my voice.

He replaces the handkerchief in his pocket and takes a step back. "It's no big deal, EJ." He winks and when his mouth tips up in a smile, it's somehow different. This one seems more personal. Sweeter, even. "Don't let any more lockers attack you, okay?"

He turns to head in the direction of his next class, and before I realize it, I call out, "What if it happens again?"

Those emerald eyes lock with mine. "Then you'd better call me, and I'll bring my mighty steed—er, handkerchief—to the rescue."

This time, when he walks away, I'm left staring after him and feel like I've caught a glimpse of the real Knox Montgomery. The one beneath the swoon-worthy grins and undeniable charm.

4

Emma Jane
PRESENT

Inhaling a deep, fortifying breath, I clutch my legal pad to my chest and turn to face Knox, forcing myself to meet his gaze.

The thing about encountering someone from your past, someone you were never able to get closure with, is when you see them, there's always this tiny ache in the center of your chest. As if your heart recognizes that person without you articulating a single word; it immediately recalls the agonizing pain it once endured. The pain might ease with time, but it will always remain; it will *never* cease to be a vulnerability.

For me, that's Knox Montgomery.

Attempting to maintain a professional façade, I raise my eyebrows politely in question. "Sir?"

He doesn't immediately respond, instead choosing to regard me carefully, almost analytically. As if he's the guy from those *Terminator* movies or something, cataloguing me and noting my weaknesses.

I subconsciously move a hand to smooth down my slim black pencil skirt but catch myself in the nick of time.

He Loves Me...Knot

Clearing my throat, I repeat, "Sir? You wished to speak to me?"

A corner of his mouth shifts, tipping upward but it isn't one of those humorous smirks. No, this one sends an ominous shiver down my spine.

"Why don't you have a seat?" He gestures to the chair nearest to where he remains at the head of the table.

Warily eyeing him, I stride over to a chair and perch on it, placing my pad and pen on my lap.

"In all the gin joints in all the world..." One corner of his mouth tilts up in what some might classify a harmless smile.

It's not. It has Big, Bad Wolf written all over it.

And he thinks I'm his Red Riding Hood.

Think again, Montgomery. My eyes narrow slightly. "You needed to speak with me?" I redirect him in an overly polite manner.

He laces his fingers together and leans back in his chair as if he doesn't have a care in the world.

"You realize your job is on the chopping block?"

I hold his stare for a beat. With force, I strive to maintain a controlled tone while simultaneously calming my erratic heart rate. "I'm aware you're restructuring and we must all pass qualifications to be eligible to keep our positions."

His eyes bore into mine. "And how do you feel about that?"

"It doesn't matter how I feel about it, sir. It just matters that I do my best—as I always do—and provide proof that I'm qualified to hold my current position."

There. That sounded cool, calm, and professional.

"You've got your eye on the VP position."

I refuse to rise to the bait because I'm not about to

show all my cards to him. Especially since I don't know his entire agenda.

Green eyes narrow at my lack of response before he finally breaks eye contact, thumbing through some papers in the binder before him. "Your file holds not one poor assessment, Ms. Haywood." His stress on the *Ms.* grates on me, but I remain silent. "Your reviews are stellar, and you've managed to bring in a great deal of revenue to *F&F* since you've come on board."

My silence causes him to raise his eyes, and the instant they clash with mine, my skin prickles with the rise of goosebumps at the utter coldness in the depths. That cool demeanor, the icy tone is at complete odds with his drawl; it's not overly pronounced, yet just enough to give him that "Southern gentleman" vibe.

"You were recommended—by the VP herself—to move up to her position once she either retired or moved on."

This time, it appears as though he's waiting for me to respond, so I simply offer a curt nod. "Yes, sir."

Leaning back casually in his chair, he fiddles with his pen, and for a moment, I recall how he used to do that long ago. Back in high school, during study sessions.

Funny, the things the brain recalls, even after so many years have passed.

"Know this, Ms. Haywood. You will have to prove yourself to me before you'll be eligible for that promotion. But"—he waves his hand in what's supposed to be a casual gesture, but I know better—"let's not get ahead of ourselves. You have to, first, prove that you're deserving of your current position."

Great. I have to run the gauntlet because I left this jackass at the altar.

"What would you say if I told you that you couldn't

He Loves Me...Knot

have the VP position? That I was promoting someone else, instead?"

My lips instantly part to form a protest because *what the hell?* There isn't anyone else more qualified, anyone else who busts their butt as I do for this place.

I clamp my mouth shut as I fight for composure. Because it doesn't take a genius to figure out that he's baiting me.

Finally, I speak in careful monotone. "I would wonder who that particular person was, but also assume and respect that you were placing someone else in that position who'd managed to bring in more revenue than I have and also managed to maintain propriety and represent the company in the best light possible."

His lips stretch into a grin that sends shivers of unease trickling down my spine.

"Are you suggesting you represent the company in the best light possible? By being the girlfriend of an NFL quarterback?"

The bite in his tone causes my spine to stiffen further, and my posture becomes rigid.

"I'm not—"

"Because, here's the way it's going to be, Ms. Haywood," he interrupts fluidly. "You have to prove yourself. No missteps in any way. Otherwise, your job?" He waves a hand dismissively. "Gone to Ms. Mitchell."

The words slip past my lips before I can think twice. "The intern?"

His gaze hardens, narrowing on me, and his tone is wintery. "Yes. Ms. Mitchell will be promoted and you will lose your position as executive marketing and advertising assistant." There's the briefest pause. "Unless you bring in a deal with Coastal Media." Then he hammers the final nail in my proverbial employment coffin. "In no more than five months' time."

It takes everything in my power not to allow my jaw to drop open because Coastal Media is the largest media group in the southeast. We've been trying to get an "in" with them—trying to come up with the perfect pitch for a joint venture—for a while now, to no avail.

And now, apparently, it's up to me to make that happen if I want to keep my job, at the very least.

"I'll be by your office later to discuss a few accounts, the latest proposals in the works, and your current client list. We'll see once and for all whether you have staying power." He rises from the chair, and closes his binder before picking it up. "Unlike all those years ago."

With that final jab, he leaves the boardroom. And I'm still sitting here, stunned.

Not only has my past turned up, but it's also out for vengeance.

Happy Tuesday to me.

"SO, he turned out not to be a super old dude, but in a crazy twist, ended up being your ex-fiancé?" The disbelief is apparent in Becket's tone.

"Yes!" I hiss into my cell phone as I pace back and forth in my office.

Sure, the door is closed, but I'm whispering because I'm still so thrown off by what's transpired and can't afford for this news to get out. I'd immediately called Becket because he was—and still is—the only person who knows my entire sordid story.

Well, aside from Brantley and Vonn, of course. But they live in Pensacola Beach.

"What am I going to do, Beck?" I hear the slight whimper in my voice, the hint of fragility.

"I'll tell you what you're going to do, Blue." Becket's voice shifts, sounding gruff with steely undertones. "You're going to show that asshole who's boss. You understand me?" He pauses, and I nod even though he can't see me. "You're going to show him that you're the best at what you do. The best, you hear me? And you damn well deserve to be promoted to VP."

What if my best isn't good enough? I silently worry.

"And if he doesn't see it," Becket continues as though he can hear my internal thoughts, "you can and *will* be hired elsewhere."

"Right." I punctuate this with a sharp nod. "You're absolutely right." A surge of confidence begins to flood my consciousness. "I will show him exactly who he's dealing with. That he's not messing with that same naïve girl from back in Mobile."

"That's right, Blue. Now g—"

"You can start by showing me your current client list and some of the proposals you've drawn up."

My entire body draws to a sudden halt, muscles tensing, my spine stiffening. Eyes closing on a wince, I'm at least thankful to be facing away from the door—the same door Knox Montgomery stealthily opened without so much as a knock.

The silence on the other end of the line tells me Becket heard. He confirms it with his next hushed words.

"If I need to come down there, you just give me the word."

"Thanks. I have to go."

"Love you."

"Love you, too."

Disconnecting the call, I let my arm drop, clenching

my cell phone as though it's a lifeline. Firming my posture, I attempt composure and do my best to channel professionalism.

Turning around, I fix a polite smile upon my face but, at the sight of him, I feel the corners of it waver ever so slightly.

There's something so incredibly unsettling about facing the man you once loved, the man you were once ready to spend the rest of your life with, the man whose body you knew like the back of your hand.

The man who single-handedly shattered your heart into tiny fragments with his betrayal.

His lips twist in a hint of a sneer, his gaze hard, unfeeling. "If you're finished talking—on company time, no less—with your boyfriend, we need to get to work, Ms. Haywood." There's a minute pause. "For starters, I'd like to see your client list and your latest proposals."

My fingers curl into my palm, one hand making a fist at my side while the other clenches my phone tighter. I'll be surprised if there aren't imprints in the case after this.

"Let me pull it up on my computer."

Stepping around my desk, I take a seat. I place my cell phone off to one side before grasping the wireless mouse and clicking on the designated folder to print the information Knox has requested.

The printer whirs a few feet away from where it sits on the far right of my L-shaped desk, rapidly spitting out the requested papers. When I turn to reach for the printouts, my fingertips encounter Knox's simultaneously.

Apparently, someone is a little anxious to get his paws on this information.

Drawing my hand back, I watch as he grasps the papers, appearing to skim the contents before his gaze connects with mine, unnerving in its intense scrutiny.

"Why don't we sit at the table and you can fill me in on everything." He poses this, not as a question, but as more of a command, tipping his head to indicate the small, round table in one corner of my office with four chairs pushed in around it.

Without a word, I rise from my seat and walk to the table. Pulling out a chair, I slide into it and assume he'll take a seat in the one directly across from me.

Imagine my shock when, instead, he chooses the one right beside me. His proximity allows me to catch a hint of his body wash, and I recognize it as the same one he's always used. The scent which had once comforted me.

He catches sight of the slim, nondescript vase I normally keep at the center of the table and something flashes in his eyes. It takes me a moment to realize why.

The vase holds a single daisy.

Sweet sugar, I internally cuss. Because it also happens to be the same flower Knox used to leave me to find on the windshield of my car, the stem safely tucked beneath the windshield wiper, when they'd bloom in season.

They've always been my favorite flower, and now, when I pass by the small floral shop on my way into the office each day, if I see that they have this particular flower available, I'll purchase one.

Because it's my favorite, of course. Not for memories or anything more than that.

"My first question"—Knox's voice draws me from my inner thoughts and forces me to focus on the spreadsheets laying on the table—"is why you don't have this amount of ad space allotted…"

And so it begins.

5

Emma Jane
TWO WEEKS LATER

I'M DYING.

Okay, I'm not *actually* dying, but it sure feels like it right now. And there's nothing I can do about it. I'm well past my eyeballs with tasks to complete, and for the past few weeks, Knox has been hounding me like I'm on work release from prison or something. A slacker who's going to skip out or steal from the till, perhaps.

To make matters worse, my migraines have been rearing their ugly head with a vengeance lately. Today's, however, puts the others to shame. My head started to ache by ten this morning and only got worse from there. It's a full-blown migraine now, and as my terrible luck would have it, I'm out of medicine to alleviate the incessant pain. I've already drawn the blinds in my office, cursing the fact that it faces east. Of course, today would be one of those typical sunny Florida days.

Knox has also emailed me no less than twenty times already with requests and criticism—heavy on the criticism, of course. There's no way I can head home because I know that will add fuel to Knox's fire. I'm certain he'd write me up and place it in my file to document that I was found slacking on the job.

I'm also starving and forgot my lunch at home, and I haven't had time to place a food order. Heck, I barely had time to answer Becket's earlier call, checking in on me.

A knock on my door has my head snapping up from where I've been attempting to concentrate on typing out a proposal. The same one I've been working on for over an hour because my head has developed a near-deafening pulse of its own.

"Please don't be Knox," I whimper to myself.

The door opens and I instantly slump with relief.

"Hey, hey, how's my—" Becket stops short at the sight of me. Dropping the bag of takeout on my table, he circles my desk and grasps the arm of my desk chair to swivel it toward him. Bending at the knees, he reaches a hand out to tuck some of my hair behind my ear, his features etched with concern.

"Blue?"

"Migraine," is all I manage to utter. I don't normally get them but, when I do, it's because I'm under extreme stress.

Immediately, Becket reaches into his pocket and pulls out a small, square pill box. "Here, take these. They're the natural, anti-inflammatory enzymes Pres swears by."

He opens the tiny container he normally carries the pills in for when his throwing shoulder acts up. Plucking out two tablets, he hands me my water thermos perched on the far corner of my desk. I down them and pray for relief as quickly as possible.

Becket's friend from college, Presley Hendrixson, is a naturopathic doctor and chiropractor. She helped me a great deal shortly after I moved here, with wellness supplements and vitamins. She and her husband are expecting their first baby soon, and Becket has far exceeded the threshold of excitement and preparation for the little one's arrival.

Which is why, through squinty eyes, I question him wearily. "What are you wearing?"

As if just now recalling what he has strapped to the front of him—one of those soft baby carriers—his lips curl up in an easy grin. "I'm getting ready for the baby." He announces this with such confidence and pride that I'd laugh if I knew it wouldn't make my head hurt more than it currently does.

"I just installed the car seat in my SUV, too, so I'll be ready for uncle duties." He shakes his head with a grimace. "Man, that sucker was a bitch to figure out."

I lean back farther in my chair, letting my eyes fall closed. Barely withholding a wince as a sharp, searing pain slices my skull, I reach up to massage my temples.

"Blue, you need to go home."

"Am I interrupting?"

Without meaning to, I flinch, releasing a whimper at the sound of Knox's voice in my doorway.

My eyes flash open and lock with Becket's, and I instantly recognize the fierce protectiveness and a hint of anger within their depths. If I weren't feeling like utter crap, I'd say something to get Becket to calm down and just leave me be.

Right now, however, that's the least of my worries because I'm rapidly nearing the point where my migraine is inducing nausea.

"No need to draw out the big guns, there, Fun Police." Becket moves around the desk to approach Knox, a friendly smile on his face as he prepares to pour on the charm and smooth talking he's perfected over the years.

He holds out a hand to Knox. "Becket Jones. Nice to meet you."

When their handshake lasts a second or two longer than normal, I can't help but wonder if the two of them did that typical *let's see who can squeeze the other's hand harder* thing.

"I was concerned about your employee here working so hard that she doesn't have time for lunch. Not only that, but she's battling a near-debilitating migraine now. The best thing for her is to head home and get some rest." Becket peers over at me, and I offer a weak smile, attempting to get back to my task at hand and focus on the computer monitor.

"I hardly think a little headache warrants the need to leave work early."

Please don't push this, Becket, I beg silently. I know he means well, but I don't want Knox's backlash from it.

"Well, I think she'd be more productive if she were able to leave early and rest at home. Then she could get back to one hundred percent and tackle the immense workload you've saddled her with."

Ouch. There's no way Knox missed that little jab.

"Plus," Becket lowers his voice conspiratorially, "I was discussing ad space at our stadium, and I have a connection who would offer it at a bargain price."

A wave of nausea suddenly hits me with violent intensity, and I rear back in my chair, the bottom wheels sliding back from my desk. I rush past both men, praying I can make it to my restroom in time.

"YOU OKAY?"

Becket's voice calls out from the other side of the door.

Leaning over the sink, I cup some water in my hand and rinse out my mouth yet again before I manage to force out a weak response.

"I'll be right out."

Paper towel in hand, I pat around the corners of my mouth and attempt to smooth down my hair. Exiting the restroom, I'm met by my best friend.

"You're going home." His tone brooks no argument.

A resigned sigh escapes me as I walk back to my desk. "I can't and you know this." With dread, I note that it's only twelve thirty in the afternoon.

I can practically feel Becket bristling with irritation as he follows me and we both stop short at the sight of Knox, still standing in the doorway.

He runs a hand over the back of his neck before sliding both hands into the pockets of his dark, pinstriped suit pants. "You need to go home. You're sick. Why don't you just come in early or stay late tomorrow to make up for it?"

I falter, surprised by his offer. Surprised and…suspicious.

"Only if you agree to write that in a memo and we both sign it with a witness. Because I don't want this to end up in my personal file as an unauthorized absence."

Knox releases a laugh that sounds a bit surprised. "I'll have my secretary draft it right now. Be back in two minutes." With that, he exits, leaving me to stare numbly after him.

"Let's get you packed up." Becket redirects me and I start gathering my belongings and placing them in my briefcase.

He guides me around my desk, his palm at the base of my back. "We'll get you settled in bed, and you'll feel right as rain by morning."

"Thanks, Beck."

"Anything for my favorite girl." He winks at me.

"Here we go." Knox reappears with two papers and a pen in hand and walks over to my small table. "Just need your signature on both and one copy is yours."

Becket reads it over before offering a short nod. With a quick scrawl of my signature and Becket's as the designated witness, I stuff my copy inside my briefcase and mutter a subdued, "Thank you," to Knox.

Becket offers the bag of takeout. "Here, man. Won't be needing this since she's so under the weather. Enjoy."

Knox grasps it numbly, and Becket guides me out of my office, palm at my back protectively.

And once again, Becket saves me from Knox Montgomery.

6

Knox

I'M unable to tear my eyes away from the sight of Becket Jones's hand at the base of Emma Jane's spine. The way he dotes on her, the natural way he touches her, affection is obvious in his actions. Like she's his.

Hell, of course she is. I mean, there's been speculation over the years, but this seems to confirm it.

And what the hell was that thing he had strapped to his chest?

I tried to continue to be a hard-ass, but it became undeniably evident that she was in pain. When she abruptly fled, her pale face in obvious distress, for the restroom attached to her office, I knew I had to give a little.

Gazing at the empty doorway after they've already gone, I can't deny my lingering concern. The possibility that I played a role in causing her to fall ill…well, it doesn't sit well with me.

With a glance down at the paper in my hand that holds our signatures, I hesitate a moment, as a part of me realizes how ridiculous it was to have to document an employee going home sick for the day. But I did this and…

No. I mentally shake off the errant thoughts trying to cloud my vision. *She* did this. She's the one who set this in motion years ago.

When the opportunity to purchase—and turn around—another business came along with the bonus of also being the workplace of Emma Jane Haywood, there was no way I could pass it up.

Now, I just need to keep my head in the game.

———

"STILL BUILDING YOUR EMPIRE?"

I exhale loudly. "It's called business, Wells," I reply as I talk to my best friend, Wells Kennedy, using my hands-free Bluetooth.

I turn left as I navigate my way through the streets of Midtown, Jacksonville to the house I closed on a few weeks ago. It'll serve as an income property once I finish all the improvements I have planned.

"It's called burying yourself in your work, living and breathing it, and never having an actual life."

"Is there a point to all this?" I ask in monotone.

"You're still trying to prove something, to prove to her that you—"

"That's enough." My tone is sharp with finality.

Wells falls silent on the other end, and I pull into my driveway. When I put the car into park, I lean my head back against the headrest and inhale deeply.

My friend's voice is subdued when he speaks again. "Look, I get it, but you and I both know that you haven't had any real relationships—nothing lasting—since *her*."

My eyes fall closed wearily. "And?"

"And," he leads in, his voice softening slightly, "I want to know if you'll finally be able to bury the past this time, when you're done undertaking *F&F*. Will you be able to move on from her once and for all?"

"Of course." I declare this with much more confidence than I feel.

For the remainder of the evening, long after Wells and I end our call, his words linger in my mind. *Will I be able to move on from her once and for all?*

I sure as hell hope so.

Knox

HIGH SCHOOL
TENTH GRADE

"Excuse me."

A prim and proper female voice interrupts me as I'm reaching inside my locker for my calculus book. Turning, I find Emma Jane Haywood standing there, eyeing me pointedly.

My lips curve into a wide smile. "Ma'am?"

She huffs out an annoyed breath, grasping the metal door of my locker and moving it from where it's fallen wide open, blocking hers.

"If your locker is right beside mine, could you possibly make some room for those on the"—she eyes me up and down critically, as if finding me distasteful—"leaner side?"

"Leaner?" I cock an eyebrow, which doesn't faze her the least. Figures. Her father owns, or had a hand in building, just about everything in Mobile. She probably had a golden pacifier as a baby. "I'll have you know"—I lean in toward her—"that I'm lean in some ways, but where it counts the most, I'm considerably *heavier*."

Her pupils dilate before she gasps in outrage and elbows me aside to get to her locker.

Watching her, I admire her profile as she manages to get her locker open and retrieve the necessary textbooks.

I lean down, bringing my lips to her ear and whisper huskily, "Same time tomorrow, EJ?"

Her head snaps around, and she narrows her eyes at me dangerously. "It's Emma Jane." To anyone else, they'd assume she was ticked off. But I know different. She's intrigued.

Slamming my locker shut, I wink at her before turning to head off to class. "Later, EJ."

I grin when she makes a frustrated noise. *Yep*, I chuckle silently, *I reckon she's into me.*

Then I promptly make a U-turn when I realize I'm headed in the wrong direction for calculus.

7

Emma Jane

Present
JULY

"It's about time you called me, Sweet Pea. I was beginning to wonder if you'd forgotten all about this dapper young man."

I grin at the sound of my granddad's voice. With my cell phone at my ear, I exit the café located in the lobby of our office building, my large latte in hand and briefcase strap draped over my other shoulder.

"Now, who is this dapper young man you're referring to? I can't say that I recall knowing anyone like that…" I trail off, teasing.

"Ah, my dear girl." He chuckles softly, and I'm bombarded with exactly how much I miss him.

It's a blessing he's in good enough health to fly in and visit me from time to time since I haven't been back to Mobile since that fateful day. But I miss going to see him at his house, the Haywood Mansion. After my grandmother passed away, he'd opened the mansion up to events, claiming he wanted to see life take over the home once again. My grandmother had loved to entertain and throw parties, and by holding weddings and reunions and such gatherings there, he always said it made him feel closer to her.

Sobering as I near the bank of elevators, I consider the other employees nearby before I lower my voice. "Have you heard who took over?"

The silence that greets me on the other end tells me everything I need to know. Quickly checking the time, I see that I have a few minutes to spare so I step off to the side where there's slightly less foot traffic and listening ears.

"Granddad," my tone is hushed, "why didn't you say anything?"

"It wasn't my place."

Heaving out a frustrated sigh, I shake my head. "You didn't think it was your place to tell me, your own granddaughter, that the guy who ripped my heart to shreds would be my new boss and owner of the company?"

He simply sighs in return. "Sweet Pea. Y'all have to work things out on your own. I can't interfere."

Right. We always come back to this. Grandma had always preached about fate and not intervening, letting it work itself out.

Granddad still believes Knox and I will, someday, work out our differences. One would think after eight years, he'd realize it wasn't going to happen.

"Other than that, how are things? How's Becket doing?"

At the mention of my best friend, my shoulders feel less weighted down. "He's great. Working hard as always."

"Ah, he's a good man." I can hear the smile in Granddad's voice.

My brow furrows as a curious thought dawns on me.

"Granddad? Why haven't you ever asked about me and Becket and whether we're dating?"

"Because I know you're not." His answer comes readily before his tone softens. "And because you're meant to be with someone else, of course."

Of course, I muse internally with a touch of sarcasm.

He quickly changes gears, inquiring about my upcoming work projects. Before I know it, it's time for me to head up in the elevator and I end our call since I'll lose cell signal.

For the entire ride up to my floor, his words run on a loop in the back of my mind.

"And because you're meant to be with someone else, of course."

"ALISSA *WHAT?*"

This is one of those times when I hear what the other person says—loud and clear—but I'm far too deep in shock for the words to register.

"Alissa went into premature labor so they're monitoring her at the hospital right now. She's officially on maternity leave." Alissa's friend Jackie, who works down on the eighth floor, offers a sympathetic smile.

Probably because she knows I'm barely keeping up with the workload Knox's dumped on me as it is. Without my assistant, I'm up a creek without a paddle.

But this pales in comparison to Alissa, of course. Damn. This stress is making me selfish now, too.

"But she's doing okay?"

"Oh, yes," Jackie answers. "She's just on bedrest and they're ensuring she and the baby are all right."

"Thank goodness." Especially since Alissa's not due for another month.

"Well, I've got to get back to work. I just wanted to be sure you knew."

She backs away hesitantly, as if she senses my growing sense of despair. As if I'll suddenly decide to hold her prisoner and saddle her with some of this work.

Which isn't such a bad idea now that I consider it.

"Bye, Ms. Haywood." Damn. Jackie darts down the hallway. So much for that idea, even if it's dripping in pure desperation.

The stack of files sitting on my assistant's desk draws my attention, and my entire body slumps as if recognizing defeat.

Looks like this is going to be a really long Thursday.

"I KNOW I'm supposed to be on board with the whole, 'Oh, our boss is the big, bad Grinch,' thing, but can I please have a quick time-out on that?"

I eye Madison over the rim of my coffee cup as we sit in the company café on what she deemed an "enforced ten-minute break" for me, but begrudgingly heed her request. "Go ahead."

She nods. "Okay then." With a quick glance around, she leans in closer and lowers her voice. "If I were on the market for a man—"

I frown in confusion. "Which you are."

She holds up a finger. "If I were on the market for a man who's crazy handsome, has a sexy broodiness, and can rock a suit like nobody's business, I'd be all over Knox Montgomery like white on rice."

At her extended pause, I raise my eyebrows in expectation. "But?"

Madison scowls. "Well, obviously I can't because he's

off-limits since he gets all Grouchy Smurf on you."

As it turns out, she's never witnessed an interaction between Knox and me, so she only has my account to go by.

Amused, I tip my head to the side. "Are you finished?"

She scrunches her nose in consternation. "I think so."

"Well…" I exhale wearily, covering my face with my hands after noting the time. "I have to head back upstairs and get to work."

"That would be a wise choice, Ms. Haywood." The deep voice causes me to jerk in alarm, and my hands drop from my face to land in my lap.

The instant my gaze locks with his, I find myself drowning in the same pair of green eyes that were once filled with love.

Now, however, they're filled with cool disdain. And even after all this time, there's a sharp pinch in the center of my chest, as if my heart still recognizes the man who broke it.

Mentally shaking off the melancholy, I rise from the chair and push it in and Madison follows suit, her eyes volleying nervously between Knox and me.

I force myself to maintain cool confidence as I stride past him without a word.

As Madison and I toss our empty coffee cups in the trash bin at the door before exiting the coffee shop, she whispers, "Never mind. I get it now." She lets out a disgruntled sound as we head to the elevators to take us to our designated floors. "Another corporate suit without a personality."

We enter the empty elevator car and press the numbered buttons for our floors. She looks over at me with an odd expression, as if she wants to say something but is unsure.

"Go ahead. Say whatever you're thinking."

Her lips twist in hesitation before she exhales loudly. "I just swear I felt something else in that interaction back there."

Instantly, my spine stiffens in alarm, but I don't respond, and Madison presses on.

"Like there's a tension that isn't simply dislike. Like it's se—"

The sound of the elevator arriving at her floor interrupts, and I can't withhold the tiny breath of relief that spills past my lips.

Unfortunately, my friend catches my little tell as she exits the elevator. She places her hand on the doors to stop them from closing and eyes me curiously.

"You're not telling me something."

I press my lips thin to contain the words practically fighting their way out. But now is not the time or place. So, all I can offer my friend is a simple, "Later."

Understanding, she nods with an encouraging smile. "Go show Grouchy Smurf how Haywood rolls." She backs away and the elevator doors begin to close.

Laughing, I smile. "Will do."

Once I'm enclosed within the quiet confines of the elevator and it begins ascending, I sag against the wall as weariness washes over me.

I should have gotten a few extra shots of espresso in my coffee.

"I OWE YOU BIG TIME, TIM."

"Enough to get me box seats to the Super Bowl?"

I can't restrain a smile. "I'll see what I can do. Fingers crossed the Jags make it that far."

"Ah, don't doubt our boy's team now," Tim says playfully. "Anyway, I'll get everything taken care of, Emma Jane. And don't work too late tonight."

"Thanks, again." I press the button on my desk phone to disconnect the speakerphone. I can't, in all honesty, promise not to work too late because, as I take account of the vast number of files on my desk, I know I'll be here far too late.

I'd contacted Tim in our legal department, because I'd needed some assistance with a few of these contracts. He's been helping me out, going above and beyond.

I think he could hear in my voice, when I called him earlier, that I was on the cusp of becoming a blubbering mess if I didn't get a little assistance with everything. But I can't let Knox find out I'm struggling because I know he'll take that as me not being able to hack it and immediately dismiss me from being eligible for that promotion. Or worse, he'll fire me.

Walking around my desk, I petulantly grab the daisy from the vase sitting on my table, and give in to my childish urge. While plucking the white petals one by one, I murmur beneath my breath, "Stab him in the junk, don't stab him in the junk, stab him in the junk, don't stab…"

When the final petal drifts to settle with the others on my table, I'm not satisfied with the verdict.

With a weary sigh, I return to the chair at my desk, massage my temples, and take a sip of my now-tepid coffee to try to give myself a necessary jolt of energy.

It's nearly five o'clock and I'm nowhere near where I need to be, progress-wise. Knox has enforced a weekly update each Friday morning to prove I haven't been slacking. I still have a dozen more proposals to finish, yet I find myself dragging, mental exhaustion beginning to take over.

There isn't enough coffee in the world for today.

8

Knox

"Mr. Montgomery, you have a call on line one from a gentleman who says he's your granddad?"

The questioning lilt to my secretary's voice over the telephone intercom causes the corners of my mouth to tip up.

Especially since my own grandfather had passed away years ago.

"Thanks, Karen."

I grab the receiver of my desk phone and dial line one. "I wasn't aware I had a granddad."

A jolly laugh greets my ears in return. "Now, son, you know you've had one since the day my granddaughter decided you were good enough to date."

His referral causes my entire body to tense, and that nagging ache in the center of my chest to kick in again.

"Are you calling to talk business or…" I trail off, hoping the old man will grant me a reprieve.

"Just wanted to check in. It's been a few months since we last talked." His tone isn't necessarily reprimanding so much as it contains a subtle layer of guilt.

"I've been up to my eyeballs with work, trying to turn this place around, but"—I run a hand down the length of my tie wearily—"I should've called."

"Now, son"—he chuckles lightly—"I know you've been busy. I just don't want you to lose sight of the reason you're there."

Bristling at his words, I can't help the scowl that comes over my face. My voice is clipped and there's no disguising the defensiveness in it. "This place was operating like a sieve and I'm turning things around."

My response is greeted with a beat of silence.

"Is that why you're really there?"

Swiveling my desk chair around to face the expanse of windows overlooking the St. Johns River, I stare blindly at the traffic traveling over the Acosta Bridge.

"Sometimes, perspective comes with time."

A derisive sound spills from my lips. "You sound like a fortune cookie now."

"Ah"—he chuckles—"but it's accurate."

"Not in this case," I mutter.

He sighs. "Knox, just..." He hesitates slightly. "Try to remember that not everything is what it seems."

I release an exasperated breath. "I'm sorry, but I need to get back to work." I can't do this with him. I respect the old man, but it doesn't mean I want to listen to him drone on with cryptic comments.

"I understand, son. I'll let you go. But"—his tone softens—"do try to stay in touch better, please?"

My shoulders slump because I know I've been slacking. "Yes, sir."

"I'll look forward to talking to you soon."

"Likewise, Granddad." My lips part to say goodbye, but before I can do so, he interjects gently.

"Remember to make your father proud."

That's the nail in the coffin.

"*SHIT!*" I mutter beneath my breath and toss down my pen.

Shoving away from my desk, I scrub a hand down my face. My palm rasps faintly against the short strands of my beard. I've been staring down at the same damn papers for God knows how long, my mind overloaded with conflicting thoughts.

My concentration went up in flames as soon as I ended the call with Granddad. The simple mention of my father, the man who'd left me to inherit two of his businesses with the stipulation that I complete my college education, causes the weight of guilt to wash over me and linger with a nagging persistence.

My father would never have approved of my plans. He certainly wouldn't approve of the way I'm doing things—with how I'm handling Emma Jane and holding her position over her head.

Shooting up from my seat, I stride over to the office windows and brace my palms flat against the glass. I peer down at the glow of lights from businesses and cars, both the Main Street and Acosta Bridges alit now that the sun has finally set.

Yet here I am. Still at work by nightfall. Leaning my forehead against the cool glass, I let my eyes fall closed with a sigh.

"Remember to make your father proud."

If I'm going to do that, I know exactly where I need to start.

And sending an email won't do.

Quickly, I shut down my computer and pack up before locking my office door. Once I'm in the elevator, instead of pressing the button that would take me to the parking deck, I press a different floor.

One that will take me to a certain brunette's office.

Strolling down the hallway, the silence is near deafening, and I realize what an idiotic idea leaving a quick handwritten note for her is.

My first surprise is the discovery of light spilling out from beneath her closed office door. Still, nothing could have prepared me for the sight that greets me when I knock softly before turning the handle and opening the door.

It stops me dead in my tracks. For more than one reason.

The sight I'm faced with is a testament to how hard I've been pushing her. Emma Jane's head lies on one arm upon her desk, hair the color of mahogany falling around her in soft waves, and there's a shadowing of dark circles beneath her eyes. Her pale red lips are parted ever so slightly, and there's a slight crease between her brows, as if she's worrying about something even while asleep.

I've caused this. I've made her exhausted to this extent, yet determined not to leave her job in fear of losing it.

Her granddad is right. My father, the man I've always emulated and looked up to, wouldn't be proud in the least. That's a truth I can no longer deny.

I draw to a stop a foot away from her. My throat grows tight the longer I gaze down at her. There's no denying I still find her incredibly beautiful. That small, extremely subtle diamond stud on the side of her nose makes the corners of my mouth tip up. I recall exactly when she'd decided to do that and how furious her father had been.

"You can't do this," I murmur to myself beneath my breath, my attention still riveted by the sleeping woman within arm's reach.

Fuck. The protective wall I'd built up against her is rapidly crumbling like a damn landslide. What had been a firm, solid foundation for my anger, resentment, and—most of all—hurt, is disintegrating. Because I know without a doubt, I don't want to come out of this hating myself, nor can I stomach the idea that my father's looking down on me with utter disappointment.

With a sigh of heavy resignation, I know what I need to do next.

9

Emma Jane

Someone is smoothing back my hair from my face in a delicate caress.

"EJ, wake up," a male voice whispers huskily. My sluggish brain vaguely registers the fact that this voice sounds familiar.

My eyes slowly flutter open, and I discover a sideways Knox, peering down at me. Except this is a deep contrast to how he normally regards me. There's no mask in place. No barrier. His expression is unguarded and it's almost like it used to be.

Then, my sleepy haze subsides and I realize where I am.

And the fact that my new boss has discovered me sleeping on the job.

Snapping to an upright position, I run my hands over my hair in an attempt to ensure I'm not too terribly mussed-looking.

"I, uh, I'm sorry. I was just going over the…" I trail off, tossing a frenzied glance down at the name listed on the file lying on my desk: Jags stadium. "The account for the

Jags stadium," I finish, trying to infuse more confidence in my tone.

Knox takes a step back and slips his hands into his pockets. "Go home, Emma Jane. It's late."

My eyes dart to the clock on the wall. *Seven o'clock.*

Holy crap.

"Oh no." I scramble for my cell phone sitting off to one side of my desk.

I was supposed to meet Becket for dinner. Scrolling through my phone, I see the text and voicemail notifications that I evidently didn't hear during my unplanned nap.

Becket: Hey, I'm sorry, but I have to cancel for dinner. I'm wrecked from trying to beat Dax's best sprint time. I should have known better than to challenge that dude. Rain check on dinner, though, and I'll be sure to take you to Luigi's, and you get all the prosecco you want.

My lips curve up slightly at Becket's words.

"Everything okay?"

Letting out a slow exhale, I nod. "I thought I'd stood up Becket for dinner but he—"

Wait. Why am I even bothering to tell him anything?

"I'd better head home."

"Right." Knox looks like he wants to say something, but instead, he turns around and quietly exits my office.

I pack up my things and slip my briefcase over my shoulder, grabbing my keys to lock up my office. Stepping out, I pull the door closed and lock it. Just as I turn around to head down the hallway leading to the bank of elevators, I find a man standing before me.

My hand flies to my chest in alarm. "Sweet mother of —You scared me!"

"Sorry." Knox offers a smile that hovers between hesitant and sheepish. "I, uh, figured I could walk you out and make sure you're safe." He waves a hand, gesturing to the empty offices and cubicles around us. "Especially since this place is a ghost town now."

"Um, sure. Thanks." I start down the hall.

We enter the elevators and ride down the eleven floors in silence and I find myself attempting to concentrate on the sound of the nineties pop hit traveling softly through the speaker above us. Anything to get my mind off my proximity to Knox, to how good he still smells even after a full workday, to his mere presence and the heady awareness I always have of him.

The doors of the elevator open and a huff of breath escapes me as I step out into the parking deck, intent on making it free and clear of him and this strange pull he still has on me.

"Good night, Mr. Montgomery." My heels click in rapid staccato on the cement.

"Emma Jane." The way he utters my name, not as a question, but more of a command to stop. Yet it's also laced with something more.

I draw to a stop, my back still to him. "Yes?"

"Would you like to have dinner?"

With you? I question internally. *Why?*

"We can discuss work, if you like."

My shoulders droop fractionally because the last thing I want to do is discuss work, let alone with the owner of the company where I'm employed. My exhaustion is bone-deep.

My lips form the start of a polite refusal. "N—"

"Or we can just be two people who happen to be

exhausted after a long day of work, who are starving and don't really want to…eat alone."

It's that right there that does it. That infinitesimal facet of vulnerability in his voice gets me. Like he knows exactly how lonesome it can be to eat alone.

But I need to be smart. I can't fold like a deck of cards.

Shaking my head, I pivot slightly and eye him with wariness. "I don't think that's wise," I say slowly.

"Please?" He waves a hand in gesture. "We can go to a crappy fast food place if it makes you more comfortable."

I study him, trying to determine what his game plan is, yet come up with…nothing.

Except the sound of my stomach rumbling angrily.

Nodding, I tip my head to the far left. "My car's right over there. I can follow you."

"My truck's here." He waves, indicating a black truck parked a few yards away.

"Okay."

"Okay," he parrots softly, a small smile playing on his lips.

Breaking the spell, I turn back in the direction of my vehicle. "See you in a few."

Knox

HIGH SCHOOL
TENTH GRADE

"You can't possibly be serious."

"As serious as Ms. Franny when she makes her collard greens and cornbread." Hell, at the mention of the woman who has a small street side café in downtown Mobile and side dishes people travel far and wide to partake in, my mouth waters.

I've just asked Emma Jane Haywood out.

Well, I've asked to take her night fishing with me.

She stares at me as if I'm a few sandwiches short of a picnic. "Night fishing?"

"Yes, ma'am." I use my smile on her, the same one ladies seem to have a weakness for. God knows, it helped me when I forgot to finish my project last semester in geometry class.

Something's wrong, though, because that same smile has zero effect on Emma Jane.

I run a hand through my hair nervously, only to panic

that maybe I've messed it up and now it's doing something crazy.

"Night fishing." I tip my head to the side and try harder on my smile. "Out on the bay. I'll bring some of my mom's potato salad."

Her eyes grow squinty. "You do realize that everyone knows night fishing means making out?"

"You say that like it's a bad thing," I tease, acting offended. "I brush and floss daily."

Emma Jane makes a frustrated sound and shakes her head, muttering while she rummages through her locker for her books. "Sweet Jesus, give me strength."

Finally finding what she needs, she withdraws it and slams her locker shut with astounding force. Then she whirls around on me, her eyes alit with fiery indignation, and it causes me to take a step back.

"You want to go night fishing?"

I glance around, unsure if this is a trick question. "Yes," I answer slowly.

"Fine." She holds up a finger when my lips part to respond. "But know this, Knox Montgomery. I will be taking part in the fishing, and there will be *no* kissing involved."

I think she's done, but when my lips part again, she holds up that index finger once more.

"And if I not only catch more fish than you, but also don't let you under my skirt, you can't pout and leave me out there alone to find my own way home."

"*What?*" I can't help but stare at her as if she's lost her mind. "I would never…" The expression on her face, the flicker of hurt that crosses it, tells me that's happened to her.

What kind of dick would… *Oh, shit*. I know exactly what kind of dick would do that. It explains the shit talking in the locker room after practice a few months ago. I'd wondered why she and Patrick Hallerton had broken up so abruptly.

"Repeat after me." She raises her eyebrows, and damn, I love the way she gets stern and serious with me. "No kissing and no leaving me."

"No leaving you and no open-mouth kissing."

Her lips form a thin line and if I wasn't paying close attention, I'd miss the signs of the faintest quiver at the corners. "Knox."

I take hold of the book and notebook she has in her hands. She doesn't immediately release her grip until I tug again.

"What are you doing?"

Placing her items on my own stack, I wink at her. "You should know when a gentleman is about to carry your books and escort you to class."

"But your next class is all the way—" She stops abruptly and looks away.

But she's already given herself away.

Grinning down at her, I nudge her playfully. "Ah, now how do you know where my next class is?"

She refuses to answer, so as we fall into step, on the way to her English literature classroom, I continue. "Besides, I've been helping Mrs. Shermack organize her filing cabinets. She's a fan of gentlemanly acts, so she'll be cool if I'm a few seconds late, once I tell her I was escorting a lovely lady to class."

We get to the classroom entrance far quicker than I'd like. Emma Jane is the first girl to make me antsy to be around her. I figured she wasn't actually a snob, but skittish after her relationship had ended with Patrick. And I'm sure my reputation with the ladies isn't helping things.

She turns to me, eyeing me expectantly, and reaches out for her books.

I raise and hold them single-handedly out of her reach, raising my brows. "Agree to go night fishing with me."

"Agree to no kissing," she counters.

"I agree to no open-mouth kissing."

When she scowls at me, I add, "No open-mouth kissing, certainly no leaving you, and I'll bring my mother's potato salad and my famous pork ribs." Another thought hits me. "Also, I think you should reconsider using the saying 'under my skirt' because I'm pretty sure it belongs back in the 1950s."

She rolls her eyes before suddenly creasing her brow. "Wait. You have famous pork ribs?"

I nod. "One taste and you'll never want to let me out of your sight." I pause and don't know why I softly tack on, "It was my dad's recipe."

Her features soften and she lays a hand on my arm. "I was really sorry to hear about your dad."

I flash a weak smile because, even though it's been a year, it still sucks losing him unexpectedly to a heart attack. "Thanks."

The warning bell rings, alerting us that we only have a minute before the final bell will ring and class will start.

Her gaze searches mine and she rolls her lips inward before finally saying, "Saturday. I can only stay out until eleven thirty."

My mouth stretches into a wide grin, and I hand her books to her. "Deal."

As she accepts them from me, I quickly lean down and kiss her cheek.

Her eyes flick up to mine in surprise, and I back away, excitement and anticipation pulsing through my veins at her acceptance of our date.

"I can't wait 'til Saturday."

I turn and head off to class with the biggest smile on my face and the strangest feeling rushing through me.

Dad once told me he knew my mom was the one for him but couldn't explain it. He simply *knew*.

I feel like I've embarked on that same discovery just now. Because the exact moment I pressed my lips to the smooth, silky soft skin of Emma Jane's cheek, a sensation ran through me with a faint whisper echoing through my mind telling me she's "the one."

10

Knox
PRESENT

"What the hell are you doing? Dinner?" I mutter disgustedly to myself.

I have a white-knuckled grip on the steering wheel of my truck as I navigate through downtown Jacksonville. My eyes flicker to the rearview mirror to ensure Emma Jane's still following me.

I'd be lying if I said parts of me aren't conflicted—one part hopes she isn't behind me and one part praying she is.

Blowing out a long breath, I turn on the radio, instantly scowling when the song that comes on is The Script's "Nothing." A song that I'd listened to far too many times to count, the lyrics were seemingly written for me, speaking of still being in love with a woman and wishing he could somehow make her change her mind, and take him back…

I shake off the bothersome thoughts and pull up to the new restaurant I'd stumbled upon a few weeks ago. It overlooks the St. Johns River and the nearby bridges with their eye-catching lighting.

Parking, I exit my truck, lock it, and walk over to where

Emma Jane's parked. Her door opens and I'm instantly faced with the sight of her sleek, tanned legs. She clearly favors open-toed heels, and my breath catches as she exits the vehicle in the wraparound style dress that, while professional in appearance, hugs her curves perfectly.

I clear my suddenly dry throat before gesturing toward the restaurant. "I assume you've been here before?" *With Becket*, I silently tack on to the end.

"Actually, I haven't. Though I've heard great things about it." A smile plays at the corners of her lips. "Surprised he hasn't dragged me here since he's big on eating healthy."

Right. *He*, automatically meaning Becket.

My mouth flattens into a thin line at the mention of the other man. "Well, you'll be able to tell him all about it." Tipping my head in the direction of the restaurant, I wave for her to precede me. "Shall we?"

I'm sure it's wishful thinking on my part, but I swear there's a softness, a tinge of affection that crosses her features when she responds.

"We shall."

"I THINK I've managed to eat my weight in the form of the salmon poke bowl."

Emma Jane leans back in her seat, folding her hands across her flat stomach while wearing a lazy smile on her lips. Her empty bowl is a testament to how hungry she'd been.

"Glad you enjoyed it."

She laughs softly. "I guess that's what happens when you forget to eat lunch."

My face drops with dismay at the additional reminder

that I'm the reason she's pushing herself so hard. She must recognize how I interpreted her words because her eyes go wide and her lips part.

I hold up a hand to stop her. "Don't." With a derisive sound, I lift a shoulder in a half shrug. "It's my fault for putting so much on you. Especially when you're going at it alone, without an assistant."

She averts her gaze, and peers down at the linen-covered table for a moment. Reaching out a hand, she traces an index finger through the condensation on her water glass, and flashes a forced smile. "I'd be lying if I said it hasn't been a bit challenging."

"I was thinking about that, actually." I lean forward, resting my forearms on the table. "The intern, Keri Mitchell, might be able to help you with the workload. She has to finish assisting with another department before I can move her, but…"

Emma Jane's blue eyes lock with mine, and a mixture of surprise and relief lines her features. "I would appreciate that," she responds slowly, almost cautiously.

Nodding, I take a sip of water, attempting to stave off this sudden feeling of nervousness. "No problem."

Emma Jane's lips part. "I—"

"Would either of you care for anything else?" the waitress inquires kindly.

I look at Emma Jane in silent question, and she shakes her head with a polite, "No, thank you." I echo her response, and reach for my wallet.

"Oh! Wait, I can—"

The waitress takes my credit card and darts away, while I level a look at Emma Jane who appears at a loss.

"Consider it a business expense. A thank you for all your hard work."

She rolls her lips inward, as if unsure how to respond, before she murmurs, softly, "Thank you, Knox."

After we exit the restaurant and head to our vehicles, parting for the evening, I can't help but feel a tightness in my chest at the distressing knowledge that the night is drawing to an end.

Then I recall the fact that this is what Emma Jane does when it comes to me.

She walks away.

11

Emma Jane
AUGUST

"I need to know your current distribution numbers, please."

I'm on a conference call with Nike, discussing cross-promotion ads, typing notes as fast as possible when a subtle noise draws my attention.

Knox enters my office, laptop beneath his arm, the sleeves of his deep-blue dress shirt rolled up to just below his elbows, no suit jacket, and those neatly tailored pants accentuating his slim physique.

So distracted by his sudden presence, I nearly miss what he has in his other hand.

A single daisy in a vase.

Without giving me so much as a glance, he casually slides the vase onto my table. Absently, I realize that it's my vase which I hadn't noticed was missing. He must have snagged it when I wasn't in my office and dumped the wilted, dying flower that had been in it since I'd been far too busy to remember to stop by the florist to replenish it.

The fact that he remembered, though, is exceedingly unsettling.

"Emma Jane?"

My head snaps around at the voice coming through my speakerphone and it takes me a moment to comprehend that I'd zoned out from the call.

"Y-yes." I frantically flip through my brain like an old-school Rolodex, filtering through what is being discussed on the other end of this call.

Jackpot.

"*F&F* can offer a greater audience range, especially according to the latest surveys. The women who are starting out on their fitness journey can be intimidated by the extremely fit women portrayed in your ads. However"—I rise from my chair, gesturing with my hands as I hit my stride—"with our cross-promotion, utilizing our models, and integrating your merchandise, I believe we could have an ad set that's relevant and engaging not only to readers, but also to your potential and current customers."

Out of the corner of my eye, I notice Knox's attention is centered on me with its full, unnerving weight.

Fifteen more minutes pass before the call finally wraps up, after we decide the next step will be to have our legal departments work together to finalize our agreement. It's only then I release a long, slow exhale, still staring down at my desk phone.

After a moment, it happens. It hits me.

I've managed to tentatively secure a deal with Nike for cross-promotion. Something that no one else has been able to accomplish.

Sure, it won't be official until the ink is dry, so to speak, but I can't help but feel a sense of pride at this accomplishment.

"That was remarkable, to say the least."

Knox's remark draws me from my internal happy

dance and my eyes lock with his. I detect something within the depths of his green gaze that makes me think he's impressed.

But it's the slight hint of softening I'm beginning to feel toward him that makes me uneasy. Because it doesn't change anything—it doesn't change his game plan.

My future with this magazine is still on the line.

Tearing my attention away from his perusal, I take a seat and compose an email to Tim in legal, attaching my notes. While typing, I address Knox. "I'm going to give Tim these notes and finalize my part and then we can go over the new media proposal."

"Take your time." His response is low, deep, and husky sounding. Intimate almost.

Focus, I reprimand myself. *Don't let him distract you.*

Finally, once the email's sent off to Tim, I pull up my files for the new media proposal between *Fit & Fashion* and one of the big television networks.

I'd been trying to grease the wheels for the past few years to set this deal in place. I'd been speaking with Coastal Media representatives about well-placed television ads featuring *F&F*. Now that our deal will soon be finalized with Nike, barring any major snags, it makes this deal look all the more appealing to Coastal Media. It gives us that powerful thing called *leverage*. Because if we're good enough for Nike to partner with…

"All right." I direct my attention to Knox as I stand, walking over to my table with my laptop and the other file in hand. "I wanted to discuss this section with you…"

Four Hours Later

He Loves Me...Knot

"HOLY CRAP." I let out a long exhale and lean back from the table scattered with papers and both our laptops. My eyes shift to rest on Knox beside me. "I think we just came up with a pretty incredible proposal."

My lips curve slowly into a grin that widens further when he mirrors my excitement, a handsome smile spreading across his face. There's something odd about seeing him with a beard. I'm slightly bereft at how it masks the face I'd once come to know so well. Yet, it also emphasizes the fact that he's different now. Like a stranger.

"I'd have to agree with you."

It's as though neither of us can bear to break the connection. To break the tenuous truce. Because I know he's going above and beyond to help me while I'm down an assistant. Yet I have to force myself to ignore that little flip my stomach gives when he looks at me this way.

I must remember who he is and what happened that June day. I must remember how he eviscerated my heart, my hopes for a future—my hope for a future with *him*.

Shaking off the moment, I avert my eyes and glance at the clock. "I should head home. It's really late."

"Right." His hurried response tells me he's feeling a bit thrown off as well.

"Well, why don't I—"

"How about I—"

We both shift out of our seats, leaning forward, reaching for a particularly hefty file situated between us on the table. Drawing to a sudden halt when our fingers make contact, I realize how close we've become, the nearing proximity of our faces.

My gaze travels over his face, along that strong, chiseled jawline, and when Knox's lips part, my breathing stutters. Because these lips once loved me, once caressed every single inch of my body. These lips once whispered naughty things while—

"Answer your phone, hot stuff."

We jerk apart at the sound of Becket's voice on the special ringtone he recorded for my phone. Damn him. I'd forgotten I'd turned on the ringer during lunch. I hadn't wanted to run the risk of missing his scheduled call to tell me the news about the gender of Presley's baby, knowing he'd be over the moon and dying to tell me.

Knox's expression clouds as Becket repeats himself, demanding that I answer my phone.

"Hey, Beck." I inwardly cringe at how breathless my voice sounds.

"Hey." There's a pause before he speaks, and his voice is lower, hushed. "Did I interrupt something?"

"No. Not at all." My words come out rushed in short, staccato bursts. "Just finishing up with work."

Crap. He's going to see right through this.

"Blue…" His tone sounds odd, teetering between amusement and concern. He lets out a loud sigh. "Just tell me you're being smart."

"Totally. I'm about to head home."

"We're still on for our FWOB night tomorrow?"

I can't resist a smile. Our Friends Without Benefits night out started as a joke but it somehow stuck. We get together and discuss the challenges of finding a normal person to date; one who wouldn't immediately try to sell a story to the paparazzi, in Becket's case or, in mine, one who wouldn't find himself intimidated by me being so driven in my career.

"All set for tomorrow. You promised me Luigi's, remember?"

"Of course, I do." I hear the smile in his voice. "Be careful heading home. I'll call you in a bit to make sure you made it home safely. We can firm up plans for tomorrow and I'll tell you about that gala I'd mentioned."

"Sounds good. Bye."

"Later, Blue."

Once I end the call, my eyes fall on Knox, and I find him studying me carefully. Redirecting my focus, I busy myself, gathering everything from the table and placing it neatly on my desk.

"Well." I hear Knox rise from his chair and snag his laptop from the table. "I've got to get my things and head out. I'll, uh…" He hesitates, and I lift my eyes to see him shift his stance, as if he's nervous. Sliding a free hand into his pocket, the other arm holds his slim laptop, and he tips his head to the side. "I can walk you out."

"That's not necessary."

"I think Becket would agree that it is," comes his quick response. The slightest smile tugs at his lips, and he gives a little shrug. "And I'd rather not have an NFL quarterback after me if something happened to you."

I press my lips thin and try to scrounge up an excuse, but come up empty. Finally, I nod. "Okay."

"Okay," he repeats softly before he exits my office.

Only after his soft footfalls on the carpeted hallway fade do I allow myself to slump back into my desk chair with a loud exhale. Staring up at the ceiling, I whisper softly within the silence of my office.

"You've got to be smart, Emma Jane. You can't go soft just because he's suddenly being nice to you."

My eyes fall closed as I try to firm up my defenses against Knox Montgomery.

And when he arrives at my office door to escort me down to the parking deck, it would be a lie if I said I've succeeded.

12

Knox

WHAT THE FUCK AM I DOING?

This question is on repeat, flitting through my mind the entire walk back to my office. It continues as I pack up my belongings, and even while I make my way back to EJ—*er*, Emma Jane's office.

The damn lines are getting blurred, and I have no one to blame but myself. Still, there was no way in hell I could've stood by and allowed her to overwork herself to the point of sickness again. Because, regardless of our past, I never want to see her like that—so ill and devoid of the usual liveliness she possesses. Certainly not because of me.

In silence, we step onto the cement floor of the parking deck and, upon spotting her vehicle nearby, I continue walking in its direction. Noticing she's stopped, I pause and turn to her with a questioning look.

"This is your car, right?"

She doesn't immediately answer, her own gaze lifting to something past me before she pastes a tight smile on her face. "Yes. That's mine." With quick steps, she strides right past me and presses her key fob to unlock her vehicle.

I hasten my steps to catch up to her and reach out to open her door. Her eyes flicker to mine briefly before she mutters a subdued, "Thank you."

The way she moves, slipping her briefcase onto to the passenger seat of her car, the way the fabric of her dress stretches over her hips and molds her perfect ass, nearly elicits a groan from deep within me.

Running a hand down my face, I pinch my eyes closed briefly, attempting to regain composure.

"You don't have far to go, do you?"

Her question is odd, the slight hint of expectation in her tone. Regarding her carefully, I tip my head in the direction of my truck, the black GMC a few yards away.

"My truck's right over there."

Surely you recognize it, considering how many times you rode in it, a voice whispers internally. *Considering how many times you rode me in it.*

Fuck.

Emma Jane fidgets with her keys before offering me an overly bright smile. "Well, thanks for all your help. Have a good night."

"Night."

She slides inside her car, and I push her door closed, then step back as she starts the engine. With a small wave, I turn and head over to my truck. It takes every single ounce of willpower to resist turning back, to resist the urge to look behind me.

Though I succeed, as I fasten my seat belt, put my truck in gear, and exit the parking deck, I can practically feel my willpower eroding at an alarming rate.

Knox

HIGH SCHOOL
TENTH GRADE

"Knox," she protests breathlessly.

"I can't help it." I tug her closer as we lie back on the tailgate of my truck, snuggled in the large sleeping bag to ward off the slight chill in the night air. "I love kissing you." I dust another soft kiss over her lips. "Almost as much," I break off for another kiss and whisper, "as I love you."

Hesitantly, I lean back to peer down at her. My chest is painfully tight as I try to gauge her reaction.

It's been six months since she first agreed to go night fishing with me and we've basically been inseparable ever since. I walk her to class; she always waits for me to finish baseball practice, doing her homework as she sits in the bleachers when the weather permits.

Her eyes are wide and her lips, rosy from my kisses, part slightly. "Oh, Knox," she sighs.

"Is that an 'Oh, Knox, I love you, too'? Or an 'Oh,

Knox, you're an idiot'?" I prod, attempting to inject teasing into my voice.

The corners of her mouth tug upward, and with agonizing slowness, her lips form a smile.

"I love you, too." Her gently spoken words wash over me and a whoosh of relieved breath escapes from my lips.

Resting my forehead against hers, I let my eyes fall closed. "I love you so much, EJ."

She presses her mouth to mine and we get lost in the kiss, falling captive to the powerful euphoria of our love.

And I know deep within my soul that this girl is mine forever.

13

Emma Jane
PRESENT

"Beck," I complain, cradling my phone between my shoulder and cheek as I enter my condo. I quickly slip off my heels before setting my briefcase down on the dining room chair. "You said you wouldn't buy me another dress."

"I couldn't resist ordering it. Plus, it's for a good cause. You know I always go to the Mayo Clinic's fundraiser gala."

With a sigh, I shake my head. "You really need to find a girlfriend."

"Who needs a real girlfriend when I have you? You nag me enough that I feel like I have one," he jokes.

I roll my eyes. "Very funny."

Becket's tone sobers. "You know the Mayo Clinic's important for me."

"I know," I reply softly. He'd lost his mother to ovarian cancer years ago and the Mayo Clinic here in Jacksonville went above and beyond in helping to give Mrs. Jones more time with her sons before she finally succumbed to the disease.

"What's the date so I can mark it in my planner?"

I pull out the thick booklet, flipping to the designated month as Becket informs me, and jot down a quick reminder. As I slide the planner back inside my briefcase, a soft knock sounds at my door.

It's late, nearly eight thirty at night. "Becket?" I hiss quietly.

"Blue?" comes his exaggerated whispered response, laced with humor.

"Someone just knocked on my door," I whisper because while the management of these condos claim these units are "soundproof," they are not. At least not entirely.

"So check and see who it is." Becket hurriedly adds, "Through the peephole, of course."

I pad across the sleek hardwood floor to approach the door, and lift to my toes to peer through the peephole.

My entire body freezes, my heartbeat stuttering.

Knox Montgomery is on the other side.

Spinning around, my hand flies to my chest, palm flat over where my heart is pounding. "Becket!"

"Why do you keep whispering my name?" His voice is tinged with humor. "Are you trying to upgrade to friends *with* benefits?"

"Stop!" I hiss, rushing away to put more distance between myself and the door. I whirl around to stare at it in horror when another knock sounds. "He's here. At my *door*." I swallow hard and my anxiety increases when Becket doesn't immediately offer a response.

"I'm assuming I know who *he* is."

"You do."

"Huh," is all he says for a moment. "Well, I can tell you one thing for sure."

The mischief in his tone is evident and has me preparing for an eye roll.

He Loves Me...Knot

"And what's that?"

"He ain't a Jehovah's Witness wanting to talk about Jesus, nor is he deliverin' a welcome casserole or—"

Yes, I was right. Eye roll. "I got it."

"So open the door."

"But what does he—"

This time Becket cuts me off. "Well, Blue, when a man likes a woman—"

"I'm hanging up now."

I receive his husky laugh in response before he quickly utters a soft, "Blue, be careful, okay? Unfinished business can be tricky."

"I will," I utter softly. "Love you, Beck."

"Right back atcha."

I end the call and toss my phone on the couch just as another knock sounds on my door, this one softer, seemingly more tentative, almost half-hearted.

My feet carry me soundlessly to the door, and one hand grasps the cool metal of the door handle. My hand reaches up to unlock the deadbolt, and I cautiously open the door a crack.

My stomach gives that little lurch when I see him standing before me, still wearing the same clothes from earlier, perfectly tailored suit pants and button-down shirt with the sleeves rolled up. His dark hair appears mussed as though he's run his hands through it multiple times.

Emerald eyes lock with mine. "EJ."

I lean against the doorjamb, not opening the door fully, curious as to why he's here.

Scared as hell as to why he might be here.

"Knox." My voice comes out wispy, slightly breathless sounding.

He drags a hand through his hair and shoves the other

into his pocket. Shaking his head, he briefly glances down at his shoes before his eyes return to me.

"I don't know why I'm here...*no*." He shakes his head again with a deprecating quirk of his lips. "That's a lie. I know why I'm here."

His expression sobers, and his gaze, laden with barely veiled heat that radiates through me, nearly singes me with its intensity. "It's because there's still something here." He waves a hand, gesturing back and forth between us. "Something powerful and I don't know what it is, but for some reason I just need..." The urgency in his tone fades, and I find myself holding my breath, waiting for him to conclude his thought. There's a beat of silence before he finishes, and his tone is husky, holding a heartfelt tenderness. "You." He swallows hard, his eyes searching. "I need you."

Vulnerability lines his features as he waits for my response.

My words feel like they're lodged in my throat, so unsure whether I heard him correctly. Finally, I manage to speak and repeat his words with a questioning lilt at the end. "You need me?"

Slowly, he dips his head in a nod, his eyes locked with mine. "Yes."

"What about"—I break off with a slow exhale—"our..." *Past*, I silently tack on.

Knox steps closer and lays a palm against the doorframe. "I don't care." He leans in, bringing his lips a hairbreadth away from mine. "I just want you."

My eyes flicker between his lips and those green eyes, which watch me with intensity while I war with myself internally. Every part of me wants to give in, but a fraction of one. There's one part that continues in a standoff.

My heart. The one he shattered years ago.

The funny thing about the heart is that even *it* can be conflicting, because there's a tug-of-war happening within mine. One part vividly recalls Knox's betrayal and the pain he inflicted, while the other recalls just how much I loved him.

Startling Knox, I launch myself at him, flinging my arms around his neck. I tug him to me, and my lips collide with his in a tempestuously feverish kiss.

And it's clear which part of my heart won the battle.

14

Knox

THE MOMENT SEEMS to drag on for an eternity, watching various emotions flicker across her face while I wait for her response.

She's going to kick me to the curb, I know it. I shouldn't have come here. Shit, I sure as hell shouldn't have turned pseudo-stalker and gotten her address from her personnel file.

But I did, and there's no turning back now.

Just as I'm mentally trying to figure out a way to save face and determine how I'll make it through work days with her, she completely stuns me when she wraps her arms around me, tugs me close, and kisses me.

The second our lips meet, all bets are off. Neither of us hold back.

My hands thread through her silky hair, and I use the slight leverage to tilt her head to the side and deepen the kiss. I walk her backward, farther inside, and kick the door closed behind us.

She steers me back against the door and her hands are all over me. They graze along my shoulders, her palms gliding down the firm wall of my chest before slipping around to grip my ass—as if she's as overwhelmed with a fierce desperation to touch me, to revel in the feel of me again, as I am her.

I tug her closer and skim a hand down her body before slipping my fingers beneath the hem of her dress to toy with the thin strap of her thong at her hip.

When I rock my hardened length against her and she releases a tiny moan, this spurs me on as our tongues slide and stroke against one another, taking part in their own carnal war. I shift my hand to the front of her panties, and when I find them damp with her arousal, it sends another sharp burst of desire radiating through me.

Tearing my lips from hers, I trail wet kisses along the slim column of her neck as I slip a finger beneath the damp fabric of her thong, dipping inside her wet heat.

Holy shit. She's drenched, coating my finger as I work it in and out of her. I add a second, and her hands grasp my shoulders, clutching tightly as she throws her head back. Her lips part, her breath rushing out in tiny pants.

Looking down at her like this, my chest constricts. Her eyes flutter open. She peers up at me for a moment, and I can see the haze of lust ebb slightly. My movements still as I watch her, her teeth nibbling at the corner of her bottom lip, illustrating her sudden nervousness.

"Knox? Are you sure about this?"

I know what unspoken question she's posing.

But don't you hate me?

Right now, I'm sure about this. More sure than I've been about anything. Even if it's the dumbest fucking thing I do and will probably set me back in getting over her and finally moving past what she did. All I know is I don't want to leave. I don't want to go back to my place alone.

I don't want to pass up the chance to have one more moment like this with her.

As for her unspoken question, I don't know how she can't fathom just how impossible that is. Because even after everything that's transpired, one thing is certain.

I could never hate the only woman I've been able to picture as my wife.

I withdraw the hand that's threaded through the hair at her nape and move my palm to cradle the side of her face. My eyes lock with hers, and as I graze my thumb over her full bottom lip, I don't break eye contact.

"I'm sure." I search her expression. "Are you?"

I hold my breath, waiting for her answer. "I'm sure…" She averts her gaze, focusing on my lips. "Because it's a one-time thing."

Her eyes flicker up to mine, as if awaiting my reaction, my response, to affirm her statement.

A one-time thing. Although her words weren't spoken in a callous manner, they send shards of unease rolling through me.

"Right," I agree hollowly.

Her lips curve upward slightly, and she places both palms flat against my chest. Rising to her tiptoes, she presses a kiss to the side of my throat, near the base, and I suddenly feel my knees grow weak.

Long ago, she used to do that when we'd make love because she knew it was my "spot."

I flash a mischievous grin. "You didn't just do that."

Her smile widens, those beautiful eyes sparkling, as she taunts, "Oh, but I did."

"That's it." I bend slightly and scoop her up, tossing her over my shoulder in a fireman's carry, and revel in the little squeal she lets out. "You're playing with fire, and now you've got to pay the price." I punctuate this with a swat of

He Loves Me...Knot

her ass as I head down her hallway, finding what I assume is her bedroom.

"Knox!" she exclaims with a mixture of surprise and amusement.

Entering the room, I walk to the bed. The soft light from the moon cascading in through the small slats in the venetian blinds sets the room alight with a soft glow.

Gently laying her back on the bed, I quickly rid myself of my shoes and climb onto the bed to brace myself above her on my forearms.

I reach out to slide some stray strands of hair away from her face, and she peers up at me with a tender quality I hadn't realized I missed.

Dipping my head, I dust a light kiss across the bridge of her nose before I do the same to her lips. It's a soft, tender kiss; our lips graze against one another in a languid caress.

We continue like this until finally, her palms press against my chest, drawing me to a stop. My eyebrows arch in question.

She doesn't respond. Instead, she guides me to shift off her. Once I'm lying on my back, she straddles me, her fingers instantly going to work on the buttons of my shirt.

Her eyes take on a playful glint. "You won't be needing this."

My hands glide up her legs, bunching the material of her dress to bare her thighs and slide it up her body. She pauses in her task, raising her arms to rid herself of the fabric, leaving it to drop to the floor beside the bed.

And promptly robs me of my breath.

The black bra encasing her breasts has a lace border along the top edge, and when I finally manage to tear my eyes away to admire her stomach and lower, a laugh erupts from me.

Her panties are hot pink and have "I'm a badass on Fridays" printed on them.

She appears confused before looking down once she realizes what's caught my attention. With a slightly sheepish smile, she tips her head to the side. "Well, I kinda was today."

"Indeed, you were."

I drag my index finger between the hollow of her breasts and down the center of her flat stomach, then lower to toy with the waistband of her panties.

"I don't think we'll be needing these."

"You first." She tugs at the sleeve of my now unbuttoned shirt. I carefully lift and she helps rid me of it.

"And these"—a smile tugs at the corners of her lips as she rises to her knees, still straddling me, and unfastens my belt—"pants are completely unnecessary, too." Unbuttoning them, she glides the zipper down before gripping the waistband of my pants. "Lift up."

Her simple command sends a surge of arousal rushing through me, and I oblige, allowing her to remove my pants with my socks following suit, both joining our other clothes on the floor.

"I suddenly feel very underdressed." With one hand, I reach around to unclasp her bra.

"Still have that skill, huh?" Her eyes question me, though her tone is playful, recalling how I'd mastered it with her.

"Still have it."

Only with you, part of me wants to add.

Something shifts in the depths of her cerulean gaze, as if she wants to ask that same thing, as if she's wondering how many times I've exhibited this "skill" with other women. But I don't want that tonight. Don't want the past rearing its ugly head. I only want this moment.

Sliding the straps of her bra down her arms, I discard it and cup the weight of her breasts in my palms, reveling in the feel of her nipples tightening. When she arches her body to press more fully into my touch, something deep inside me snaps.

With one hand on her back, I guide her to lower herself, and I lift slightly, enabling my mouth to latch onto one of her nipples. I lave it with my tongue, suckling it, while I toy with her other nipple, gently plucking her hardened peak between my thumb and forefinger. Her fingers sift through my hair, tightening their grip of the short strands with a feverish desperation.

"Knox," she breathes out, her eyes fluttering closed as she rocks herself against me. I'm unable to resist a groan as I switch to her other nipple and suckle it. "That feels so good," she whispers.

Watching her unabashedly, I release her nipple from my lips, taking in her beauty. Then I drag my lips against her collarbone and murmur, "It'll feel so much better once I push inside that wet pussy while I suck on your nipples."

Her eyes flash open, lips parting on a gasp. And that's when I feel it. Even through the thin fabric of her panties and my cotton boxer briefs, I feel it.

The sudden rush of heated wetness.

From my words alone.

I know I'm playing dirty, but I can't help it. I recall with vivid clarity just how much my words—my dirty talk —would turn her on.

"Knox." That's all she has to say. One word. My name. That's all it takes, and instantly, I know what she needs.

Even after all the time that's passed, I know what she's saying.

She wants—needs—one thing.

Me.

15

Emma Jane

"Knox." My voice is laden with arousal because when he spoke those words, when he whispered those naughty things, it shifted things into high gear.

He'd always been incredible in bed, but I hadn't realized how much he'd turned me on with his dirty talk.

Suddenly, I'm flipped onto my back and stripped of my panties. Then he rids himself of his briefs before drawing our bodies closer in a fusion of heated flesh.

I can't recall anything that's ever felt this good, that's as decadent as the sensation of his body pressed against mine, all of his hard angles fitted against my softer, more lush body.

Our combined ragged breathing is the only sound in the quiet room before his mouth finds mine again in a feverish kiss. My hands glide over his body, and I'm frantic—this urge to touch every single inch of him is profoundly fierce.

He draws his lips away from mine, breaking our kiss to move down the length of my body and settle between my legs. Nudging them wider, his eyes lock with mine and when he cocks an eyebrow, I swear he's barely withholding a smirk full of wicked intent.

"I had dinner earlier, but I never did get my dessert."

He lowers his mouth to me, fastens his lips around my clit, and sucks it gently.

All without breaking eye contact.

When he slips a long, thick finger deep inside me, a loud gasp spills from my lips, and I grow even wetter. His beard abrades the skin of my inner thighs in the most decadent way.

Withdrawing his finger, he slides lower on the bed, and his words are low, gravelly, and unequivocally seductive. "I've got to taste you again." His tongue sweeps inside, delving as deep as he can, and I can't resist rocking against him. The sensation of his facial hair against my core as it brushes my most intimate parts sends delicious shivers down my spine.

My hands find my breasts, and I begin to toy with my hardened nipples while he tastes me, darting his tongue in and out. His thumb circles my clit and my inner walls tighten in anticipation of my release.

My eyes flutter closed, and my body arches as my breathing becomes more ragged as I near orgasm.

"Come for me." His hot breath washes against my skin. "Come on my tongue."

I suck in a sharp breath when his tongue delves inside me as his thumb works my clit feverishly, and my body gives in to the pleasure he's providing, clenching and releasing around his tongue. I writhe, shamelessly thrusting against his mouth, my fingers still plucking at my nipples.

Once the shudders begin to subside, my breathing still slightly staggered, Knox shifts to reposition himself above me. A bit unsure of what I'll find, I slowly open my eyes. But I should have known.

Some things never change.

Those lips of his are stretched in a wide, smug grin, his green eyes dancing. "Yep. Still got it."

With a roll of my eyes, I can't withhold the smile that breaks free. Half-heartedly, I shove against him. "Maybe it's not you. Maybe it's just that it's been a long—"

I break off abruptly, squeezing my eyes shut with a wince as my body tenses with the knowledge that I've just handed him ammunition.

Heck, I've given him the freaking Atomic bomb.

Here we go. I wait, still not brave enough to open my eyes, preparing for him to say something cocky and revel in my unexpected disclosure.

When his lips lightly skim across my forehead with a soft kiss, my eyes flutter open in surprise. I find him backing away to admire me with tenderness etched across his features.

"Same." His tone is subdued, husky, his vibrant green eyes holding mine. And it takes a moment for his response to sink in.

Wait a minute… Same? Same, as in, it's been a while since he's been with a woman?

I can't help myself. I stare up at him, practically gaping at his admission because, regardless of our tumultuous past, Knox has always been an incredibly attractive and sexy man. One who most assuredly never lacked female attention.

Before I can ponder it further, he lowers his head and drops a featherlight kiss to my lips before his mouth trails along my jawline, leading to my earlobe. His teeth toy with it as he murmurs soft, heady words. "You have no idea how hot you looked, touching yourself while I had my mouth on you." His sensual words send delicious shivers ricocheting through me. "I can't wait to slide"—he presses his hard length against me and I instinctively arch into his touch—"deep inside you." His lips continue dropping tiny, wet kisses along my neck and collarbone. "And feel you clench around my cock like you did my tongue."

My breath catches in my throat while my fists clench the bedsheets. "Then what are you waiting for?"

He leans back slightly, his features etched in surprise. "Well"—he grins—"look at who's getting all bossy."

I raise an eyebrow pointedly. "We're naked. In my bed. I think that automatically gives me the right to be bossy."

He smirks, and with a roll of his hips, his cock nudges my entrance. "Does it now?"

"If you don't hurry up and grab a—"

He shoots out an arm in the direction of my bedside table. "On it." Sliding the drawer open, he reaches in and immediately freezes, his eyes widening with what appears to be surprise. Slowly, he withdraws his hand from the drawer, a condom pinched between his thumb and forefinger.

My brow furrows. "Is there a problem?"

"This is all you have."

"What do you mean it's—" I stop, my lips forming an O. "You mean…"

"This is all you have," he repeats slowly.

One condom.

One. Single. Condom.

The universe is just cruel.

I offer a wry smile. "I guess this means you'd better make it worthwhile."

An indecipherable expression flickers across his face before his eyes crinkle at the corners. "Sounds like someone's already doubting me."

He rises to his knees, straddling me. Without breaking eye contact, he rips open the package and tosses the wrapper aside before focusing on the task of rolling the condom over the flared head of his cock and down the rigid length.

His intense appraisal holds me captive, the heat flaring within the depths as he guides himself to my entrance and presses inside fractionally, eliciting a faint gasp from me.

He lowers himself to rest his forearms on either side of me, and his hands cradle my face in a manner that's so reverent, it causes my heart to skip a beat.

"You're beautiful," he whispers before taking my mouth in a greedy kiss while simultaneously sliding deeper inside me. The combination of this—the all-consuming passion in his kiss, the way he presses deep and feels so perfect—propels me into a flurry of action.

Gripping his ass with my hands, I urge him deeper, undulating my hips. Our tongues seductively spar as he establishes a rhythm, thrusting in and out of me. One of his large hands cups my breast, and my nipple puckers more, reacting to his slightly calloused palm. He grasps my leg, just beneath the knee, and maneuvers it to drape over his shoulder, and the shift causes him to sink even farther inside me.

My lips part on a breathy moan, and my pleasure increases tenfold when I hear Knox's staggered breathing, his thrusts picking up speed. Bringing his lips to my neck, his voice is guttural, ragged with lust, as his hot breath fans against my skin. "Feels so fucking good..." His choppy breaths match my own now as I feel my body tense, fast approaching my orgasm. "God, I... *Fuck*."

Knox shifts to his knees, positioning both of my legs over his shoulders before he resumes thrusting. His movements are desperate, frenzied, and drive me right over the edge. My body stiffens right before I come apart, pleasure crashing over me in waves.

"Knox," I cry out, my inner muscles clenching around him as my hips writhe and I buck against him.

He manages to drive even deeper before succumbing to his own orgasm with a powerful shudder.

Once the slight trembling subsides, Knox gently releases my legs and drops down to brace himself above me on his elbows. A lock of hair slides over his forehead, and I'm taken aback at the sight of lingering hunger still present in his eyes.

A smile tugs at the corners of his mouth and when he dips his head to skim his lips against mine, a dangerous emotion radiates through me, causing my throat to constrict almost painfully.

There's a part of me that's grateful I had only one condom handy. Because if this is how I feel after sex with Knox after all this time, I have a pretty good idea what would happen if we went numerous rounds.

I'd be back to square one, and would find myself in love with a man who never really loved me.

Emma Jane

HIGH SCHOOL
SENIOR YEAR

"He loves me, he loves me not, he loves me, he loves me not..." My voice trails off when a muscled arm snakes around my waist and tugs me back against a firm, familiar body.

"He loves you."

I peer down at the white flower petals that remain on the daisy before tilting my head to look up at Knox when he adds, "Trust me."

"Is that so?"

"Woman," he growls playfully, spinning me around in the circle of his arms. He dips his head to kiss me softly. "I went dress shopping with you for prom. You *know* I love you."

My laughter brings an easy smile to his lips, and I know that I'd give anything in the world to make him smile like that for the rest of my days.

Suddenly sobering, I avert my gaze. "You'll have to leave soon for Auburn."

Heaviness hangs between us at the mention of him leaving for college. Knox received both academic and athletic scholarships to Auburn University and has to be settled in his dorm earlier than the average freshman due to the requirements for baseball conditioning. Auburn's about three hours away, and I'm sticking around to attend The University of South Alabama here in West Mobile.

Knox lifts my chin with his finger, tilting my face up to his. "Hey." His voice is husky with emotion, and I know it's because he's heard what people are saying about us.

They'll grow apart while they're in college.

They're just kids.

They'll find someone else.

The thing is, they're all wrong. There's no one else for me. Knox Montgomery is it.

"You know what's going to happen when we go to college in a few months?"

"What's that?" I answer in a hushed tone.

"I'm going to miss you like crazy, but we're going to email and talk on the phone when we can. And one thing's certain." He places my palm flat against the center of his chest. "My heart is yours."

16

Knox
PRESENT

The morning after—the whole "walk of shame" thing—never was my style.

Turns out, it still isn't. And it's awkward as hell.

Case in point, I wake up in EJ's bed, sprawled on my stomach, facing her blinds which now have sunlight streaming through the slats. Her trademark scent of apple blossoms surrounds me, and my mouth stretches into a wide, smug grin as the memory of last night hits me.

Until I realize I'm alone.

Pushing up on my arms, I turn my head on the pillow to scan her side of the bed. Judging by the lack of indentation in the pillow and how the covers on her side are fixed neatly, she's been up for a while. It's only now that I note the scent of coffee brewing.

I shift, sitting up slowly, and take a moment to study her bedroom in the light of day. One door leads to an en suite bathroom on one side, where she lent me an extra toothbrush last night. This was only *after* I'd promised—and followed through—on proving to her that we didn't need a condom to have more fun.

When I'd laid her doubt to rest, it'd been an intensely gratifying victory. But the moment she'd relented and offered me a spare toothbrush from the pack beneath her sink was the moment I felt like I'd managed the impossible. Like I'd won gold at the Olympics.

I won't even get into how I'd played up my exhaustion and guilt-tripped her about sending me home in the middle of the night. Not one of my more manly moments, but it got the desired results.

Sliding out from beneath the sheets, I stand and stretch before I adjust my boxer briefs to account for my morning wood. In an attempt to calm my erection, I step closer to inspect the framed photos on her walls that I hadn't paid attention to last night. There are quite a few of her and Becket. I never verified what exactly their relationship *is*, in fear of what her answer would be. I also figured it was pointless since we agreed this—whatever *this* had actually been—would be a one-time thing.

My eyes fall on a few more photos in a collage-style frame, and this time, she and Madison, *F&F*'s beauty editor, are all smiles, so infectious that I find my own lips mirroring theirs.

Until my gaze lands on the small photo at the bottom of the frame, that is. Because this one shows her with Becket, and it appears he's holding his phone up to take a selfie of them. Her smile is just as beautiful as usual, but something's off. Even without being in contact with her for the past eight years, I know her smiles, and this one's slightly forced and almost seems like it's tinged with sadness, just a bit lackluster.

I'm so caught up in my perusal of her features in the photo, it takes me a moment before I realize what she's wearing.

Her wedding dress. The one she'd complained that her

He Loves Me...Knot

father had insisted she wear in lieu of the one she'd wanted. All because of what he thought his daughter would be more "well-received" in.

That man had been a thorn in my side from day one, but I'd remained respectful because he was the father of the woman I'd loved since I'd realized love existed. He was far more concerned with how those he did business with would react or their opinions than the well-being of his own family. I still don't understand how his wife has stayed with him all this time.

I recall that conversation he'd bombarded me with as I'd been pulling on my tuxedo jacket, preparing to marry his daughter. He was the absolute last person I'd wanted to see moments before I allowed the wedding planner to ensure I was standing in the correct spot to await my bride. Little did I know, the man turned out to be a fucking omen.

Because that ended up being the shittiest day of my life.

"Hey."

Her soft, tentative voice draws my attention and I turn to find her already dressed in workout clothes and holding a mug, a tiny spiral of steam coming off the top of it.

"I have to head out and meet Madison, but I made coffee." With a tight smile, she offers the cup to me. "I wasn't sure if you still took yours the same way or not, but there are four sugars in there..." She trails off nervously, averting her eyes.

There's a pinching in the center of my chest at the fact that she recalls exactly how I take my coffee. Still.

Accepting it, I thank her and take a small sip of the warm brew while eyeing her over the rim. She looks cute in a pair of shorts paired with a tank top over a sports bra.

She reaches up to adjust her ponytail, and it takes

everything in my power to resist rushing toward her and tugging that silky, dark hair loose. To convince her to pick up where we left off last night.

"Well." She takes a step backward. "I'm going to grab my stuff and put on my shoes so, uh, if you want to just lock up behind you…"

This awkward shit is for the birds.

Quickly draining my coffee, mindless to the burn my throat is enduring, I hold the cup out for her. Once she accepts it from me, I bend and begin gathering my clothes. My only care now is getting out of here and sparing us more of this tiptoeing around one another.

"No worries. I'll be out of your way in less than five minutes."

"O-okay." She disappears down the hallway, and I hurriedly button my shirt and pull on the rest of my clothes before slipping into my shoes with record speed.

Just as I'm stepping out of her bedroom, I can't help but toss another look over my shoulder in the direction of that one photograph of her and Becket with her in her wedding dress.

I should've been the guy beside her in that damn photo.

I'M MUDDING and taping in preparation of painting my kitchen when Wells calls. Some days, I think my best friend has some sort of weird telepathy for when I get my ass in a bind.

Descending the ladder I've been perched on for much of the morning since I left EJ's, I grab my phone from the smooth surface of the newly installed granite countertop.

"Hey, man." We've been missing each other since both our workloads had increased quite a bit lately.

"Please say you're painting or are finished painting."

A laugh escapes me because Wells hates mudding and taping. The last time he helped me was with vaulted ceilings over eighteen feet in height at my Mobile house, and, well, my buddy is decidedly not a fan of heights.

"Not quite."

He exhales loudly. "Damn. Well, I was planning to head your way just to get a breather from this place. Plus, I know you'd asked me to look over the financials and legal terms on a few things."

"That'd be great, man. I appreciate it."

"Except I'm not mudding and taping. I'll paint, but that's it."

"Noted." I tug open my fridge and grab a bottle of water. Uncapping it, I take a swig. "When will you be here?"

"Probably by about five tonight." He pauses. "You just purchased that place a few weeks ago."

My brow furrows, unsure of where he's going with this. "Yeah?"

"And you're already doing prep work for painting."

"Right." I draw out the word slowly, still not following.

"You ripped out all the carpeting and installed hardwoods throughout the entire place—yourself—and installed all new kitchen cabinets. Did I miss anything?"

"I built an eight-by-two island in the kitchen and added a half bath to the first floor."

"Exactly."

I drag a hand over my face wearily. "I got up way too early this morning, after not getting much sleep last night, so you're going to have to spell it out for me."

When he doesn't immediately respond, I realize what I've basically just admitted to.

Fuck.

"All right." Wells's tone is dripping with smugness. "First off, the last time you ended up finishing the major renovations in Mach speed was shortly after that day in June that we never discuss. I'm wondering if I should find it curious that you're reverting back to being Superman HGTV-style when you're there, in Jacksonville, operating as current employer of a certain woman."

My lips part to form a response. "I ju—"

"Or the other more intriguing fact that you were up early this morning—didn't sound too happy about that part, by the way—and mentioned not getting much sleep last night, to which there was definitely a hint of pride in your voice."

"I'd forgotten how great it was to be best friends with a lawyer," I respond drily and I'm greeted by his laughter.

"I'll be sure to stop and grab some beer on my way."

"Sounds great. You have the address of this place?"

"Got it plugged into my GPS."

"Great. Drive safe."

"Will do."

Emma Jane

HIGH SCHOOL
SENIOR YEAR

The salty spray hits my face as we speed across the waters of the Gulf on the jet ski, the brightness of the full moon lighting our way. I'm holding Knox tight, and I relish the feel of the hard wall of his abdominals beneath my grasp.

We approach Sand Island, the small uninhabited strip of land with a thick line of trees blocking the view across the expanse of it. Knox slows the jet ski as we near the shallow waters before he kills the engine and hops off. After helping me down, he reaches for the small anchor and walks the jet ski up the shore a bit before ensuring it's secured.

When he lifts up the seat and reaches inside to withdraw a folded beach mat, I'm overwhelmed with a mixture of nervousness and excitement.

Knox holds out a hand for me and when I take it, his gentle, yet firm grip helps to soothe some of my nervousness.

Once he unfolds the large mat and places it on the sandy shore, we lie back upon it and admire the night sky glittering with stars.

"I hoped the weather would cooperate for tonight."

At his hushed tone, I turn to face him, only to discover that he's already watching me. My breath hitches at the combination of affection and tenderness in his eyes.

"You planned this?" I inquire softly.

"I wanted tonight to be perfect."

It's our last night together before he leaves for Auburn early tomorrow morning.

I shift to my side and face him fully. "You know what everyone's saying, right?"

He turns his attention to the starlit sky above us, and his jaw clenches and unclenches. "They're wrong."

I release a small sigh and whisper, "But what if—"

His head turns abruptly, and his eyes lock with mine, shimmering with a fierce intensity. "Do you believe that I love you?"

"Of course."

"And do you love me?" He searches my features, and I wonder if he's worried that I don't.

Rising to rest on my arm, I lean over and place a soft kiss to his lips before I whisper again, "Of course."

"Then nothing will happen."

I duck my head, averting my eyes, unable to resist voicing my main worry. "But the girls at college are prettier and more…experienced than I am."

His hand cups my cheek, lifting my face up to force me to meet his gaze. "You are my everything, Emma Jane."

I'm overwhelmed by my insecurity over our future and sorrow at the fact that he'll soon be hours away from me. Those emotions, intertwined with my love for him, propel me to act. Slinging my leg over his body, I straddle him and press a tiny kiss to his lips. "I love you, Knox."

His lips curve beneath mine. "I love you back."

When he takes my lips in a kiss, it starts out gentle and oh so tender before rapidly turning hotter and passionate. His fingers tangle in my hair, and he angles my head to deepen the kiss. Knox grows hard beneath his board shorts, and my own bikini bottoms provide no real barrier against the feel of his arousal.

I rock my hips, and a low groan rumbles through his chest before he tears his lips from mine. My chest rises and falls as I draw in ragged breaths, and I peer down at him, wondering why he stopped. Knox's hands move to my hips, applying a little pressure as if he wants me off him, but I resist.

"What are you doing?" I frown.

"EJ." He tips his head back against the mat and his eyes fall closed with a wince. "I don't want things to get too out of hand."

"You don't"—I swallow past the sudden lump in my throat—"want me?" The confusion is apparent in my voice.

His eyes flash open. "I want you too much. I just—" He breaks off to drag a hand over his face with a sigh. "I don't want you to do something you'll regret."

I place my hands on my hips, and the movement causes me to shift where I'm still straddling him, eliciting another groan from Knox. "Listen here. I love you and I want this." I wave a hand to indicate our surroundings. "It's a perfect night. Beautiful. What more could you ask for?"

"A bed." Knox answers this matter-of-factly. "Not a freaking beach mat."

"Well, I love you and I love this mat." I lower myself

and begin to press tiny kisses along his jawline. "And I want you to make love to me on this mat." I press my lips to the base of his neck, and he makes a rough sound in the back of his throat.

"I didn't bring anything," he whispers. "I didn't plan this, EJ."

"It's okay. I trust you." I nibble on his earlobe and revel in his sharp intake of breath. "You can, uh, pull out," I offer shyly.

His hands frame my face, and he steers me back slightly to peer up at me. "Are you sure?"

He knows I've never done this before, and I understand why he's hesitant. But he needs to realize how much I love him, and that I want to end this chapter of our lives—post high school, pre-college—like this.

"I'm sure." I punctuate this with a brush of my lips across his.

With a gentleness that's utterly breathtaking, he proceeds to love me, to carefully and slowly love my body with his hands and mouth before he takes my virginity. And I realize something's changed.

Knox owns my whole heart, but now he's ingrained in my soul, too.

17

Emma Jane
PRESENT

"Holy shit."

"For real." I stare back at Madison where we sit on a wooden bench.

We've just finished our outdoor yoga class here in the center of the large park near the waterfront, and I started to fill her in on what happened last night between me and Knox.

I haven't delved any deeper, nor have I divulged anything about our complicated past. Since she'd joined the *F&F* team two years after I had, I'd never felt a need to do so; I hadn't thought it was pertinent information. I certainly didn't think I'd ever be given a reason to bring it up.

Her lips curl slightly, eyes shining with humor. "Guess you didn't tell him to namasté away."

I shove at her playfully. "You're hilarious." Taking a sip of water from my thermos, I turn my attention to the various parkgoers who are jogging or walking their dogs, enjoying the early morning. "It was just a one-time thing, anyway. So no big deal."

"Right. And it's not going to be weird that he's also the current owner and person in charge of your employment?"

Or that we used to do what we did last night all the time? Every chance we could? That we once talked about our own happily ever after?

Her eyes light up even more as she nudges my shoulder with hers. "You have to dish. How was it? Did it start with the whole, 'After working so late tonight at the office, I just couldn't get you off my mind' kind of thing? Or did he show up at your door and shove his way inside and go all alpha male on you?"

Staring back at her, I'm not sure how to answer. "Wow." Raising my eyebrows, I ask, "Did someone just subscribe to *Showtime After Hours*?"

Madison makes a derisive sound. "I need to live vicariously through *someone*."

We fall silent for a moment, both of us lost in our thoughts.

I don't know what makes me say it, but the words just spill out. "It was nice."

My friend rears back with a horrified look. "Nice?" She shakes her head so forcefully I find myself worried that it might come off. "No. Absolutely *not*. Nice should never be a word that goes along with a night full of sex."

"Well, we didn't have a night full of sex, really…"

She shifts abruptly to face me, and folds her legs to sit cross-legged on the bench. Jabbing an index finger in my direction, she commands, "Start from the beginning, when he showed up at your door, and go from there."

"He showed up and told me he wanted me, that he needed me. We agreed it would only be for one night." With a wry smile, I add, "And it *was* only once, anyway, since we only had one condom."

She cocks her head to the side and frowns as though

she hasn't heard me correctly. "Wait a minute. You only had *one* condom?"

"Right. Because I'd forgotten to buy more since I haven't exactly had any 'gentleman callers' in a while. At least, not since Jeff.…" I wrinkle my nose, recalling the last guy I'd dated who'd turned out to be less than stellar.

"First of all"—Madison holds up a finger—"Jeff was a douche." She holds up another finger. "Second, Knox didn't have a condom with him?"

"No," I answer hesitantly.

"Huh. Interesting." She narrows her eyes. "Don't you find it odd that a man of his caliber doesn't carry protection? He's smart and freaking hot. You *know* he must get serious action."

"I guess I hadn't thought about it." I shrug. "I was too busy trying to survive the awkward morning-after situation with him."

"So how did he deal with the only-one-condom thing?"

"It wasn't a big deal. He just—" I break off and instantly feel the rush of heat flood my cheeks as I recall the way Knox had brought me to orgasm countless times throughout the night.

"Ah," she says knowingly. "He improvised."

Nodding, I release a sigh and bring my leg up, setting my foot on the bench and wrap my arms around my knee. "He did."

"So how firm are you guys on it being a one-time thing?"

"Firm." I punctuate this with a nod. Because I know it's necessary that we never cross that line again. It's far too risky.

"Well, I know what this calls for."

I flash a curious glance at my friend. "I'm almost afraid to ask."

"Girls' night out."

Squinting my eyes, I give her a sharp look. "You'd better not drag me to that place in Midtown again where the guy goes around sketching people and they all basically look the same with apple cheeks."

"He was really sweet, though!" she protests with a laugh.

"He extorted twenty bucks from us!" I remind her.

"Fine, I promise I won't drag you there."

"Good."

"I have it on good authority that this new pub is a great find. And"—she leans in conspiratorially—"we can find you a guy you won't have to worry about facing at work."

Great. Madison has it in her head that she's going to play matchmaker and find me a guy. The day after...*yeah*. So I respond the only way I possibly can.

With a vast amount of enthusiasm, of course.

"Yay."

Whoops. Guess I failed.

"OOOH! I think I've found one for you."

I've heard Madison claim the same thing at least five times already tonight.

I'm more interested in the preseason game and the fact that the Jags are down by six points and it's in the final quarter. Not to mention that sack Becket took looked downright brutal. His teammate, Diego, got face-masked to hell and back, and I'm shocked his head didn't literally snap off.

"*What?!*" I gasp in outrage at the television displayed above the bar where we currently sit in the new pub. At least Madison hasn't let me down there. However, when it comes to "finding one" for me, she's striking out.

"No, seriously, Emma Jane. This guy is freaking *hot*. Dark blond hair and a great smile." Madison's voice turns dreamy.

My eyes remain glued to the television where Becket's currently looking for a receiver. My entire body tenses when I see him getting rushed by the defensive players, but suddenly, he darts off, and I realize all that speed work he claims has been kicking his ass is paying off. Because he's running like the freaking wind.

"Go, Beck, go!" I chant beneath my breath. When he scores the touchdown himself, my whoop of delight is joined by the other patrons who are tuned into the game, as well.

Grabbing my phone, I quickly shoot off a text to him.

Me: You nearly gave me a heart attack with that sprint move, buddy. I'm sitting with Madison in some new pub in Midtown and cheering you on. Now, hurry up and win the game. Love you.

I know he won't get my message for a while but I want him to know I'm watching and thinking of him.

"And wait...it looks like he has a tattoo on his arm of a...barbed wire with a skull and crossbones or something. Sexy." Madison's still going on about the guy she spotted, apparently.

"Oh-*oh!* He's noticed us." She leans in closer and hisses with urgency, "He's coming over here."

"Super." I'm praying the Jags's kick for the extra point doesn't get blocked. "You can talk to him, and I'll continue watching my best friend play football."

Clearly not pleased with my response, Madison starts,

"You're a sad excuse for a Southern belle. You're supposed to—"

"Well, hello, ladies."

That voice. Oh, dear God. That voice.

I know *that* voice.

My eyes pinch closed with dread because if that voice belongs to who I think it does, that can only mean someone else isn't too far behind.

"Long time no see, Emma Jane *Haywood*."

Emma Jane

THE UNIVERSITY OF SOUTH ALABAMA
SENIOR YEAR

"Things are still good between y'all?"

My head snaps up at the odd tone in my best friend, Katherine's voice.

"Yes," I answer slowly. "Why wouldn't they be?"

"No reason." She shrugs casually and pokes at her salad.

We met for lunch across the street from campus. After this, I need to head back to the library to do more studying since Knox and I have a phone date later tonight.

I roll my eyes. "Well, obviously there's a reason. Otherwise, you wouldn't have asked." Sometimes Katherine can get so snooty over things.

Katherine and I grew up together, our mothers had grown up together, and we went through debutante school and cotillion together. I've known her my whole life, and sure, she was prissy and didn't appreciate the tiny diamond stud I'd recently had my nose pierced with, but she's always been there for me.

However, I've begun to grow weary of her constantly second-guessing Knox's loyalty to me.

"I just think of him being the typical handsome baseball player on campus, girls flocking to him at every turn, and wonder…" She trails off with a shrug and her insinuation makes me bristle with irritation.

Knox has never given me any reason to doubt him. Plus, with the appeal of Facebook catching on, people have begun to post pictures and tag people like crazy. I basically know what he's doing before he even gets to call and tell me himself.

I raise my chin and announce primly, "You don't have to wonder about anything."

What she doesn't know is I found a receipt in his wallet when he was home over Thanksgiving break. He'd asked me to grab a few more dollars out of it when we were filling up the coolers with ice to go night fishing.

The receipt was from a jeweler, and the amount on it had sent my eyebrows practically flying to my hairline.

I haven't mentioned it to anyone because I don't want to get my hopes up in case I'm mistaken, but there's honestly no other explanation.

Knox is planning to propose.

"What's got you smiling like the cat that ate the canary?"

My attention snaps back to Katherine who's eyeing me with interest.

Shaking my head, I avert my gaze to my salad. "Nothing, just excited to see Knox for Christmas."

18

Knox
PRESENT

"Tell me again why we're here instead of tossing back beers at my place?"

Wells shakes his head at me. "Because you wouldn't wipe that lovesick look off your damn face, and I spotted this place on my way into town." He gives me a little shove. "Now quit being a cheap ass and order us a round."

We weave through the crowded pub, which opened just a few weeks ago. I hadn't had time to check it out but, begrudgingly, I'm glad Wells insisted we stop by. It has a casual feel to it and plenty of mounted televisions for sports enthusiasts to watch their teams. Currently, it's tuned to the Jags's away game against Washington.

Huh. Wonder if EJ is watching this at home.

Finally landing a small high-top table, Wells and I settle on the barstools and are quickly greeted by a waitress who takes our orders. Glancing around the place, something catches my eye and I swear I see a flash of hair that looks just like— *Shit*. I need to get it together. I can't deal with wondering if every dark-haired woman I see is EJ.

"Here you go." The waitress delivers our beers before

fixing a smile on us. "Let me know if y'all need anything else."

"What we need to do is find you a new woman to distract you from your recent foray into the past."

"Foray?" I repeat sarcastically.

He grins. "I'm a highly-educated guy. I can use foray."

With a chuckle, I take a long drink of beer. "Right."

He directs his attention to our surroundings, scanning the other patrons. "What we need is a woman who is obviously easy on the eyes—"

"Obviously," I add drily.

"And smart, but not desperate. One who knows what the score is."

I stare at Wells with disbelief. "What the hell are you talking about?"

"Ah-ha. Bingo." He turns back to me, wearing a proud grin on his face, and reaches out a fist for me to bump.

"Right. Bingo." I bump my fist to his, then draw back to inspect my hand. "Shit," I mutter.

"What's up?"

"Must have gotten a splinter when I was trying to sand part of the new crown molding I nailed in earlier today." Glancing up, I shake my head at the dim lighting of the pub before I slide off my barstool. "I'm going to head to the bathroom and see if the lights in there are better so I can get it out."

I don't catch Wells's response, if he has one, because there's a collective cheering from the majority of patrons watching the game.

As I enter the bathroom, I find my myself wondering again what EJ's doing tonight.

FOR FUCK'S SAKE.

"Leave the guy alone for two minutes and he disappears," I mutter under my breath as I take in the sight of our table, now short one beer.

Wells's, of course.

The dick left mine behind unattended.

Scrubbing a hand down my face and over my jaw, I scan the pub for my friend. After failing to find him in the crowd, I'm on the verge of texting him to find his whereabouts when I catch sight of the back of his blond head, and shock instantly reverberates through me.

Of all the women in the city of Jacksonville, he not only found the two women who work for me, but also the one I'd slept with last night.

The one who kicked me out, albeit politely and with coffee, this morning.

Madison's friendly smile is fixed on Wells, and the two seem to be conversing while Emma Jane's attention is trained on the television mounted above the bar. By all appearances, she looks like a typical fan who's on edge because of the football game currently playing. But I notice the rigidness of her posture.

As I near them, only two steps away, Wells tosses out casually, "So what did you ladies do last night? Anything fun?"

"I had to catch up on some work. Nothing too much fun. But Emma Jane, here…"

Emma Jane's head whips around and she gives her friend a glare, ripe with warning. Just as she's about to turn back to watch the final minutes of the game, she notices me and pales, eyes going wide.

"I see you've met Wells." I greet Madison with a polite smile. "Good to see you, Madison."

Surprise etches her features before she returns the smile. "Good to see you, too, Mr. Montgomery."

"Knox," I correct, "please."

"Knox." She nods before continuing. "Wells has been entertaining me with stories of Mobile."

"Ah, yes. It's a beautiful place."

God, this is awkward.

"Emma Jane once called Mobile home." Wells raises his eyebrows in her direction, but she doesn't acknowledge him. "Isn't that right, Ms. *Haywood*?"

It doesn't take a genius to realize that he's using her last name pointedly, considering she would have been a Montgomery.

If she'd followed through with her own wedding and hadn't chosen to skip out on it, of course.

Emma Jane suddenly whoops in delight and turns to high-five the guys to her left. She reaches for her cell phone, typing frantically, her lips curved into a smile, happiness radiating from it.

Because Becket Jones has just thrown a winning touchdown in the nick of time.

"You've moved on to bigger and better things, I guess."

Wells is getting started on what I foresee as a dangerous roll, but in his defense, he was the one who saw me at my lowest. The only one I allowed to see me that way.

"Guess Knox, here, couldn't begin to compete with a guy who throws a football for a living."

EJ spins around in her seat so suddenly that it takes all three of us by surprise, and we rear back slightly. Her expression is one of absolute rage, her blue eyes narrowed dangerously at Wells, lips pressed thin with irritation.

She practically grinds out the words from behind clenched teeth. "Listen here, *Kennedy*. You of all people should know not to run your mouth when you don't have all the evidence at hand."

Slipping off the barstool, she grabs her small purse and phone before she eyes Madison. "I'm going to get some air." Glaring at Wells, she adds, "The stench of animosity is stifling," before she stalks off.

I track her movement as she heads toward the exit. Regardless of what's just transpired, I'd be lying if I said she doesn't look hot as hell in her blue form-fitting sundress.

A hand shoots out in front of my face, fingers snapping, and I turn to glare at Wells.

"What?"

"You looked like you were about to drown in your own drool. I was saving you." His smug grin grates on my nerves. "You're welcome."

Stepping in, crowding him, I eye Wells hard. "You didn't have to be such a dick to her."

He makes a face. "I'm your best friend. I'd be remiss if I didn't give the woman who—"

Madison's face, leaning in farther, eyes volleying between us, draws our attention. She raises her eyebrows, her face a mask of innocence. "The woman who…?"

"Don't." I address Wells, my tone lethal and heavy with warning.

"Eviscerated his damn heart."

"Great," I mutter with irritation. "While you're at it, you can tell her about that time I was in the first grade and cried after coloring the wrong section on a color-by-numbers worksheet."

"I didn't even remember that." Wells pauses. "But that's pretty pathetic. Are you sure you want me telling that story to people?"

I drag my eyes from the door EJ exited through

moments ago to glare at my friend who's clearly enjoying giving me shit if the mischievous amusement sparkling in his eyes is anything to go by.

"I'm getting some air."

"Yeah, you'll be getting something all right."

I don't bother to respond to Wells's wisecrack. I stride across the pub, intent on exiting and finding a certain brunette.

Once I step outside onto the sidewalk and into the oppressive Florida humidity, I spot her a few feet away, peering into one of the windows of a shop which is now closed. My feet carry me closer, and the moment she notices my reflection in the window, the hand not holding her purse clenches tightly into a fist at her side.

"Are you here to dish out more insults on your friend's behalf?" She poses the quiet question without turning to face me. Instead, she remains facing the darkened shop window.

"No." I shake my head slowly. "I'm here to apologize."

She releases a slow exhale, and her eyes close briefly before she turns to face me. "There's nothing to apologize for." She offers a pathetic excuse for a smile. Even a fool would be able to see that it's laced with intense sadness. "Your best friend's supposed to stick up for you, just like Wells did." Emma Jane drops her eyes, studying her feet which are encased in simple white sandals. "You're lucky to have him." Her words are spoken so softly, I strain to hear them.

"You"—I swallow past the tightness in my throat—"have Becket."

Her gaze rises to mine, and she regards me with a look I can't decipher. "You're right. I do." There's a brief pause, and this time, her smile, though small, is more genuine than before. "He's a guy who's ready and willing to beat the tar out of everyone who's ever hurt me."

It makes me want to beat the shit out of *him* because he has that right.

I used to have that right.

"Knox." Her voice draws me from my thoughts and our eyes lock. "I know our past is messy, to say the least, and we agree that last night was an oddity—a one-time occurrence—but I think the smart thing to do is to try our best to go back to regarding each other in a professional capacity only." Her features are drawn tight with concern. "It just seems like fate is screwing with us a bit."

I nod curtly. "You're probably right. It's smart to keep things professional."

She worries the bottom edge of her lip, watching me cautiously before returning the nod. "Good."

We regard each other in silence for a beat before I shove my hands in the pockets of my khakis and take a step backward. I need to head back inside the pub and find Wells and hopefully tear him away from Madison.

"Night, Emma Jane." I spin around, not waiting for her to respond, and head down the sidewalk.

But I catch the faint sound of her voice behind me.

"Good night, Knox."

My feet feel like they get significantly heavier with every step I take that puts more distance between us.

Fucking fate.

Knox
SENIOR AT AUBURN UNIVERSITY

HOME FOR CHRISTMAS BREAK
THE HAYWOOD MANSION

"You're going to wear a freaking path on the floor, man."

I ignore Wells as I pace back and forth, because my nerves are beyond frayed. They're absolutely shot. Running a hand through my hair, I try to calm my racing heart as nervousness pulses through my veins.

"I hope like hell she says yes," I mumble.

"Knox." Wells's tone gains my attention. "You know she will. That woman loves you."

I've been planning to do this while I'm back home in Mobile for Christmas break and want it to be perfect for EJ.

We're both in our final year of school, and she's been spreading herself thin since she'd been accepted into the accelerated degree program. She'll be graduating with both her bachelor and master's degrees in business and marketing.

My father left me a considerable trust fund and businesses to my name, but I won't be able to do anything until I have my degree in hand. Still, I'm confident EJ and I will do well professionally and financially.

Pausing my pacing, I withdraw the small box from the pocket of my dress pants and pop it open once again. I hope like hell she loves this ring.

"Ah, hell. Here comes trouble," Wells mutters beneath his breath, and I don't have to look to know who he's referring to.

"Well, if it isn't two of the handsomest men in Mobile," Katherine remarks, striding into the empty ballroom.

Her heels click against the smooth floor as she approaches. Her hair is perfectly coifed, her black dress likely costing an ungodly amount, and she has the same smile gracing her lips that never quite reaches her eyes. I've never understood how she and EJ are such great friends. They're so different, and while EJ is genuine, sweet, and sometimes—mostly when it pertains to her father—a bit of a rebel, Katherine is a young version of Martha Stewart.

Just add her having a giant stick up her ass into the mix.

"Katherine." I nod politely.

"Nervous?" She arches a brow.

I shrug it off. "Not really. Just want everything to be perfect." My eyes scan everything from the pristine white linens covering the tables to the crystal goblets and polished flatware at each place setting. "She deserves it," I finish softly.

"Of course. Nothing but the best for Emma Jane." My eyes dart back to Katherine, my body tensing in response to her odd tone, but she's already turned away, inspecting the large room.

Suddenly, she fixes her attention on Wells. "Be sure to save me a dance, okay, Wells?"

Without waiting for his affirmation, she spins on her heels and exits, the clicking of her stilettos resounding throughout the room. The voices of arriving guests drift in from the foyer.

"That woman is no good."

Wells mutters this beneath his breath, and I silently agree before the sight of something else catches my eye through the large oversized windows. Or, more specifically, *someone*.

It's show time.

19

Emma Jane
PRESENT

"You planning to enlighten me about everything at some point?"

Madison gently poses the question in the back of the cab we take home to my place.

"Not much to tell," I say with a sigh. Dragging my gaze away from my window, I turn to her. "Once upon a time, we were in love. Then I found out he didn't really love me, and I left."

"After you walked outside, Wells mentioned something about you"—she breaks off and hooks her fingers in air quotes—"eviscerating Knox's heart."

I scoff in disbelief. "Right. That's almost believable."

She studies me curiously. "Isn't it?"

"No." My tone brooks no argument.

Madison exhales loudly. "Okay, fine." She reaches over and links my hand with hers. "We shall continue to consider Knox Montgomery pond scum."

I give our joined hands a squeeze, mustering up a smile. "Thanks."

Turning back to stare sightlessly at the passing scenery,

I lean my head against the cool glass of the window, and my eyes fall closed.

I thought I'd managed to escape to Jacksonville years ago.

Never would I have predicted that my past would find me here.

Damn fate.

Late September

"DID YOU GET IT?"

My head snaps up in startled surprise at the male voice at my office door. "Becket!" Flashing him a stern look, I warn, "Didn't I tell you not to sneak up on me like that?"

He merely offers his trademark smile and strides on in. Instead of directly approaching me, he heads over to my table and plucks the daisy that's on the verge of death out of its small vase and tosses it in the nearby trash bin. Walking to the restroom attached to my office, I hear him dump out the old water and replenish it, only to emerge with the vase holding a fresh daisy. He walks toward me and winks.

"Not only do I bring you a flower, but I had a dress delivered. Did you get it?" He glances around in search for it.

I gesture with my pen, directing him to look behind him to where the garment bag is hanging from the hinge of the closet door. "It's right back there."

He grins excitedly like a kid at Christmas. "Do you like it?"

I can't help but smile in return. "Yes, Beck. It's absolutely gorgeous." I school my expression to be one of utter sternness. "But I told you, you have to stop buying me these expensive dresses."

"But I love spoiling my favorite girl."

"Maybe you can just hurry up and find a g—"

"Ms. Haywood, could I see—" My attention is drawn to my doorway, again, to find Knox. "Oh. I'm sorry. I didn't realize I was interrupting." His eyes dart back and forth between me and Becket.

"Becket was just ensuring I received a delivery."

I eye Becket, who suddenly drops into one of my chairs. He stretches out his long legs and crosses them at the ankles.

"I also made sure to replenish her vase." He waves toward the center of the table where the new daisy now sits in water. He dusts invisible lint from his shirt. "Because I'm sweet like that."

Oh, dear Lord.

I flash an apologetic look at Knox. "Becket was just leaving." Giving my friend a pointed look, I prompt, "Isn't that right?"

With a smug grin, he reaches his arms above his head and laces his fingers together before sliding them behind his head. "Not at all. I was just about to give you some great business-related news."

Staring at my best friend, I clench my teeth. "Really?"

"I'd love to hear the news, as well." Knox strides over and slides the other chair over to face Becket before taking a seat.

"Well, it just so happens that the owners of the stadium are going to be at the gala tonight to benefit the Mayo Clinic." He lifts his shoulder in a slight shrug. "Perfect opportunity to strengthen the new business partnership."

"Right," I murmur, eyeing Becket suspiciously because

I know my best friend and this is most assuredly going somewhere.

"The thing is, Mr. Montgomery…" Becket lowers his arms and waves to himself with a self-deprecating chuckle. "Business talk and the savviness that goes along with it aren't my forte. Not like Blue, here." He nods at me with a wink before redirecting his attention to Knox. "And you, too."

Oh, hell no.

No, no, *no*.

"I mean, we all know what I'm good at." Becket goes as far as to pat his throwing arm lovingly. "And that's tossing a football around."

My face is a mask of disbelief intermixed with a large dose of panic along with a *What the hell are you saying?!* tossed in for good measure. Because Becket Jones graduated at the top of his class, not only in high school but in college, too.

This impressive athletically inclined man didn't walk away with a degree in underwater basket weaving. He graduated with a degree in civil engineering and assisted his alma mater, the University of Florida, with their campus expansion.

My eyes narrow on my best friend, and I feign a look of confusion. "Huh. That's so odd." I twist my lips in an exaggerated frown and tap a finger against them in thought. "I once had this best friend who drew up plans for his own house and then did a bunch of the labor himself." I cut him a sharp look. "Even got into trouble with his coach for it."

Becket's expression is one of exaggerated amazement. "*Wow*. That friend sounds really impressive. You should probably worship the ground he walks on." Then he flashes me a wide, toothy grin.

Bless his heart, he might not live to see his next birthday at the rate he's going.

"Anyway," he addresses Knox, "I have two extra tickets to the gala tonight if you'd like to bring a 'plus one' with you and join us." His grin widens, and I swear, if he smiles any bigger, his face will split in half. "Like one big happy family."

I'd really like it to split.

Right. Now.

"That's very," Knox responds almost cautiously, as if he's suspicious of Becket's offer, "generous of you."

He's not alone because I'd sure like to know what's up my best friend's sleeve.

Becket claps his hands together so suddenly that it causes both me and Knox to jerk in surprise. "Great! It's settled then." He jumps up from his seat. "I'll leave your tickets at the front desk in the Omni Hotel lobby, and we'll see you at seven tonight."

Without pausing to wait for Knox's response, he strides over to where I'm still sitting at my desk, stunned, and drops a loud smack of a kiss on my forehead. "Pick you up at six thirty, Blue."

I can't manage to do more than stare after him as he exits my office. Finally, I brave a look at Knox, who appears amused.

"Is he always like that?"

Slowly shaking my head, I murmur, "Not normally."

He rises from his chair and walks toward my desk. "I came to see how everything was coming along for the new ad space."

I wish I could say that I'm paying attention to what Knox is saying right now, but I'm not.

Normally, I might be transfixed by the sight of his dark gray pinstriped suit pants that fit him perfectly, showcasing his strong, muscled legs or the black button-down shirt with the sleeves rolled up like usual, accentuating his forearms sprinkled with dark hair. But none of that has snagged my attention.

Instead, it's his hands.

"What did you do?" I blurt out, staring at him.

Knox appears confused, brow furrowing. "What did I do?"

"To your hands." I wave the tip of my pen toward him, circling it to encompass what I'm seeing. "What happened?"

Startled, he lifts his hands, turning the palms upward, and looks down at them before chuckling softly. His eyes slowly lift to mine, appearing a deeper, more mossy green color, and it's like all the air has been sucked from the room.

Knox's gaze is heated. "Had a little mishap while I was installing new baseboards in the kitchen."

I can tell with just one look that he knows—that he recalls exactly how much I used to love watching him work with his hands, making or fixing things.

Instantly, I'm taken back in time to when he purchased his first home along Mobile Bay.

"It's not much to look at now, but it has great bones, the foundation is stable, and I know I can do a lot with it." His excitement is contagious, and I smile back before he opens the front door and leads me inside.

"Oh. Wow." I don't know what to say because I sure hadn't expected this sight.

"Now don't get discouraged," he tells me hastily. "Just picture this. I'll knock out this wall…"

I remember watching him tell me his plans, my eyes cataloguing the way he spoke so animatedly, and becoming mesmerized by his energetic attitude.

He'd worked on that house nearly every day after he got home from working his day job. I'd helped him measure tile for the backsplash he'd installed in the kitchen and bathrooms. I'd watched him in his worn-out jeans that had holes scattered here and there and a plain white T-shirt that clung to his damp chest and back. I'd admired him while he'd furrowed his brow in concentration on a particular task, and I knew one thing.

There wasn't a sexier sight to behold.

And I'd told him so. Many, many times. And those times were usually followed by fierce lovemaking.

Knox's eyes bore into mine as if he can see my thoughts.

Way to go, Emma Jane, at being completely transparent, I berate myself.

The breath I've been holding in whooshes out. Because I'm now picturing him down on his knees with the denim of his faded jeans stretched taut over his ass, the muscles flexing in his arms as he works.

"Are you okay?" His voice is gravelly and subdued, and I know he's detected the flush that's spreading across my face.

Clearing my throat, I release the pen my fist has been strangling to death and attempt a calm, collected demeanor.

Steepling my fingers, I raise my eyebrows in question. "Me? Oh, I'm fine. So, you're"—I tap my fingertips together—"renovating a place here?"

His lips tilt up at the corners. "Yes. I bought a place in Midtown." He pauses for a beat. "And I've installed all new hardwood floors."

"Oh, really?" My voice comes out sounding strangled. So much for maintaining composure. Because now I'm picturing him installing hardwoods. And recalling the last time he did so.

And exactly how we christened those particular hardwoods.

In every. Single. Room.

Jumping up from my chair, I grab my stainless steel water thermos and hold it to my chest. "I need to refill this and forgot I have an appointment. I'm supposed to go talk to Tim in legal." I scoot around my desk quickly and dart over to the door. "I can send you an email to update you on all prospective and filled ad space, if you'd like."

Stepping across the threshold of my doorway, I offer an overly bright smile before I dart down the hall on my way to see Tim.

For the appointment that doesn't exist.

"SO YOU TOLD him you had an appointment with Tim and then you…?"

"Ran as fast as these heels would carry me." I lift my foot to show Madison my shoes.

"Oooh, those are cute! Are they new?" A crease forms between her brows. "Remind me again what size those are because I have a dress that would look great with—"

"Madison!" I let out an exasperated sound, my hands flying to rest at my hips. "Focus!"

With a sigh, my friend shakes her head at me. "Fine. Quick recap." She ticks off each finger as she goes. "Becket played some sort of screwy matchmaker and offered tickets to Knox." Cocking an eyebrow, she adds, "With a plus one."

"Right."

Ticking off another finger, she continues. "Then Knox

was talking to you, and you got mesmerized by his hard-working hands that installed…"

"Baseboards," I supply quickly, and there's no disguising the dreamy quality to my voice.

Madison stares at me. "You're literally scaring me right now."

I rear back slightly. "Why?"

My friend cuts me a look. "You just mentioned baseboards the same way Belle mooned over the beast's library." With a wrinkle of her nose, she adds, "Baseboards, Emma Jane. Base. Boards."

I begin pacing back and forth in her office. "I can't help it! It's my weakness. Back when we were…" I falter, abruptly drawing to a halt.

Madison crosses her arms and peers up at me speculatively from her chair. "Back when you were…?"

It's with hesitance that I part my lips to answer, but I'm interrupted by the sound of a voice speaking over the intercom of Madison's phone.

"Ms. Kilpatrick?"

Her head whips around to stare at her desk phone before her wide eyes lock with mine. "Yes, sir?" she answers, tentativeness apparent in her tone.

"I was trying to locate Ms. Haywood to go over a few things and Tim said she's already finished up their"—he pauses and my eyes fall closed in a wince at the insinuation of falsehood—"appointment some time ago. If you happen to see her, can you tell her I'd like to go over three proposals, in particular, with her."

I shake my head repeatedly and make a cutting motion with my hand near my throat, silently begging my friend to cover for me.

"Uh, I'll be sure to pass on that message." Madison's

voice is overly bright. "Should I end up running into her," she tacks on hurriedly, "which I haven't."

Then she does the unthinkable in her nervousness.

"Maybe you should try to text her? She always has her phone with her."

My jaw drops at my friend's suggestion, and there's a beat of silence on the other end of the line.

"Well, I appreciate that, Ms. Kilpatrick." The humor lacing Knox's tone is apparent and I'm praying it's because he finds Madison's response amusing and classifies it as nervousness. "I'll have to do that."

"Have a great day, Mr. Montgomery."

"You do the same."

Just when we believe we're in the clear, the unthinkable happens.

My phone—the phone I'd set on the hard surface of Madison's desk—begins to vibrate.

Loudly.

"Oh and would you tell Ms. Haywood that text message is from me, please? Thank you, Ms. Kilpatrick." And the line disconnects.

Clearly, my reprieve has come to an end.

It's time to pull up my big girl panties and get on with things.

Knox
THE WEDDING PLANNING STAGE

"I hate to break it to you, but your dad's going to lose his shit."

I can't help but laugh because it's in typical EJ fashion to make a move like this.

She's dyed a streak of her hair blue. Sure, it's subtle, but still. Her father's always been obnoxiously domineering. I tolerate him—barely—for her sake, but I despise the way he treats and speaks to the women in his life. Hell, I can't stand the way he thinks of women, period. It's demeaning.

"But it's my something blue," she protests mischievously.

I frame her face gently with my hands, gazing down into the depths of her cerulean eyes. "I love it, but then again, I love everything about you."

"Is that so?" She gives me a sly smile and runs her hands down my damp T-shirt, dusting some sawdust from me. "Well, it just so happens that I love everything about you, too." She tugs at the hem of my shirt, and her eyes sparkle with mischief. "Especially when you're in handyman mode."

Her words bring a smile to my lips because every time she comes over to my place after work and I'm in the midst of renovations—whether I'm cutting boards to build the base for the island in the kitchen or installing the cabinets—she gets a certain look in her eyes and can't keep her hands off me.

Don't get me wrong. I'm not complaining. It's just surprising since most women turn up their noses at a guy liberally coated in sawdust and sweat. Not so with EJ.

"I can't help it." She reaches around and swats my ass playfully. "I happen to be madly in love with the man I'm going to marry."

The way she peers up at me, with so much love shining in her eyes, nearly robs me of breath. She's so damn beautiful.

Soon—in exactly two weeks—she'll be my wife.

20

Knox
PRESENT

I'M NOT sure how long I sit, staring at my phone after I disconnect the intercom call to Madison Kilpatrick. I figured when I couldn't find her, she'd be with her closest friend and co-worker.

"What's got you smiling like the cat that ate the canary?" Wells walks into my office without knocking and closes the door behind him.

I give him a look, shaking my head. "Did you even ask my secretary if I was on a call? Or in a meeting?"

He grins. "I just had a lovely chat with your secretary. She told me you were in here working by yourself, and you didn't have any appointments until later, once you tracked down"—his smile widens—"Ms. Haywood."

"Remind me to update Karen on who she's supposed to disclose my schedule to from here on out," I mutter.

Wells slumps into the chair across from my desk. "So what's the deal? Did y'all hook up in the copy room?"

Making a face, I cock an eyebrow. "You've been watching too much TV."

"You're avoiding my question."

Sliding my chair back, I prop my shoes on the edge of my desk, fold my hands behind my head, and focus my attention on the ceiling. "I'm not sure what's happening." With a sigh, I go on. "There are moments when it's like no time has passed, like we're still the same people we were before…"

"And today you had one of those moments?"

My eyes close, and I recall exactly when I realized Emma Jane remembered when I'd done the renovations on my house in Mobile. When she recalled exactly how hot it had been that summer—more than just the temperatures had escalated.

"Did I ever tell you how sexy you are when you're"—*she points a finger at me and circles it to encompass my current attire*—*"all sweaty and manly like this?"*

"Is that so?"

Her eyes flare with heat, and she steps closer, raising a hand to gently brush sawdust from my chin. "Oh, honey. That's a fact."

We'd christened that house so many times, in every single room. I recall thinking that was what it was all about. That love like that, like ours, was the kind I'd always heard stories about. One that would last.

My eyes flash open at the harsh reality of how wrong I had been.

Turning to Wells, I raise my eyebrows in question. "Feel like spending your last night here as my date to a gala?"

He places his palm against the front of his suit. "Why, Knox Montgomery. How the tongues will wag."

Jesus. "We were invited by Becket Jones."

His expression is wiped clean of all humor, and his gaze narrows on me. "We were invited by the man your ex-fiancée is rumored to be shacking up with?"

"That's right." I proceed to fill him in on the entire conversation that took place earlier in Emma Jane's office.

He leans back farther in the chair and strums his fingers on the armrests contemplatively. "And what do you think about this? Is it an olive branch?"

Pressing my lips thin, I carefully consider Wells's question. "I'm not entirely sure that's the case. Possibly. But more than anything else, it felt like he was almost..." I trail off, unsure if I want to actually voice the words.

"Playing matchmaker," Wells finishes for me.

I simply nod and avert my gaze, pondering the idea. Silence falls over us for a moment before he finally speaks.

"What if he is? And what if all these rumors about them have been just that? What does that mean to you?"

Wearily, I run a hand down my face before I raise my troubled eyes to his.

"Hell if I know."

"YOU OWE ME FOR THIS," Wells reminds me yet again. "I say two crawfish boils at your place might make it even." He gives me a pained expression. "Because you know I hate wearing a damn tux."

I offer him a dry look. "Yet you travel with one at the ready."

"One must always be prepared."

With a laugh, I add, "Need I remind you that I *always* host the crawfish boils?"

"Well, that's true, but I—" He breaks off abruptly, most likely catching sight of a beautiful woman. "Oh my. I'd forgotten how well she cleaned up."

It's on the tip of my tongue to ask him who he's referring when I follow his line of sight.

And promptly lose all ability to form words.

She's exquisite. Her dark hair is twisted up in a way that makes it look effortless and touchable. Her eyes are more striking than usual, accentuated by darker makeup, and her lips are a subtle, soft shade of red. Her mouth parts with a smile as she talks with an older couple, and while the woman looks vaguely familiar, I don't pay any mind because I instantly feel the warmth from Emma Jane's smile, even if it isn't centered on me. But what's really the most showstopping of all is her dress.

The dress is a deep shade of blue, made of a shimmery fabric with wide straps on the edge of each shoulder. The front dips down in a thin, sharp V, but not too much to be indecent. With a cinched waist, it flares down to the floor.

"On second thought, I think she looks rather pitiful in that getup."

My head snaps around and I stare at Wells. "*What?*"

He smiles and gives me a slight shove in the shoulder. "Just checking to see if you managed to find your ability to speak."

Before I can respond, we're interrupted.

"Great to see you, Knox." Becket holds out a hand, his warm smile greeting me. I accept his handshake. "And your plus one..." His smile widens as he takes in the sight of Wells. "I can honestly say I expected a plus one of the female variety."

Wells eyes Becket. "Are you saying I don't measure up?"

Becket laughs. "It's safe to say you both measure up a little too well, from the looks of it." He tips his head to indicate a group of ladies nearby who are obviously discussing us.

"Wells Kennedy." My friend holds out his hand for Becket, and the two men exchange a quick handshake.

"I'm his plus one out of obligation since I've been in town to check financials and contracts."

"Ah, I take it you're from Mobile, too?"

Wells cocks his head in question at the inquiry, and Becket merely shrugs. "Just assumed, since Knox and Blue are both from there, as well."

Wells's eyebrows rise slightly and he flashes me a quick look. "Yes, I'm from Mobile, just like Knox and *Blue*."

Ah. I know what he's getting at, and I can't say that I blame him. It grates on my nerves, too. The fact that this guy has a little nickname for EJ.

I mean, Emma Jane.

Shit.

"I'll let her know you've arrived." Becket offers an easy smile before turning and calling, "Blue?"

Blue. God, that nickname is going to make me grind my teeth into dust.

"Want to come over and say hi to our friends?" Becket asks, and the way he's turned prevents me from seeing past him to gauge her reaction.

If I thought she was gorgeous while standing about twenty feet away, it pales in comparison to how breathtaking she is once barely three feet separate us.

Right now, right here at this moment, drives home the fact that she's turned into an elegant, poised woman. So vastly different from the one I once knew who would rebel against her strict, overbearing father and dye a streak of blue or purple in her hair or get her nose pierced.

Sure, back then, she'd been refined and knew the proper etiquette for social events and outings, but she always had a hint of wildness within her.

Now, I can't help but wonder where that wildness went. If it was extinguished, much like the way she killed our love, our future plans, our—

"Knox? Becket was just asking how long you'll be in charge of the company before you hire a new CEO?" Wells prompts.

Great. I've been zoning out, going all maudlin about the past.

Doing my best to exude a calm, cool composure, I slip my hands in my pockets and offer a shrug of nonchalance. "I'm hoping everything will be firmed up within a matter of a few months." Tipping my head in Emma Jane's direction, I add, "Assuming we can get our prospective deals finalized."

Becket drapes an arm around Emma Jane's shoulders, and my spine immediately goes rigid in response as a fierce surge of jealousy pulses through my veins. "I foresee my girl, here, knocking that out of the park. And"—he flashes a pointed look at me—"earning that promotion."

She laughs nervously. "Beck, now's not the time to talk business."

He shoots her a look of confusion. "But weren't you just talking to the editor of—"

"I could use some more champagne," she interrupts, and the two of them have some weird silent conversation.

Finally, Becket winks and gives us an apologetic smile. "Excuse me, gentlemen." He plucks her glass from her grip. "I need to get the lady a refill."

"I think I'll follow you and get myself a drink," Wells pipes up, and before I can say anything, he and Becket disappear in the crowd.

"Well." Emma Jane clears her throat and smiles politely. "You and Wells are making good progress with looking everything over?"

"Yes," I answer, watching as she fiddles with the clasp of her small wristlet purse. "It's been trying at times, but things are coming along."

"That's great." Another polite smile.

I fucking hate it. I don't want a polite smile. I want a real one, dammit.

Silence falls over us—awkward silence, at that—and the words spill out.

"Remember the time we went to some debutante ball, and you were pissed at Annabeth for calling you and your newly dyed hair an 'abomination,' so you tampered with the punch she insisted on having even though no one liked it?"

"And it turned her teeth red for days," she finishes with a laugh, her lips parting in a wide smile at the memory. Shaking her head, her eyes sparkle with humor. "It was the best revenge." Her expression sobers slightly, and her brows draw together, her head tipping to the side. "But you took the fall for that instead of me," she adds softly.

My smile mirrors hers, genuine and softened with the fondness of memories. "I didn't mind taking the heat so my girl could escape the wrath."

Her eyes study me thoughtfully. "You were forced to clean the administration offices for a month."

I lift a shoulder in an off-hand shrug. "Wasn't the worst punishment I ever suffered." I cock an eyebrow and flash her a smug grin. "Plus, I believe someone crept in after hours while I was cleaning and gave me extra incentive to finish up faster."

She laughs and shakes her head before her features cloud. "Knox, I—"

"They're playing our song." Becket reappears and snags her wrist, drawing her attention. "Dance with me, please, gorgeous?"

She frowns. "But I thought you were getting me a champagne?"

"Oh, I'm sorry." He offers her a look of faux dismay

before brightening. "Knox and Wells can watch over your purse because"—EJ appears stunned as Becket slides the strap of her small wristlet over and off her wrist—"you're going to need to bring your A-game for this one."

Becket tosses the purse at me, and luckily, I catch it. I watch the two walk away, hand in hand.

"Why don't we snag that table over there?" Wells gestures to an available table that's on the outskirts of the ballroom. I follow him, carrying Emma Jane's purse, and set it on the table.

We take our seats, and Wells sets our drinks down before he reaches over and flicks open the clasp of her purse.

"What the hell are you doing?" I hiss incredulously.

He flashes me a bored expression before taking a sip of his drink. "Just look inside." He averts his eyes to the dance floor where Becket and Emma Jane are dancing.

I feel torn between curiosity and guilt. But, as I tap a finger to the side of the small purse, nothing is jostled out except for her slim cell phone. A tiny zippered square, which I assume is a wallet, is still tucked inside, and I want badly to see what's inside.

And if she decided to carry a condom with her tonight.

With what feels like lightning speed, I reach in for the small wallet, but my finger snags something else.

And I stop dead in my tracks.

Because what I originally thought was the inner fabric of the purse isn't. It's a handkerchief. With a monogram.

With my initials on it.

21

Emma Jane

"So this dance was a ploy of some sort, wasn't it?"

"I don't know what you're talking about." Becket's answer is accompanied by the telltale sparkle of amusement in his dark eyes. Which means he's full of it.

"Becket," I warn.

"Blue," he parrots back with a wide grin. "Just let me work my magic."

With a laughing roll of my eyes, I let him spin me out and back before he dips me with flair.

It's his—well, really *our*—go-to dance at events like this.

Pulling me closer and smiling down sweetly, he presses a kiss to my forehead, and as we sway, he murmurs, "You still keep that handkerchief in your purse, don't you?"

Drawing back in surprise, I stare up at him. "How do you know about—" I shake my head. "Never mind. You're Becket Jones. You always meddle."

His eyebrows rise expectantly. "You mean I help people?"

With a little laugh, I shake my head. "You set it up so

he'd find my handkerchief." Suddenly, a thought stops me. "Wait. How would he find it *inside* my purse?"

He just gives me a look.

"No." My eyes narrow. "He wouldn't."

"No, he wouldn't." I relax instantly. "But I bet Wells would."

My eyes widen with alarm. "Becket, he can't—"

He dips his head, our gazes lock, and from others' perspectives, we probably appear like two lovers, engaged in an intimate conversation.

Not squabbling like we actually are.

"Blue." The way he murmurs my name gains my attention because his tone is softer, gentled. "When the past knocks on your door, it's because there's unfinished business."

"But you're—"

"Helping it along so you can finish it." He levels me a look. "Because you and I both know he's the one man who still has a hold on your heart."

"THANKS FOR A WONDERFUL NIGHT. Even if I did have to wear this getup, it was worth it." Wells and Becket shake hands like old friends.

"Saw you chatting up that one blonde in the red dress." Becket grins and wiggles his eyebrows at Wells.

"And that's my cue." I offer my goodbyes with a tired smile before addressing Becket. "I'll wait for you in the lobby." Turning, I take one step in the direction of the exit of the ballroom. Only about a third of the original crowd remains, either dancing or chatting at the numerous round tables.

"Wait." Becket's voice stops me. "I'm thinking of doing the after party."

Slowly spinning on my heel, I narrow my eyes at my friend. "The after party?" I repeat slowly.

Becket hates after parties of any kind. Heck, he's repeatedly preached to me about how much he abhors them.

"Yeah, an after party. So"—he nods to Knox and Wells beside him—"these two gentlemen would be honored to see you home, I'm sure."

"Of course, we would," Wells instantly agrees. "Oh, wait!"

"Let me guess," I suggest in a bored tone, "you forgot that you suddenly have an affinity for after parties too?"

Wells doesn't answer me. Instead, he addresses Becket. "Mind if I tag along?"

"Not at all."

"Well, let's head out then."

I stand here stunned because my best friend just gave me the heave-ho.

"Bye, gorgeous." He drops a quick kiss to my cheek. "Call you later." And the two of them are gone in a flash.

Leaving me with Knox. Again.

With a weary sigh, I open my purse and withdraw my cell phone. "Look, don't feel obligated. I can get a cab or a ride with Lyft."

As I scroll through my phone for the app, Knox's softly spoken words drift over me.

"I'd be honored to take you home."

My eyes lift to his, and all I witness in the depths is sincerity.

He tips his head toward the entrance of the ballroom, only a few feet away, and I now notice the first few notes of a song I once loved. Knox's expression turns almost bashful.

"One last dance?" He holds out an upturned palm.

Indecision wars within me until something gives way. I'm not certain whether it's my weakness for the old Elton John song, "I Guess That's Why They Call It the Blues" and the way the musicians aren't butchering it like most tend to do, or if it's the fact that I actually want to dance with Knox. To simply pretend we don't have a past and tons of baggage between us.

Sliding my phone back inside my purse, I snap it closed. When I slip my hand into his, his features soften, eyes crinkling at the corners with a small smile forming on his lips.

After leading me to the dance floor, he pulls me in close, and it's like that moment when you're on the verge of solving a new puzzle and you have maybe half a dozen pieces left. The picture is there—evident—but still incomplete. But you know where those pieces need to go, and things slip into place with ease.

That's what I feel when I dance with Knox—when his hand falls to rest at my hip, the way he grasps my other hand in his, the way we fit together so perfectly.

I don't think anything of it when he dips his head just so, and his jaw brushes lightly against my cheek. The short yet soft strands of his beard take part in a tantalizing dance across my skin.

"Remember when you found out Elton John was coming to Mobile, and you just about went crazy trying to save up the money for tickets to see him in concert?"

My eyes fall closed at the memory, but also at the way Knox's husky voice sounds melodic and intimate.

A smile plays upon my lips. "And you surprised me by scoring front row tickets." My eyes open, and I lean back slightly to peer up at him in question. "How did you manage that, by the way?"

His eyes are alit with what appears to be humor and possibly affection. "A guy's gotta have some secrets, doesn't he?"

As though someone's just tossed ice cold water on me, his words wake me from a daze.

Secrets. Boy, he's not kidding.

I draw to a stop, pulling from his embrace, and fix a polite smile on my face.

"Thank you for the dance, but I'm calling it a night."

Desperate to put distance between us, I walk as fast as I possibly can without breaking an ankle in these heels. And the irony is not lost on me.

Yet again, I find myself walking away from Knox Montgomery.

Emma Jane
WEDDING DAY

"Do you think…I can't…" I'm having great difficulty voicing coherent thoughts. Not to mention, I'm also on the verge of hyperventilating.

I relented and let my best friend inside the room, hoping she'll be able to help me regain composure and figure out what I should do.

"Calm down." Katherine pats my back soothingly. "You had no way of knowing. Especially since you've been so wrapped up in work and wedding planning."

Something in her words, in her tone, brings my eyes up to clash with hers. "I had no way of knowing," I repeat numbly. "Meaning…you knew?"

Her smile is sympathetic yet pitying. And that speaks volumes.

Frantic, I nearly rip the engagement ring from my finger and slam it down on the small table off to the side of the room. I stand, my chest heaving with heavy breaths, and stare down at what I'd thought was a beautiful token of the start of our lives together as a married couple.

Now, though, all I see when I look at this diamond ring is betrayal and lies.

And devastating heartache.

22

Knox

PRESENT
OCTOBER

"What the hell are you doing at a florist this early in the morning? Did someone die?"

Why did I blurt out where I was to Wells? Sweet Jesus, it's Monday morning, and my head's still not right after how things ended between me and Emma Jane the night of the gala.

"Just let it go," I mutter into my cell phone with clenched teeth.

"I'm over here at the office—been here since five this morning—and I could use something to distract me from the messages from the city council about how hellfire and damnation will be brought upon the lovely city of Mobile if we allow a grocery store that offers primarily organic foods to be built in the downtown area. The same downtown area whose population is growing in vast numbers."

"The same downtown area that only has one old, rinky-dink grocery store," I supply, shaking my head as I peruse the various flowers in the shop. "That's why they need more freethinking people on the council. People who aren't against any form of growth or addition but still appreciate ways to keep the quaint and historical relevance of the city."

"Exactly." Wells pauses. "Think you'd consider running for councilman? And what are you doing at the florist again?"

I make a face even though I know he can't see it. "Not a chance. And I'm getting a dai—"

That sneaky fucker.

"Ah." There's no missing the smugness in his tone. "A flower for your Southern belle. Just like old times."

"That's enough out of you."

He just laughs. "I'll let you get to your flower picking. Good luck."

We end our call and I finally spy a lone daisy in the top portion of one of the refrigerated sections. I open the door and reach up to snag it when I hear a female voice.

"Good morning, Pete."

"Morning, Ms. Emma Jane." I can hear the warmth in the shop employee's voice. It doesn't surprise me that the older man has taken to her since she's always had a way about her that makes everyone like her. "I saved one for you, and it's—"

He stops, and I know it's because he's just noticed me. Grasping the stem of the flower, I pluck it from the container and close the door to the case before turning around.

"Oh, dear." This comes from Pete.

"Oh." My eyes land on Emma Jane and I watch as her eyes flicker back and forth between me and the flower I'm currently holding. Finally, she turns to Pete and offers an overly bright smile. "Thanks anyway, Pete. I'll check back tomorrow." With a quick wave, her heels click in rapid staccato and she's gone.

Heading over to the cash register, I hand my card to Pete who looks a bit torn between confusion and dismay. "Not to worry." I wink. "It just so happens this flower's intended for her."

"Oh, I see." His expression relaxes instantly, and he lets out a relieved sigh. "Thank heavens." He slides my card through the reader, and a soft smile plays at his lips. "When she stops in, she's like a bright ray of sunshine, and I hate to disappoint her on the rare occasions I don't have a daisy for her." With narrowed eyes, he gives me a sharp look while we wait for the credit card slip to print out. "You're on the up-and-up, though, aren't you?"

Am I? I'm caught off guard by his question. "Yes, sir."

He eyes me hard before ripping off the receipt and sliding it across the counter for my signature. Pete hands me a pen, and I accept it, but he holds tight, waiting for me to meet his gaze again.

"It doesn't take a genius to know that lovely woman's been hurt by a man. I also know she's not the modern type who shacks up with some young buck. She's a white picket fence woman."

I once thought the same thing, I muse to myself.

Long after I exit the shop and head to the office with a flower in hand, Pete's earlier words stay with me.

"That lovely woman's been hurt by a man."

I'm dying to know exactly who hurt her.

And wonder if she realizes just how much she once hurt me.

"GOOD MORNING. AGAIN."

I greet Emma Jane, stepping into her office, and place the daisy in her vase. I fill it with water from her small restroom off the corner of her office before placing it on her table.

"Thank you." Her tone is subdued and almost tentative.

"You're welcome." I take a seat in one of the chairs facing her desk. "I also have good news. You have an assistant again."

Her shoulders slump in relief. "Oh, thank God." She flashes me a pained smile. "Lord have mercy on this poor woman because she's going to have her work cut out for her."

There's a knock on the open door, and we both turn to find Keri Mitchell, the intern and Emma Jane's new temporary assistant, standing there.

"Come in," I wave her inside and gesture to the chair beside me. "Take a seat and we can fill you in on everything."

Emma Jane smiles at Keri. "I can't tell you how relieved I am to have some help again. I hope you aren't intimidated by a bit of a larger workload than normal because"—she waves a hand toward three thick files on her desk—"we're in the process of trying to close a few deals and executing some proposals."

"I'll leave you ladies to it." I rise from my seat. "I look forward to seeing the upcoming proposals in the next few weeks." With a polite nod and smile, I leave the office.

I can't lie and say the disappointment of no longer having an excuse to work closely with Emma Jane and offer a helping hand doesn't weigh heavily on me.

"I KNOW. LOVE YOU, TOO."

I step forward into the office a few days later, watching as Emma Jane sets her cell phone aside, already jotting notes in the margin of some printouts.

"How's everything working out?"

Her head snaps up in surprise before she regains her composure. "Oh, everything's fine. Thank you."

I reach back and pull the door closed behind me. Stepping closer to the chairs facing where she's seated at her desk, I lower my voice. "I just wanted to check and see how things were going with Ms. Mitchell."

"Everything's coming along well. She's been a huge help." Emma Jane drops her pen and leans back slightly. "She's gone above and beyond, in fact, and asked me to increase the work I've been giving her." She gives a little laugh and shakes her head, a stray strand of hair coming loose from her loose bun. "Guess that's what being a young twenty-something is all about."

"Ah, now." I smile while slipping my hands in my pockets to prevent the further urging of my fingers to slide that piece of hair behind her ear. Because I know if I touch her in any way, it'll be all over. "You speak like you're an old fogey already."

"I turned thirty last year." She makes a face. "It's all downhill from here."

"But you just keep getting more beautiful as you go."

I have no idea where the hell that came from, but it's clear that I've managed to startle not only myself but her as well.

Clearing my throat, I avert my eyes to her table where there's a pathetic, wilted daisy. "You should have told me. I would've picked one up for you."

Silence greets my comment, and it lasts so long that I

finally turn to look at her. She continues to study me and then parts her lips to respond.

Just when there's a knock on the door, and it opens.

"Ms. Haywood, I have the—" Keri falters slightly. "I'm sorry." Her eyes dart back and forth between me and Emma Jane before tentatively offering, "Should I come back later?"

"No," Emma Jane answers quickly. "I believe Mr. Montgomery and I are finished." She shoots me a questioning look.

With a brief nod, I make my way to the door. "I'll touch base with you on that proposal later, Ms. Haywood."

23

Emma Jane

Sweet Jesus, give me strength.

I repeat this internally as I track Knox's exit from my office. He looks so good in that gray suit paired with an emerald-green tie that brings out his eyes. I was instantly transfixed the moment he entered the room.

With effort, I drag my eyes away from him and fix my attention on my assistant. I offer the young woman a smile. "Thanks for all your help with everything, Keri. You've been a lifesaver."

Keri runs a shaky hand over her mousy blond hair which is pulled back in a severe ponytail. She ducks her head and murmurs, "It's my pleasure."

She's dressed in a prim and proper pantsuit, further accentuating her overly thin figure. I'm not sure how to get this poor woman to relax around me, but every interaction we have has me feeling like I instill a near frightening nervousness in her.

"We present this proposal to Mr. Montgomery in a few weeks and this deal could really impact *F&F*—in a great way—so I want to be sure we have all our ducks in a row."

"Yes, ma'am. Absolutely." She takes a seat across from me with her legal pad and pen poised to jot down important notes.

"All right, so we need to…"

"THANKS, AGAIN, KERI," I say with a grateful smile. "Have a great night."

"You, too, Ms. Haywood."

She exits my office after a long day of work, and I chuckle softly at her insistence on calling me Ms. Haywood instead of Emma Jane. From the start, I'd told her to feel free to call me by my first name, but she insists on being more formal.

I'm setting the file on my desk when a male voice catches me off guard.

"Know where I can find my workaholic best friend? The one who forgot about our FWOB date tonight?"

My head snaps up, and I stare wide-eyed at Becket. "Oh, no!"

I'd completely lost track of time, and the fact I was supposed to meet Becket for dinner at six thirty had slipped my mind.

It's close to seven right now.

He grins. "Oh, yes." Becket places a palm over the center of his chest and lets out a dejected sigh. "The wound cuts so deep."

Covering my face with my hands, I slump over my desk. "I'm so sorry. I've been trying—"

"To do your job," he finishes for me, the teasing gone from his voice. Instead there's understanding. "I get it."

Suddenly, he's gently tugging my hands away from my

face and I find him crouched beside me. "Hey, it's okay. I promise."

"But you had reservations and everything." My lips twist with regret and self-recrimination.

He raises an eyebrow. "Do you really think Luigi's won't let *me* make another reservation there?"

With a tiny laugh, I shove at his shoulder. "So humble."

He grins and reaches up to tuck some stray hair behind my ear. "Now come on and let's get you some dinner." Helping me up from my chair, he adds, "One cannot live on coffee and sweet tea alone."

"Speak for yourself," I tease.

Once I've gathered up my belongings and I lock up my office, we head toward the bank of elevators. "Want to order in Chinese?"

A ding sounds, and a door opens for us. Heading inside, I lean against the wall, tip my head back, and close my eyes. "Sounds good."

"Your place?"

I open my eyes and nod wordlessly, knowing my place is closer than Becket's. He murmurs his assent and pulls out his phone to begin looking up the restaurant to place the order for delivery.

As the doors begin to close, an arm suddenly shoots out and stops them. Instantly, prickles of awareness roll through me at the sight of the hand whose fingers have telltale nicks and scrapes from home improvement projects.

I just can't seem to catch a break, and part of me wishes Knox would go back to regarding me with hatred and anger all the time. It was far less complicated then.

"Hey, man," Becket greets Knox. "Working my girl to the bone, again, huh?"

I feel the weight of Knox's eyes on me, but I can't bring myself to look at him.

"I got her an assistant."

Becket laughs. "Well, you should know better. Blue always—"

"Takes on more than her fair share of the workload."

My breath catches at Knox's words because it's not so much his response as it is the way he says it. With affection…and maybe even the barest hint of pride.

"I was placing an order for Chinese delivery. We're heading back to her place if you want to join us."

My eyes fly to Becket who's purposely avoiding looking at me.

"Uh, I don't want to intrude." Knox's polite response is a total out.

Becket needs to take it.

Take it, I plead silently. *Take. It.*

"No intrusion whatsoever." My best friend gives a dismissive wave. "The more the merrier."

I'm literally staring a hole in him. Because not once in the eight years we've been friends and holding our Friends Without Benefits date nights have we invited anyone else along.

Never. It's been like an unspoken rule.

Which apparently has changed.

"Just tell me what you normally order, and I'll submit it right now with ours." He holds his phone and fixes an expectant look on Knox.

"Sweet and sour chicken," we both answer in unison.

I freeze, realizing I spoke without meaning to. That I've shown my hand—that I distinctly recall what specific dish Knox had normally ordered for Chinese takeout. My eyes fall closed in embarrassment and dismay.

"Sweet and sour chicken it is." My best friend's voice is heavy with amusement.

This dinner night has trouble written all over it.

"WHY ARE you getting out my nice wine glasses?" I hiss at Becket, returning them to my kitchen cabinet.

He merely reaches over my head and plucks them back out, holding them over my head out of reach. "Because we should have wine with our dinner."

"It's after seven at night."

He frowns at me with exaggerated seriousness. "Do you have a curfew I'm not aware of?"

Narrowing my eyes, I pointedly ask, "And are *you* having wine with me?"

"You know I don't drink."

Folding my arms across my chest, I level a look at him. Because *I* know this. Yet... "Then why are you getting two wine glasses?"

His mischievous grin irritates me even more. "For you and—"

"No." I wag a finger at him. "No, no, no." Pressing my palms against his chest, I shove to no avail since he's a Mack truck compared to me. "Go sell your crazy somewhere else."

The doorbell rings and I hear Knox thanking the delivery person.

"The food's here," Knox calls out, his footsteps sounding along the hardwood floor as he draws close to the kitchen.

Becket's eyes grow wide with surprise and my stomach drops. Because I know that expression.

It's nothing but trouble.

"I just remembered that I have something urgent to do. Sadly, I'll have to take my dinner with me."

My hands fly to my hips while I glare at him. *Hard*.

He simply grins back sweetly. Dropping a quick kiss to

my cheek, he turns and roots through the bags Knox placed on my kitchen counter. Once he finds his meal, he abruptly announces, "Gotta run. You kids have a great night."

With that, he's gone, leaving Knox and I standing in stunned silence.

He cocks his head to the side quizzically. "What did he have to do?"

"Something urgent," I answer in monotone. Because it's obvious Becket was full of crap.

"Huh." He nods slowly, and his eyes dart around the kitchen before returning to me. "Look, if you want to eat alone, I understand."

"No, it's fine."

He studies me, those emerald eyes searching, poring over my features. "You don't have to be polite. We're both off the clock."

I exhale loudly. "If you really mean that, then you won't mind if I change into my sloppiest yoga pants and T-shirt and pour myself an extra-large glass of wine with my dinner?"

The slow smile he gives me begins to turn my insides to mush until I force myself to mentally shake off the effect. "If you're okay with me losing this tie."

I offer a faint, tentative smile. "Sounds like a plan. I'll be right back."

IT'S NEARLY NINE O'CLOCK, and the exhaustion of the day is fully catching up to me. Knox and I have actually had a nice dinner. We've stuck to safe topics, luckily. He's been telling me about the house he purchased in Midtown and the improvements he's making. The pride in his eyes, the way they light up while he talks about everything, makes it impossible not to be drawn in and entranced by him.

Exactly what I can't allow to happen.

When he helps me clean up, he notices the stack of mail I'd brought in earlier when the three of us had arrived here. I hadn't paid attention to it since I'd been so thrown off by Becket inviting Knox over in the first place.

"I got this in the mail the other day as well."

I turn in question and find him holding a letter with a familiar return address label. My grandfather's address.

Immediately, dread churns sickly in the pit of my stomach, because Granddad calls me. He never sends me anything formal in the mail.

My eyes flick back and forth between what appears to be an envelope for a formal invitation and Knox's eyes. "What is it?" I manage to get out.

He appears to hesitate. "An invitation to your father's sixtieth birthday party."

Spinning around to face my sink, I grip the edge of it, my knuckles turning white.

"Why would he invite me?"

"Why wouldn't he?" He sounds confused by my question. "You're their daughter."

Tears gather in my eyes, and I swallow hard past the lump in my throat. "I haven't spoken to my father in eight years." Knox should know this. Being a businessman in Mobile, it's a given that he does business with my father.

My admission is met with silence.

I know Granddad means well, but he should know that if I were to show up, my father would raise all sorts of hell.

"Neither have I."

It takes a moment for Knox's words to sink in. I raise my head in shock, still facing away. "What?"

He lays a gentle hand on my shoulder. "I haven't spoken to your father, aside from a random greeting when we cross paths in public, in years."

Why? It's on the tip of my tongue to ask him this. But I don't because I can't afford to open that door I've kept locked tightly all these years. Due to Knox's unexpected and sudden arrival in my life, it already has cracks in it, and feels warped, as if it fails to close securely.

"Are you going?" I ask in nearly a whisper.

"I am." He pauses briefly. "Your granddad wrote a note in mine, asking me to please consider coming."

My lips curve upward slightly as I recall Knox always having a soft spot for my granddad.

"If you want to go, I can…" He hesitates. When his hand drops from my shoulder, the loss is instant, and I feel like I'm barraged by a sudden draft of cold, bitter air. "I can drive over with you. So you're not alone."

I shake my head sadly. "I haven't been back in so long." My voice cracks, and I clear my throat to try to cover it up. "He disowned me."

"You're his daughter, EJ," he murmurs quietly. "Nothing can change that. Plus, it's been a long time. He may be a stubborn old coot, but I know he loves you."

I let out a humorless laugh. Because I distinctly recall my father's text messages that fateful day. Love came long after business and his public image.

"At least open it and see."

Knox's outstretched hand holding the envelope comes into view. I cautiously accept and stare down at the invitation before I open it.

Out falls a small, folded note and I instantly recognize my granddad's handwriting.

My dearest Emma Jane,

I know you're wondering why I didn't call and talk to you about this. Your father's experienced some challenges and his perspective has changed on many things. He's still a stubborn mule, but his mind is not as narrow as it once was. I'm asking you to strongly consider coming into town for his birthday celebration I'm having at the house. It would be so nice to have you back home. And before you ask, no, your father doesn't know I sent this to you. But I believe that it would make his birthday more meaningful to have you present.
Please consider coming, Sweet Pea. If not for him, then for me.
All my love,
Granddad

"Some things never change, huh?" Knox murmurs.

My mouth curves upward in a weak smile. "If you're referring to the fact that my granddad still calls me Sweet Pea, then no."

There's a beat of silence, and I know what he's going to ask before he voices it.

"So what do you think?"

Staring down at the invitation in my hands, I shake my head. "I think I'm scared." A derisive sound bubbles up from my throat. "Which is shameful that a grown woman should feel that way about the possibility of attending her own father's birthday party."

"I'll stay by your side." His offer brings my eyes up to meet his. "I'll make sure everything goes smoothly." He clears his throat and steps back to drag a hand through his hair, mussing it slightly. "Plus, I have plenty of room at my place, to save you from having to stay at a hotel."

"Knox," I breathe out. "I don't think that's wise."

A crease appears between his brows, and it instantly evokes a powerful urge for me to press the pads of my fingertips to his skin and smooth out that wrinkle. "Why not?"

My shoulders slump. God, this man can be dense. "We have a past." I wave a hand between us. "We have so much unfinished business. It's just…not smart."

"We've been fine lately. We've worked well together. We're…" He hesitates before finishing with, "Friends."

Friends. Part of me is grateful that he thinks of us that way, especially after all that's gone on. But for that same reason, it also angers me.

I'm not certain I can truly be friends with someone who's dealt such a devastating blow to my heart. The old adage about forgiving and forgetting is unfathomable to me because I don't believe it's possible to erase the memory of the pain Knox inflicted on my heart. Which means the smart thing to do is to politely decline his offer.

As it turns out, I'm not smart at all when it comes to this man.

24

Knox
NOVEMBER

The drive to Mobile goes smoother than I expected.

"I can't believe they went out of business," Emma Jane muses about the one bait and tackle shop a few miles away from where she grew up. "That was where we'd get our supplies to go crabbin'."

I can't disguise the way my mouth curves up in a grin. Since we've crossed into Mobile city limits, her Southern accent has made a bit of a comeback.

It makes me wonder if anything else will return along with it.

"I'm glad Ella Mae's alteration shop is still doing well," she murmurs, facing her window.

She falls silent the closer we get to my house, likely recalling all the memories it holds. Once I pull up the driveway and park, we exit the vehicle.

Emma Jane closes her passenger side door and pauses to appraise my house.

"It looks beautiful." Her eyes find mine before they dart away. "I love the flowers you planted along the front."

I tear my gaze from the scattering of daisies, their

bright white petals contrasting with the vivid yellow centers, and open the back door to get our bags. "I planted them a while ago. Thought they'd give the place 'curb appeal.'"

When I say I planted them a while ago, I mean I did it a few months after you left. When I still had hope you'd come back.

I grab our things and carry them up the sidewalk leading to my house. After I punch in the code on the keypad to unlock the door, I open it for us to step inside.

Once I give her a cursory tour, I show her to the guest room where she'll be staying. It, along with the guest bathroom, are the only doors left open. Wells helped me with that as soon as I knew she was going to accompany me on this trip.

I set her bags on the bed and wave a hand to encompass the room. "This is yours." I point through the doorway to across the hall. "The bathroom is there. Help yourself to any food in the kitchen. Watch whatever you want on TV. I have to unpack and catch up on some emails." With that, I rush out of the room, to leave the increasingly intimate confines of this space.

This was an idiotic idea, offering to let her stay with me. It's difficult enough being around her when we're at work or out at social gatherings, fighting to escape from beneath the fierce, impenetrable blanket of attraction when she's near. Especially after that one night…

As soon as I step one foot over the threshold, she utters a subdued, "Knox?"

I stop but don't turn around. "Yes?"

"Thank you. For letting me stay here." She pauses. "Especially…after everything."

Like you leaving me at the altar? Without an explanation?

My hand tightens on the straps of my laptop and duffle bags draped over my shoulder while my other hand absently rubs at the center of my chest where there's a sharp, searing pain.

"You're welcome."

I head down the hall to what is now my master suite and close the door.

Only then am I able to breathe easier.

"LET ME GUESS." Wells pauses like he's deep in thought for a moment. "You're making stir-fry. With extra water chestnuts."

For a split second, I pause stirring the vegetables in the pan, my eyes narrowing slightly in irritation. Cradling the phone between my cheek and shoulder, I add more soy sauce.

"You did, didn't you?" *Shit.* He keeps going without even waiting for my answer. "Seduction by water chestnuts. Brilliant." Wells chortles with laughter.

"Is this the only reason you called?" My bored tone is obvious.

"No, actually." He sobers, sounding more serious now. "I called because I wanted to know exactly what the hell you're doing."

"What are you talking about?"

He releases an exasperated sigh. "Come on, man. You brought your ex-fiancée back to your house when she could've just as easily stayed in a hotel."

"Not that easily if the talk is true about how many people are coming in from out of town for Davis Haywood's birthday party."

"Not buying it."

I flip the dial, turning off the heat on the stovetop.

Placing the lid over the stir-fry, I turn to lean against the counter across from the stove.

"Nothing to buy. Her granddad sent us both invitations and personally asked us to attend."

"Right," he remarks dubiously. "And y'all had to drive together for, what? Nearly six hours? She couldn't drive herself?"

I drag a hand down my face, my patience running thin with his questioning. "Look, it's done, okay? She's here. I'm here. We're both going to the party. End of story."

"Where are you sleeping?"

My head falls back, and I stare up at the ceiling in confusion. "Where do I normally sleep, Wells?" I ask with weary exasperation.

He falls silent for a beat until he finally releases an, "Ah, I see."

I refuse to fall for his trap so I don't respond.

"Someday, you'll have to figure out what to do with that room."

"I've got to go and eat dinner." My steely tone finally seems to get through to him.

"Fine." He sighs. "But you know I'm right." There's another pause, and his tone softens. "Just be smart."

I make a sound of affirmation and hurry to end the call.

Be smart. I'm not sure if I've ever truly been able to do that around Emma Jane. My heart's always taken the lead.

Turning, I stare out the large sliding glass doors leading to the porch and dock, with the gleaming waters of Mobile Bay at the shoreline down below, and find my mind wandering.

"Your dad's going to shit bricks, EJ," I muse, shaking my head at the streaks of blue in her hair.

She shrugs. "Whatever." Reaching up, she smooths a hand down over her hair. "I love it." With a mischievous grin, she adds, "So does Granddad."

"Of course, he does," I say with a laugh. Her granddad dotes on her and I can't say that I blame him. I tug her closer, framing her face with my hands, and gaze down into her blue eyes. "I love you."

She smiles up at me and it's one I cherish because it's brimming with emotion, her eyes alight with love and crinkling at the corners with happiness. "I love you, too, Knox." She presses a sweet kiss to my lips. "Always."

Always, she'd said. After knowing her for what seems like forever, I know how to decipher when she's lying and telling the truth. And back then, she'd been telling the truth.

Hell if I know what made it all change.

25

Emma Jane

"Did you pack the prophylactics?"

"Becket!" I hiss, darting a glance at my closed bedroom door. Not that I believe Knox can hear my friend over the phone, but still.

"Hey, I'm looking out for your best interests."

"Go an' tell me more tall tales," I respond drily.

He pauses for so long that I frown with concern. "Beck? Are you there?"

"Did you just hear yourself?"

"What are you talkin' about?"

Amusement is laced in his tone when he speaks. "You're going back to your roots. I already hear it." He chuckles softly. "I sometimes hear traces of that thick Southern accent when you'd get fired up over something you were working on. Or when you're laying on the charm at an event you attended with me."

"That doesn't mean—"

"Anything? Sure, it does. It means a lot."

"Like what?"

Before he can answer, a knock sounds and Knox's voice carries through the closed door.

"I'm making stir-fry if you want some."

Moving the phone away from my mouth, I call out, "Okay, great. Thanks."

"I once heard all great things start with stir-fry," Becket declares.

I throw myself back on the bed with a small groan. "Beck, stop."

He inhales sharply in dramatic fashion. And I know what's coming next. "I bet you a ten spot he throws in extra water chestnuts for you. Even after all these years, I'm sure he remembers you love extra in your stir-fry."

"A ten spot? Really, Beck?"

"What? Those little water chestnuts might just be game changers."

"For heaven's sake." I make an exasperated sound. "I'm hanging up now."

"But wait! You haven't blessed my heart yet. Isn't that how it's done in the Deep South?"

If I roll my eyes any harder, I'm certain they'll get stuck.

"Goodbye, Becket."

I end the call, toss my phone down on the bed beside me, and continue to stare up at the ceiling.

"I have a surprise for you." Knox's excitement is evident, his grin contagious, as he leads me down the hall of his house.

He'd finally finished all the renovations he'd planned and had been working on a "surprise" for me. A wedding present of sorts, he'd said. Part of me wondered if he'd set up a nursery or something. Granted, neither of us were ready to start our family quite yet but we'd talked about trying in a few years, once I'd gotten settled with my job at *Southern Charm Life-*

style. I'd had my sights set on working hard to gain a promotion in advertising and marketing. It went against many of the old-school "belief systems" that I wanted to have a job and be successful in it, to contribute to our household and future, but I'd always been a rebel when it came to that sort of thing.

When his surprise for me had been a home office setup in one of the spare bedrooms, I recall vividly how confused I'd been.

It increases exponentially when he mentions, "This way, you can have a place to do your work."

"But I don't...work from home."

He shrugs. "Well, maybe when we have a baby. You'll obviously have to slow down a bit then, right?" His smile, the obliviousness, stuns me.

The nature of my work, the contracts, the proposals... The aspects of my job, especially if I were to continue working my way up and gaining more responsibilities, made it crucial that details of deals not be compromised in any way, that no information be exposed to the public. Everything was kept under lock and key at the *Southern Charm Lifestyle* offices. And he *knew* that.

My wedding present from Knox was a home office.

That had been the first inkling that things weren't quite as they'd seemed. That maybe I'd somehow failed to notice the shift.

"Maybe you can do some of that monogram design stuff on the computer. Have a home business."

I recall how numb I'd felt when Knox had offered that up. Because monogram designs were an occasional hobby. Every now and then, when I'd wanted to give a special gift to someone dear to me. I didn't want to make a career of it. It wasn't a passion of mine like advertising and marketing were.

And I'd thought he'd understood—recognized—that.

Then again, I should've known my father would've had a hand in it. The man had nearly had a coronary when I'd sat down to dinner with the tiniest, most subtle diamond stud in my nose or when I'd had blue streaks dyed in my hair. Or when I'd saved up my own money to buy a used Honda Civic because I didn't want to be driving around in a snooty BMW when most of my classmates couldn't even afford the premium gas that kind of car required. My father had always tried to control me with his money—tried to tell me what to do, how to act, who to be friends with, and even what to major in when I went to college.

I'd thought that Knox was on my side. He'd stood by me when I'd declared to my father that I'd be attending The University of South Alabama because of their accelerated degree program, giving me the opportunity to work toward my bachelor and master's degrees in one fell swoop. At the news, my father had practically had a stroke and demanded that I attend The University of Alabama because that had been his alma mater. Because he wanted me to have "better choices for my circle of friends."

That really translated to him wanting me to have a bunch of snobs as friends. Shocker there. When your father is Davis Haywood, the businessman infamous for having his fingers in just about every "pot" in Mobile, it comes with so many strings and contingencies that it's ridiculous.

I still don't know why he approved of me dating Knox.

Scratch that. I didn't know *then*. Until it was nearly too late.

I shrug off the melancholy memories and pull myself up off the bed. I take my hanging garment bag from where it's draped over the chair in the corner and walk to the closet to hang it up. Once that's done, I unzip my suitcase and withdraw some of my small clothing items with the intent of placing them in the top drawer of the small dresser.

Sliding out the drawer, I set my underwear and bras inside to the far right and distractedly recognize there's a large stack of something, placed inside a small, open box, on the other side. When I move to close the drawer, the movement causes the stack to shift slightly within the box and that's when I truly notice the contents.

Photos. Of Knox and me.

I reach out, my fingertips nearly grazing the top of the box before I draw my hand back quickly. It's like Pandora's box. I want so badly to look through these photos, but I'm not certain I can handle it.

With a deep breath, I carefully push the drawer closed and step back from the dresser.

Even so, I swear it taunts me throughout the evening.

"HERE YOU GO." Knox slides a bowl in front of me after directing me to take a seat at the large dining room table.

I stare down at the contents of it, unmoving, and swallow hard.

Oh, my word.

"Is something wrong?"

My head jerks up, my eyes finding Knox looking at me oddly.

With an overly bright smile, I shake my head. "Not at all. Thank you for making dinner."

He nods and plates some stir fry for himself before sitting at the other end of the table. Folding his hands, he darts a quick glance at me.

"I, uh, usually say grace."

I know. We used to say it together. And kiss after we said, "Amen."

Knox bows his head, and I do the same, listening to the smooth cadence of his voice as he murmurs a blessing.

"Thank you, Lord, for this food, for seeing us safely to Mobile, and for granting us this time to spend with loved ones. In your name we pray, Amen."

Our eyes connect once we both raise our heads, and he offers me a faint smile as if he, too, recalls what would have come next. I work hard to fight against the urge to admire the curve of his lips and instead focus on my food.

Oh, hell.

I'd briefly forgotten what had initially taken me by surprise.

My stir-fry has extra water chestnuts in it.

26

Knox

Just as Emma Jane mechanically stabs at her stir-fry with a dazed look, there's a brief knock on my door. Before I can react, it opens and my mother's cheerful voice calls out, "The welcoming committee is here!"

Shit. With a wince, I run a hand along my jaw. I didn't exactly plan on this, and with the knowledge that my mother's always had a soft spot for Emma Jane—somehow even through everything that's happened—nervousness unfurls in the pit of my stomach at what she might have up her sleeve.

When a male voice accompanies hers, I know for a fact she's up to no good.

"Why, I know y'all are tired from the drive, so I told Caroline, here"—they emerge from the hallway, and stride into the kitchen—"we need to feed you something g—*Oh.*" Granddad stops in his tracks, eyebrows shooting up as he takes in the sight of the stir-fry, likely noticing the extra water chestnuts.

He attempts to school his expression, but fails at stifling the pleased look when he turns to me. "Son, I see you haven't forgotten certain…culinary skills in the kitchen." He sets two casserole dishes onto the table before walking around to his granddaughter and greeting her with a hug and a kiss on the cheek.

"I brought my potato salad and some fried chicken." My mother rushes over to the table and sets down her dishes. First offering Emma Jane the same greeting as her granddad, she withdraws the fork from her grasp, removing the plate as well.

Turning to me, she holds out the objects. "Put these in some containers for later, honey. And get a few extra plates, please." She smiles sweetly.

"Yes, ma'am," I mutter and acquiesce.

Within moments, the four of us are seated at my dining room table, our plates laden with food from my mother's kitchen, sweet tea poured in everyone's glasses, and Granddad leads the four of us in saying grace…again.

Once everyone starts digging in to the fried chicken, potato salad, and cornbread—and I have to admit that this beats my stir-fry any day of the week—the older two start in.

"Are you staying in Knox's spare bedroom, honey?" my mother inquires with far too much innocence.

I flash her a look of warning. "Mother."

She waves a hand dismissively. "I was just concerned because"—she turns to Emma Jane with absolutely no subtlety whatsoever—"Knox's bed is much more comfortable."

Emma Jane promptly chokes on her sweet tea.

IF I THOUGHT dinner was the pinnacle of awkwardness, with my mother and Emma Jane's granddad bouncing back and forth between their leading questions and blatant insinuations, things veered into the realm of *debilitating* awkwardness from there.

"What if you get disoriented in the middle of the night and become frightened, Emma Jane? I'm certain Knox wouldn't mind if you shared his bed. It's a California king."

"Knox, are you planning to take Emma Jane out on the water? It might be nice for old times."

"Knox, honey, you're picking at your food. You need to keep up your strength." This remark received a hard glare in return.

"Sweet Pea, are you and Knox going to do some stargazing this weekend? Because the weatherman said it'd be clear and perfect conditions."

The utterly serious expression on her granddad's face nearly does me in. Finally, I excuse myself, claiming the need to ensure the banana tree in the backyard hasn't been trimmed back too far by the lawn care workers I hired to come while I've been away. I'm certain my mother realizes what I'm doing, that it's an excuse to escape, but she can't argue since she's made many loaves of banana bread from the product of that same tree.

I follow through on my claim and am checking the leaves and stalks to ensure nothing's overcrowded when I detect the sound of the back door to the house open and close. With a quick glance over my shoulder, I spot Granddad.

Returning my attention to the tree, I note that the bananas should be ready to be cut and collected soon. I examine it thoroughly while I wait for the older man to approach. He soon sidles up beside me.

"You brought her here."

I don't turn to face him. "Yes, sir."

"I wouldn't have expected that a few months ago when we first spoke."

He's referring to when I first arrived in Jacksonville, and he called me to discuss "business." As it turned out, that had meant we would discuss business *and* his granddaughter.

Even then, I'd tried to dodge his questions with care.

"There's so much hurt between y'all, but you've come far." He pauses, thoughtfully. "And you inviting her to stay here speaks of your feelings."

I make a small derisive sound in the back of my throat. "My mother taught me to be hospitable. That's all it means."

He falls quiet for a moment. "But would she have agreed to stay here months ago? When you first got to Jacksonville?"

His sharply posed question sets me on edge. "I can't answer for her."

"Try."

Between gritted teeth, I begrudgingly answer. "No, sir."

Hell, she hadn't seemed crazy about it when I'd originally brought it up. *I* had been the one to push the offer.

"Ah-ha! Progress has been made then."

I turn to face the older man. "Progress? You call this progress?"

He nods once, perfunctorily. "I do. Because she had a choice. And in this case," he cocks an eyebrow meaningfully, "she chose you." He turns on his heel and walks away, toward the house.

It takes everything in my power not to call out after him with the agonizing reminder—the truth—that lingers.

Instead, I turn to face the water and mutter beneath my breath, "She didn't choose me when it mattered."

27

Emma Jane

I NEVER THOUGHT THEY'D LEAVE.

Throughout dinner, between Granddad and Ms. Caroline's questions and comments, both Knox and I grew more than a little uncomfortable. This was confirmed when Knox excused himself to head outside. Once Granddad came back after briefly speaking to him, he'd had an oddly pleased expression.

Knox still hasn't come back inside, and I don't feel comfortable going out there. He's made it obvious that he wants to be alone, so I head to the bedroom to get ready to turn in for the night.

After I've brushed my teeth and am crawling beneath the covers, my phone vibrates from where it sits on the bedside table. Reaching for it, there's a FaceTime request from Madison. Leaning back against the pillows, I accept the call and her face pops up on the screen.

"Hey! How's the Deep South treating you? *Oooh!*" Her eyes widen dramatically. "Have you decided to buy a truck, have a gun rack installed on the back, and fly the Confederate flag from it?"

I gasp with mock dismay. "How could you possibly leave out attending Mardi Gras balls, having crawfish boils, and inviting everyone we meet to go to church with us?"

She grins, her eyes sparkling with amusement. "Go ahead and do it. You know you want to bless my heart right now."

I can't help but snicker. "You've done pretty well at stereotyping us."

Madison's expression sobers. "So really. How are things?"

I quickly give her the rundown. After I finish the recap, she lowers her voice. "Has he come back in yet?"

"I don't think so," I reply quietly. "He must have been out there for over an hour now."

"Maybe he's pondering the meaning of life." She smirks. "Or realizing he's madly in love with you. Still."

"Not likely."

"Well, maybe not, with you so"—she pauses to lean in toward the phone for a closer look—"obviously dressed for seduction."

I stick my tongue out at her. "Very funny."

Madison smiles. "You know I love you."

"Love you, too."

"Get some rest and I'll talk to you soon."

"Night."

After we end our call, I toss my phone aside on the bed and let out a long breath. I'm tired, yet an antsy feeling is deep within me.

My eyes are drawn to the dresser—particularly to the top drawer where I discovered Knox's collection of photos.

I worry my bottom lip with my teeth and ponder if I should do it. If I should dare open it and look at the contents. If I can handle the walk down memory lane.

But maybe, just maybe, it'll be therapeutic and help me finally close that last door. Move on.

Before I know it, I'm up and my feet are carrying me over to the dresser. I carefully, slowly, pull open the drawer. Scooping up one thick stack of photographs, I carry them to the bed and settle back against the pillows to peruse my findings.

I'm thankful I'm not standing when I flip to the third photo because it would have knocked me off my feet.

Knox had taken a candid photo of me in the midst of my usual *he loves me, he loves me not* plucking of a daisy's white petals. There's a secretive smile playing at my lips and my features are so bright, so full of love for him that my breath lodges painfully in my chest.

I should put these back; I should stop right now if this is the effect one photograph has on me. But, like some sort of sadist, I keep going. When I come across our old prom and homecoming photos, I can't help but smile at how young we look, at our cheesy grins, at the way Knox peered down at me with ardent pride and affection.

Hours pass by and deep down, I know I should get some rest, but I can't manage to stop looking through the photos. Each one I pore over, whether it be of Knox and his friends after a baseball game or randomly hanging out, a photograph he took of me or those of us together, increases the nagging ache in the center of my chest. Finally, I set them aside with a long sigh full of melancholy, lined with what-ifs and questions I don't have the answers to.

What if things had been different? What if I hadn't left? What if I'd married Knox? Would we have been just as happy as we once were?

Once I return the photos to their designated place in

the drawer, when I press it closed, a strange sadness washes over me. Like I'm closing a chapter in my life. Which is crazy since I closed that chapter years ago.

I closed it the day I left Mobile in my wedding dress.

28

Knox

I should be getting rest, especially since I know tomorrow night's going to be a long one. The anxiety won't seem to ease, though, which is why I finally crept from my bedroom and went back outside to sit on the dock.

Using my foot to shift the other chair and prop my feet on the seat, I release a long breath and watch the play of moonlight on the water. I've always loved the peacefulness this place offers.

Even so, I still can't help but be torn about my decision to bring EJ here.

As soon as she stepped foot in my house, it felt like she was supposed to be here, the sense of rightness that used to be so powerful even back then. But simultaneously, I could also hear a little voice in my head say, *"This is a mistake. She'll only hurt you again."*

Running an agitated hand through my hair, I stare out at the water, allowing my mind to give way to memories.

I'm down on one knee, my hand trembling as it holds the diamond ring. My nerves are shot, not because I think she'll say no, but because

I want this moment to be so perfect for her and to say the right words, to somehow communicate how much of an honor it will be to have her as my wife.

"Ever since you came into my life, it's been brighter, better, and happier." I swallow hard past the lump of emotion. "It would make me the happiest man in the world if you would marry me." Tears escape, slipping down her cheeks, as she gazes at me. "Let's make some babies and grow old together, EJ." With her hand in mine, I pause with the ring at her fingertip, my eyes silently questioning her.

She nods, more tears raining down her cheeks, and a smile forms on her lips. The instant she murmurs, "Yes," is when it all comes together for me.

I can see it all like a movie playing in my mind. The two of us getting married, living in my house, and working hard at our careers, before we change the spare bedrooms into nurseries or rooms for the kids. Me teaching them how to fish, EJ teaching them how to swim, both of us teaching them how to cook our separate specialties.

I see our life together. One that I want with every breath I take.

I'd be lying outright if I said that a part of me didn't still want that life.

IT'S a little past two in the morning when I finally make my way back inside and head down the hallway to my bedroom. Instead of being therapeutic, the time I spent on the dock, staring at the water, managed to make me feel more emotionally raw.

The doorknob turns just as I pass her closed bedroom door. My body tenses, and I fight the urge to sprint to my own room and rush inside like a damn wuss. Instead, I stop.

She steps out and immediately gasps, a hand flying to her chest. "Oh! Knox, you startled me."

"Sorry, I was just coming back in from…" I lose my train of thought as my eyes drift down her form, taking in the sight of her. She's wearing a pair of black, loose-fitting cotton shorts with a cotton tank top in the same color, and the way her nipples are tightening beneath the top makes it evident she's braless.

My jaw clenches, my hands fist at my sides, and I channel all my willpower to resist the urge to kiss her. To just…touch her. To have another opportunity to love her.

Fuck. My eyes close with a wince as I attempt to drag in a deep, calming breath.

Wells was right. This was stupid. I should've known better.

"Are you just now going to bed?" Her voice is nearly a whisper.

I open my eyes and focus on a point just above her shoulder. Anythin other than the tempting woman standing before me.

"I tried earlier, but I couldn't sleep. I went back outside for a bit."

She stays quiet, offering no response, which causes my gaze to shift. I discover her regarding me with an expression teetering somewhere between anguished and pensive.

"Knox." She appears to choose her words with great care. "Do you sometimes miss"—she pauses before finishing, and the last word comes out as more of a faint, breathy wisp—"us?"

I pinch my eyes closed briefly and roll my lips inward to stop the words from spilling out. *All the damn time, EJ. All the damn time.*

Instead, I merely offer a curt nod.

She takes a step toward me, and I immediately stiffen. "I didn't mean to snoop, but I was putting some things in the dresser."

Shit. I forgot about the photos I'd stashed in the drawer. Wells had made me take each one of them down and out of the various frames around the house to stow them where I wouldn't have to see them all the time.

"You can have them if you want."

The words are out before I can even think. The way her head rears back, as if I've slapped her, takes me by surprise. Because it shouldn't matter—none of this should still matter to her. Not anymore.

"Y-you don't want them?" She asks this with that damn crease between her brows.

I can't do this. I *can't* fucking do this right now.

"You know what I want?" I explode suddenly. "I want it all back! All of it!" I run my hands over my head, fingers clenching in the short strands of my hair and I tug slightly in frustration. "I would do it all over again even though I know"—I break off with a weary sigh and drop my hands to my sides—"it means we don't end up together."

She takes a slow, tentative step toward me, then another one, until finally, there's barely a foot between us. We stand here, me clad only in my low-slung pajama pants and her in that tank top and shorts.

With her eyes locked on mine, she reaches for the hem of her tank top and, with aching slowness, lifts it up.

Her movements are so languid, almost tentative, as though she's expecting me to stop her. As if I could ever deny this woman. She's always had a hold on me like no other.

Emma Jane Haywood has always been the keeper of my heart and soul.

When she lifts the cotton tank up over her bare breasts before letting it drop to the floor, I lose all semblance of control. I move a hand to the back of her head, threading my fingers through the strands of her silky hair before my lips crash down on hers in a kiss that's passionate and insistent. My other hand moves to her hip, and I steer her back against the wall, pressing my body flush against hers. I'm unable to restrain the rough sound in the back of my throat at the sensation of her bare breasts against my chest. The ardent way she kisses me back, the way her tongue collides with mine, it's as though she feels the same ferocious desperation I do.

Her hands are all over me, moving from where they fist in my hair before skimming down my back and over my ass. When she grips it in her hands, tugging me even closer to press my hard-as-hell cock against her, our kiss turns molten hot.

Her body arches into mine, and my mouth swallows her moan when I rock against her. My cock is jutting against my pajama pants, aching to be set free, aching to be inside her. Caging her body against the wall, I slip a hand between us, beneath the leg of her shorts, and veer toward her center where I'm instantly greeted with scorching heat. I skim the pad of my finger along the crease of her entrance, already slick enough to coat my fingertip. As soon as I push inside, I tear my lips from hers with a hoarse groan. Our eyes lock and I take in the sight of her heavy-lidded gaze, her lips parted, breath coming in fast, harsh pants.

"Your pussy's so damn wet for me."

Heated arousal flares in her eyes at my words, and her body coats my finger with her slick arousal. Slowly dragging it out until only the tip of it remains, I add another finger and quickly slide both back inside her wet heat. The way her inner muscles clench around them makes my cock pulse with need. Her hand reaches out for me, fingers tugging at the waistband of my pants.

"Knox, please," she pants. Her hips begin to buck, and

she works herself over my fingers as I thrust them in and out of her.

"Tell me what you want." My own voice sounds guttural, rough.

Her breathing is becoming increasingly labored. "I need you." Her eyes flutter closed, and she murmurs, "Oh God," before her hand slips beneath my pants and grips my thick shaft. "I need this. I need you inside me."

I hook my fingers inside her pussy, and I'm confident she'll come soon. Instead, she takes me by surprise when she places her other palm against my chest, guiding me back against the opposite wall.

She shoves my pants down to my ankles and drops to her knees before taking my hard length in her mouth.

And I promptly lose all ability to breathe.

29

Emma Jane

"EJ."

The way Knox utters this, with a reverence of sorts, urges me on. His fingers tighten their grip on my hair when I take him even deeper, hollowing out my cheeks. I release him from my mouth with a pop and drag the flared head along my lips. Running my tongue along the slit, I revel in his harsh groan before taking him as deep as I can. My mouth glides up and down his thick shaft, and just when I think he's about to find his release, he pulls away.

I peer up at him, confusion lining my features. He merely offers me a lazy grin in return, helps me to my feet, and kisses me softly. Then he murmurs against my lips, "I need to be inside your sweet pussy."

He steps out of his pants, leading me down the hall into what had been a spare bedroom, but I assume is now his master suite. He doesn't allow me time to wonder about the room change, because he walks me backward until the back of my legs hit the bed and he strips me of my shorts.

"Get on the bed."

He utters this command in a low, silky tone while he

strokes his cock. His eyes remain locked with mine as his hand works his length, still slick from my mouth, from root to tip. As I scoot back onto the cool, cotton sheets, the sight of Knox's large hand sliding up and down his thick shaft in tantalizingly languid strokes elicits a rush of wetness to my core. I press my thighs together to try to ease the rapidly increasing pressure, the flicks of heat setting my body aflame.

"Do you want my tongue inside you?" His voice is a low growl. "Or my cock?"

My tongue darts out to wet my lips before I answer, and his eyes track its movement. "Both."

His grin can't be classified as anything except predatory. "I was hoping you'd say that."

Releasing the grip on his cock, he reaches for my ankles. He drags my ass closer to the edge of the bed, then spreads my legs apart. Our eyes remain locked while he lowers his face to where I ache for him the most. The instant he traces his tongue along the crease, my entire body goes rigid. A surge of wet arousal seeps from me, which he readily laps up.

"Watch me taste you." His whispered command elicits shivers down my spine as the sensation of his hot breath fans against me.

To resist the urge to close my eyes when he plunges his tongue inside me is the most difficult thing for me to do. The sound of his husky moans while he tastes me voraciously propels me closer to orgasm, causing my muscles to tense in anticipation. The way his short beard rasps against my inner thighs sends delicious surges of arousal strumming through me.

He releases his grip on my one leg and reaches up, using his thumb and forefinger to give the gentlest tug on my clit. Then moving his thumb in slow circles over it, he applies just the right amount of pressure to send me hurtling over the edge.

"*Knox.*" I moan his name as the waves of my orgasm crash violently over me, my hips undulating as I shamelessly ride his tongue.

Once my heart rate begins to calm, he moves up my body and braces himself above me on his forearms. His arousal presses firmly against my stomach, which gives a little flip when he lowers his head and places a tender kiss on my forehead.

I swear the effects of that kiss radiate all the way to my heart.

He moves to lie on his back beside me and reaches over to retrieve a condom from his bedside table. Quickly ripping open the wrapper and discarding it, he sheathes himself.

Without a word, I shift my position and straddle him. Surprise etches his features before he settles one hand at my hip and reaches his other hand out to tuck some of my hair back behind my ear. With aching slowness, he skims the pads of his fingers along my cheek, down the column of my throat, and over one breast, sweeping over the tip of one nipple.

"So beautiful." These two words, whispered with such reverence, nearly do me in.

Pressing a palm against his firm pectorals, I lift slightly while using my other hand to guide him to my entrance. With his tip poised at my core, I brace my hands on his chest and ease down upon his length, little by little, and my breath catches at the delicious way he stretches me.

He glides his palms up along my sides to cup my breasts, grazing the calloused pads of his thumbs over my sensitive nipples. I close my eyes, relishing in his touch. My head falls back, and I rock my hips, taking him deeper inside me. I quicken the pace, only to have him draw me to a stop when his grip tightens on my hips. My eyes flash open to find him watching me.

"I want to take it slow."

He thrusts upward while pulling me down, and I can't restrain my sharp intake of breath. Both his hands clutch my hips as he takes control, working me over his cock in a tantalizingly languid pace. I reach back to brace my palms on his firm, muscled thighs, which changes the angle and allows him to slide even deeper.

He continues rolling his hips, driving upward while pulling me down on his length in slow, methodical thrusts.

His breathing becomes more labored, and his eyes flicker down to where our bodies are joined. "I love watching the way you take me deep inside you."

My fingers tighten their grip on his thighs. "Feel how wet I am for you." As soon as I breathe out the words, his cock jerks inside me.

"*Fuck*," he groans. "I love when you talk like that."

Emboldened further by his response, the words pour out of me. "I wish you weren't wearing a condom so I could feel you come inside me. So you could fill me up with your—"

"Fuck!" He cuts me off, flipping me over and onto my back, draping my legs over his shoulders. Now, his thrusting is no longer methodical, but feverish and frenzied. I'm entranced by his expression of such fierce concentration, the way the cords of his neck appear strained. The play of muscles in his abdominals with each thrust and the strength in his biceps braced on either side of me push me closer to release.

"Touch yourself for me," he pants, his eyes a bit wild. "I want to feel your pussy clench around me when you come."

My hand moves down between our bodies to finger my clit. With a hoarse whisper, I confess, "It won't take me long."

His eyes briefly fall closed at my admission. When they flare back open, the heat in them nearly overwhelms me. "Come with me, beautiful. Work that clit." He dips his head, bringing his lips to my ear to nip at it with his teeth. "I'm gonna pretend I'm not wearing a condom, that I'll fill you up, pretend that you'll be dripping from me."

That's all it takes. His words alone send me over the edge.

"Knox," I cry out as my inner muscles spasm around him, and my hips move of their own volition, pleasure coursing through my body.

He whisper-groans in my ear, "EJ," giving two deep thrusts before a final one, and his entire body goes rigid as he finds his release inside me.

Knox buries his face in the pillow next to my head and lets out a long exhale. I feel him shift slightly and place a quick kiss to my temple before sliding off me, probably to dispose of the condom.

Already, my mind's racing with questions. What did I just do? Does this even mean anything to him? I should hurry up and go back to my room, right?

Luckily, he makes it easy for me when he slips off the bed and walks into the bathroom, closing the door behind him without so much as a word or a backward glance.

30

Knox

I EMERGE from the bathroom after cleaning myself up and grabbing a warm, damp washcloth for EJ, only to discover her scrambling from the bed, obviously trying to make a getaway.

Drawing to a stop, I narrow my eyes on her. "Leaving so soon?" I can't help the sharpness in my tone. It's not like I expected her to just up and leave after some of the hottest sex of my life.

Her head whips around, her eyes wide, startled. "I, uh"—she shrugs—"thought I'd leave you be."

"Get back on the bed." My command brooks no argument. When she hesitates, I raise my hand holding the washcloth. "I need to clean you up."

There's a soft flush that spreads across her cheeks. "I can do that myself."

I arch an eyebrow. "Get on the bed, EJ."

With a huff, she relents and returns to the bed, leaning her back against the pillows. "Fine, Mr. Bossypants."

My lips quirk at her comment, but I don't respond. I pad over to where she's lying and gently use the washcloth to wipe her clean. When I hear her sharp intake of breath, my eyes instantly find hers.

"Did I hurt you?"

"No," she answers quickly. At my pointed look, she averts her eyes before adding quietly, "It was just a little... sore since I don't"—I strain to hear the rest when she mumbles—"do that regularly."

She's still avoiding my gaze, and it's probably a good thing since I have the biggest shit-eating grin on my face. Not because she's sore, but because she basically admitted that she hasn't been with anyone regularly. Especially not since the last time we were together.

I can't deny that I'd wondered about it. *Worried* about it. *Hated* to consider it.

"I'm sorry I made you sore." With a gentle touch, I place a hand on her smooth thigh. When her eyes lift to mine, I wink. "But I can't say I'm not glad I'm the one who did it."

Her lips part, and she leans forward to shove at me. "Jerk."

My hand slips around to cup her nape and guide her to meet my lips in a soft kiss. I speak against her parted lips. "You like this jerk. Admit it." I refuse to acknowledge how much I want her to admit this.

She mumbles something that I can't quite decipher.

I lean back slightly. "What was that?"

She squints at me, but the corners of her mouth quiver as she fights a smile. "Maybe." She raises a hand and places her thumb and forefinger about a half inch apart. "Like that much."

Turning slightly, I toss the damp washcloth into the bathroom, vaguely aware of the faint sound of it landing on the tiled floor. I return my attention to her, noting the mischief in her light-blue eyes.

"I think it's a little more than that."

"Really? How much more?" Her eyes dance merrily.

I school my expression into one of stern concentration and hold my hands about seven inches apart. "Probably about this much."

I can't restrain my wide grin when I see the insinuation finally dawn on her.

She narrows her eyes and shoves at me again. This time, I catch her wrist, my fingers encircling it and tugging her to me for a deep, wet kiss. My tongue delves inside, and I know I could kiss her forever and never tire of it.

Once our lips finally part, we're both breathing heavily. When I catch sight of the time on the clock sitting beside my bed, I note the late—or, rather, early—time and groan with dismay.

"We have a long day tomorrow." I help her settle beneath the covers, ignoring her quizzical glance, before I slide in beside her. I know what she's not asking.

Why aren't you kicking me out of your bedroom?
Why do you want me to stay in your bed?

I refuse to answer her unvoiced questions because the truth of my answers is pretty damn scary.

Because I never want her to leave.

IT TAKES a moment for me to realize I'm not having a dream. That this is actually happening and it's oh, so very real.

And so fucking good.

With my eyes still closed, I thread my fingers through her hair, relishing in the sensation of the silky strands and the way it brushes against my thighs. The suction she creates with her mouth is fucking heaven, and I work hard to resist the urge to thrust deep inside her mouth.

I clench my fingers, tightening my grip on her hair. "If you don't want—"

I fail to finish voicing my warning because she suddenly creates a stronger suction and does something with her tongue that pushes me over the edge. I tighten my grip of her hair, my fingers fisting the tresses, as I erupt, shooting hot spurts in her mouth. She takes it all, sucking me dry until I'm limp and completely boneless.

Once I find the strength to open my eyes, I peer down and watch as she rises up, a smug grin playing at her lips. "Good morning."

"Morning, beautiful."

When she shifts with the intent to move back beside me, I snake an arm around her and tug her close, fitting her against me. Ducking my head, I feather a light kiss on the top of her head and close my eyes, content to simply hold her.

Hell, I'd give anything to stay here with her, just like this; forever, with no interruptions.

As if on cue, my phone's alarm goes off, alerting me to the fact that we need to get ready for her father's birthday festivities. I hadn't even realized how late we slept, but considering everything, it's really not much of a surprise.

Reaching over to where my phone's sitting on the nightstand, I silence it quickly and return to holding EJ tight.

"Damn reality and obligations. I'd much rather stay here." My tone is hushed, and I press another kiss to the top of her head.

"Me, too." Her whisper is faint, but the way she snuggles into my embrace sends warmth rushing through me.

We lie here for a while longer, and I'm on the verge of

falling back asleep when I hear her quiet voice. "I'm scared, Knox."

With a frown, I peer down at her, but she doesn't shift to meet my eyes. "About?"

She pauses. "Seeing him again."

I run a hand over her back in a comforting caress. "I promise, if he's an ass, we'll leave."

This gets her attention. Her head lifts from my chest, and my heart falters at the sight of her mussed hair and sleepy eyes. "Really?" Her eyes search mine as if in disbelief of my promise.

I cup her face with one hand and skim her cheek with the pad of my thumb. "Really."

She ducks her face and presses a kiss to the base of my throat before settling her cheek against my chest again.

Staring up at the ceiling, I smooth a hand over her hair in a caress and, lost in thought, my words spill out without any consideration.

"I'm not complaining about being woken up that way, but I didn't get to surprise you with a daisy. It's not as exciting if I give you one after we..." I trail off as what I've just admitted to dawns on me.

Emma Jane doesn't immediately respond, but when she finally does, it's barely more than a whisper. "I always loved...love getting daisies from you."

I release a rush of breath I hadn't realized I'd been holding. My lips curve up in a slow smile. "Well, then." I press a kiss to the top of her head, her hair so smooth and silky against my lips. "I'll just have to pick you one after we shower."

Instantly, her arms wrap around me, and she hugs me so tightly that it catches me off guard.

She turns her face slightly. "Thank you." Her words

are spoken softly against my neck before she presses a delicate kiss on it.

That kiss that forces me to face what I've been trying to deny all along. What I've denied for the past eight years.

I never got over Emma Jane.

I still love her—the woman who shattered my heart.

31

Emma Jane

My nerves are completely frayed and, right now, I'm fantasizing about doing shot after shot of Patrón.

Knox takes my hand in his and links our fingers together. Instantly, I have the urge to pull away because people will talk.

I dart a meaningful look down at our joined hands. "I don't know if this is smart, Knox."

He stares at me for a moment. "If what's smart?"

"This." I give a little tug on his hand. "Us holding hands." I gesture with my other hand which holds my small clutch. "Here. With all these nosy people around."

He merely shakes his head with a dismissive laugh. "Not everyone's nosy."

"Not true. I am." We both turn at the sound of a familiar male voice.

"Wells." I greet him with a small, tentative smile.

"Emma Jane." He appears amused by my uncertain greeting before he addresses Knox with a grin. "Intent on sending the wagging tongues into overdrive, I see." His eyes flick down to our hands, and when I try to withdraw mine again, Knox flashes me a sharp look and tightens his grip.

"Just making sure she doesn't dart out the back door."

Wells laughs. "Kinda like the last—" He stops abruptly, sending a flood of awkward silence rushing over us.

Turning to Knox, I smile weakly. "I'm heading to the ladies' room really quick."

Green eyes hold mine for a beat, as if he's trying to ensure I won't skip out on him. Finally, he relents and releases my hand. "See you in a few."

I nod and head off in the direction of the restrooms, praying I'll be able to weave my way through the crowd of partygoers without getting stopped and subjected to an awkward conversation.

Once I make it safely inside the restroom, I release a massive sigh of relief before checking my makeup at the vanity. Luckily, no one else is in here and I take an extra moment to stare at my reflection. I can't help but recall the last time I was here and all dolled up in Granddad's home—the Haywood Mansion—surrounded by family and a ton of guests, was for my own wedding.

The wedding my own father had a hand in destroying. Or opening my eyes, however one might phrase it. But he wasn't alone.

Knox had also played a part in it.

I'd graduated early from my accelerated degree program at The University of South Alabama. *Southern Charm Lifestyle* had been the only large magazine in the area and when I'd acquired a position there, I'd been honored to join their staff.

Then my father purchased the magazine six months later. We'd had a huge argument over that development, and I vividly recall demanding to know why he'd purchased the magazine, knowing he had plenty of other business endeavors.

He hadn't given me a straight answer, and I instantly knew why. Because he wanted another way to try to control me. To get me to do his bidding.

Knox's work was rooted here in Mobile, and I knew it would be unfair to ask him to move if I managed to acquire a job in Atlanta, Jacksonville, or even Miami. Although, at that time, another job was unlikely with my lack of work experience at the magazine.

The day of my wedding had started out as the happiest day of my life before transforming into the worst, most depressing, and heart-wrenching day.

I'd been trying to get a moment alone with Knox, but kept getting deterred in some way or another. I'd wanted to give him the small wedding gift I'd made for him; a monogrammed handkerchief I'd designed. He always talked about how his grandfather had carried one on him that his grandmother had made for him, the same one Knox had carried for years. I thought he'd appreciate my thoughtful gift.

I never got the chance to find out.

I pad down the carpeted hallway as stealthily as possible in my wedding dress, making my way toward the room where Knox is getting dressed. I never gave much thought to the whole seeing one another before the wedding bad luck thing, so I figure this will be the perfect time to give him the handkerchief.

As I near his room, I see the door is ajar before I hear the familiar voices inside.

"You need to get control of her and knock this damn career mindset out of her." I recognize my father's voice. He's been giving me crap for years about how I need to "improve myself" and become "proper wife material."

Basically, he expects me to cower to a man's bidding, get married, and not do much else except pop out a bunch of kids and have dinner prepared and in front of my husband each day when he comes home from work.

Which means I'm not surprised to hear this coming from my father. What does surprise me is what I hear Knox utter next. Silently, I plead with Knox, Tell him to take his old-school ways and shove them where the sun don't shine!

"Don't worry about that. I've got it covered. I'll work on her while we're away on our honeymoon. By the time we get back, she'll be scheduling dinner parties and my golf outings and won't pay that job of hers any mind."

The blood drains from my face, a lightheaded sensation washing over me, and I place a palm against the wall to steady myself. My other hand clutches at the center of my chest, as if I've just been stabbed.

"You'd better. Otherwise you can kiss that deal with my company goodbye."

"As I said, I've got it covered." *The calmness in Knox's voice, the casual way he declares this kills me.*

Spinning around, I rush away, thankful for the thick carpeting, which masks the sound of my escape back to my own dressing room, grateful I'd shoved everyone, especially my overbearing mother, out, citing that I needed some quiet time alone.

Once I'm safely inside, I lean back against the door, dragging in heaving breaths to try to get air into my burning lungs. Knox's handkerchief remains clutched in my fist as thoughts flit through my mind in snippets.

Knox redirecting the conversation each time I bring up the idea of applying for the position at StyleNow Magazine after hearing through the grapevine that they'd been looking to fill some positions at their new location in north Pensacola Beach. Sure, it means I'd have to commute, but that certainly isn't the end of the world. He suggested I stay at Southern Charm Lifestyle since it's close to home.

Then my father purchased the magazine shortly after I'd begun working there. I know he did this to try to execute more control over me.

Next is the home office setup Knox had made for me.

Now my eyes are opened to the fact that Knox has been placating me all along. He's been in on it with my own father.

He doesn't truly love me or respect me. I've given my whole heart to this man who wants to cage me.

"I can't marry him." My ragged whisper sounds amplified within the silence of the room, and my voice cracks with pain. "I can't marry someone who's lied to me all along."

I stare blankly at the floor, knowing that my father had attempted to stifle me and control me my entire life. Sure, I've rebelled here and there, in little ways, like with coloring my hair and my choice of school and degree and job. But I realize I've never lived. I've never actually experienced anything on my own. I've never truly stood on my own two feet and existed outside the circle of control my father held.

But now that's all going to change.

WITH MY FOCUS on dragging in deep, calming breaths, I stare at myself in the mirror and ruminate over the day's events thus far. Knox has been beside me from the time we'd arrived—early, at the request of my parents—and hasn't left my side, as promised. He kept a comforting hand at the base of my spine throughout the entire conversation with my parents and granddad.

My father's recent hush-hush bout with prostate cancer has clearly changed him. I'd been decidedly hesitant about this encounter and with good reason, considering our past. We were interrupted by some always-early Women's League members, but our conversation had gone much smoother than I'd expected.

Exiting the restroom, I nearly collide with a blonde woman in a gorgeous red dress.

"Pardon me." I step aside, intent on rejoining Knox.

"Emma Jane?"

I instantly tense, and once I take a better look at the woman, I recognize her as my former best friend. With a strong emphasis on *former*. After I'd left, every single one of my so-called friends had separated themselves from me, including her. No doubt, that had been my father's doing.

"Katherine." My eyes scan her features and it appears that she's already had some plastic surgery done, which is surprising since she's only one year older than I am. Pasting a polite smile on my face, I say, "You look well."

"Thank you." Her smile doesn't quite reach her eyes, and just as I'm about to excuse myself from the awkward exchange, she leans forward. "You had to come back, didn't you? Little Miss Perfect?"

"Excuse me?" I frown in confusion and edge away from her.

She sneers. "Did you find out the truth?"

My parents have insisted no one knows about my father's recent battle with cancer, so her question is puzzling.

Switching gears, she lifts her chin haughtily. "I must know. You and that handsome football player, are y'all—"

"Well, my stars! I dare say, my ears were burnin'."

Our heads whip around at the terrible imitation of a Southern accent. I gape at the sight of my best friend standing before me with Madison at his side.

Rushing over, I wrap my arms around them. "You're here!" Suddenly, I lean back, confusion lining my features. "Wait. How did you get in? It's invite only."

Becket flashes the slow, easy grin that's graced billboards and TV ads galore. "I'm Becket Jones."

With a laugh, I shake my head at him. "Well, I'm glad you're here."

"Are y'all together?"

I'd forgotten about Katherine who just piped up, directing her question to Becket and Madison.

Becket's expression sobers. He focuses an intense scrutiny of Katherine, who begins to fidget under his perusal. "Are you asking that question with genuine interest and not just to spread gossip?"

The other woman manages to look aghast at his question. "Why, of course."

"Not," Madison cough-mumbles.

"Ladies." Becket crooks both of his elbows, ignoring Katherine, and glances at me and Madison. "Shall we?"

We link our arms with his and allow him to lead us down the hallway to join the large crowd of people mingling.

Glancing up at him, I have to ask, "What are you doing here?"

He winks with a warm smile. "My favorite girl needed reinforcements. It didn't take a genius to figure that much out. So"—he nods toward Madison at his other side—"I called up Madison and we decided on an impromptu trip."

"Y'all are the best." A thought strikes me, and I stop to peer up at Becket in alarm. "You have a home game tomorrow night."

"Right," he agrees slowly.

"You should be at home. Resting."

He tosses Madison a look of exasperation before returning his attention to me. "We're your friends. That's what friends do. And"—he adds—"we're flying back tonight. I can sleep on the plane."

With a grateful smile, I tip my head to the side. "You know I love you both, right?"

"Of course," Madison answers with a wink. "Now lead me to the food because I overheard one of the ladies talking about shrimp and grits and this transplanted Yankee is intrigued about something called a grit."

Laughing and feeling lighter by their presence alone, I lead my two friends toward the vast array of food.

32

Knox

"Didn't realize he was on the guest list."

"Who?" After thanking the bartender for the glass of scotch, I turn back and take a small sip.

"Becket Jones."

I choke on the smooth liquor and cough into my fist. Once I manage to get myself under control, I eye Wells sharply. "*What?*"

He nods, gesturing to the right side of the room, and my eyes instantly land on the man who's currently gazing down adoringly at my—

Shit. What is she? And why is she looking at him that way?

"Those two are adorable. But I can't quite figure out how the friend fits in the mix. Maybe she's part of it? Like a polyamorous thing?" Wells muses good-naturedly.

I glare at him. "Not funny."

He shrugs with an easy chuckle. "I beg to differ." Then he turns back to me, eyes dancing with mischief. "You look like you're about to Hulk out." His attention returns to the trio. "Simmer down, man. Simmer down."

"Easy for you to say," I mutter and take a healthy swig

of my drink. "You're not competing with a guy who's lusted over by women everywhere. Envied by grown men, even."

"Pray tell," Wells says, his accent growing thicker. "Are you jealous?"

I don't respond and simply partake in my scotch in silence.

"You realize you're looking at this all wrong, don't you?"

"How's that?" I'm barely resisting the urge to roll my eyes.

"You're looking at it through the wrong lens."

I turn my head and stare at him like he's got a screw loose. My friend merely waves a hand dismissively.

"Just listen." He tips his head in the direction of where Becket, EJ, and Madison are talking animatedly and laughing. He leans in closer to me while lowering his voice. "Watch your woman. The way she smiles up at him, the way she shoves at him when he spouts off some nonsense. Is that the way she reacts to you?"

It takes me a moment to realize what Wells is getting at. Thinking back to last night and this morning, the way EJ interacted with me, the way she looked at me…

"She's affectionate with him," Wells continues, "and it's clear that she loves him. But not in a romantic way."

As I continue to study them, I suddenly realize he's right.

Unfortunately, I've also been caught staring if Becket's wide, smug grin is anything to go by. He wraps each arm around the women on either side of him, startling them in the process, and tugs them close before laying a resounding kiss on their foreheads.

All while holding my gaze.

With that same damn smug-ass grin.

Wells shakes his head with a laugh. "I've gotta say. He's something else."

"Yeah." My response is flat monotone.

"And he's got your number. Even worse." Wells pauses. "You're letting him."

With a long sigh, I toss back the remainder of my scotch. Focusing on the empty glass in my hand, I mutter, "I don't know how to take the next steps."

"Easy." My friend's quick reply startles me. "You clear up the past."

When I turn to regard him, his eyes bore into mine with a heartfelt intensity only a best friend can display. One who's been with you through your darkest of days.

"You can't move forward until you do that."

I murmur my agreement even though he's wrong. It's not the least bit easy when you have to clear up a past that includes eight years' worth of pain and anger.

Easy doesn't even begin to cover it.

"SO YOU CAME HERE with my daughter?"

I knew it was bound to happen. It doesn't make the encounter or conversation any less uncomfortable, however.

"Yes, sir." I spin around from where I was appreciating a painting on the foyer wall of the mansion.

The fact that this is the same venue where EJ and I were supposed to be married isn't lost on me.

Facing Davis Haywood again, this time alone, it's staggering to witness his thinner form and the additional gray hair he now has from his bout with cancer.

Back when the wedding ended up a bust, I distanced myself from him and his domineering ways. Mostly because I didn't want to have dealings with him, but also because seeing him, seeing blue eyes so similar to his daughter's, was a constant painful reminder of what I'd lost.

He eyes me hard. "Then what are you doing here while she's in there, being courted by that quarterback?"

I force nonchalance. "I'm surprised you care. Especially after you disowned her and"—I tip my head to the side, wrinkling my forehead in faux confusion—"discontinued business dealings with me." My features grow hard. "You've only recently admitted to your wrongdoings and to mistreating her." I wave a hand in EJ's direction. "She might forgive you, but I'm still not buying it."

Davis doesn't even address my remarks. "You've always loved her. Never quite got over her."

I rear back slightly, barely resisting the urge to flinch at his words.

At the truth in them.

Forcing a bored tone, I gesture toward the crowd of people a few feet away from us in the large ballroom, attempting to redirect the conversation. "Why don't you talk with her some more? She came all this way for you."

He falls quiet, and I take this as the prime opportunity to leave. I barely make it two steps before he speaks, his voice subdued.

"I made mistakes. I won't deny that."

I still at his words but don't turn around. His admission —the emotion in his words—is jarring, especially coming from this man.

"Eight years…getting older and then…" He trails off, his tone taking on a sudden sadness. "I regret the way I handled things."

I turn around and find his eyes trained on the ballroom. When I follow his line of sight, it's centered on

Emma Jane who's entertaining her granddad, Madison, and Becket with some story. I can't help but compare this to another time Davis's birthday party was held here. It had been right after she and I had gotten engaged.

At one point, I'd stood in this very spot and watched her interact with guests. I remember with such vivid clarity how people responded to her, even the elders who often scoffed at "That wild Haywood girl" when EJ had dyed a streak of blue in her hair or pierced her nose. She'd still managed to charm the hell out of anyone in her presence.

That particular evening, she'd been chatting with Mrs. Tilman and had even managed to get the old coot to laugh. The expression on her face when the older woman had laughed at whatever she'd said had been a mix between pride and happiness. And she'd never looked more beautiful.

No. That's a lie. She looks even more exquisite tonight. She may have poise and confidence with this crowd, but what shines through is her kindness, her heart.

I just wish I knew what made that heart stop loving me.

"I'D LIKE to thank all of you for coming tonight." Davis is addressing a hushed crowd of partygoers with his wife, Rose, by his side, and Granddad on the other. "I'd especially like to thank my daughter, Emma Jane, for making the trip here."

Beside me, she jerks slightly at the mention of her name, as if surprised by it.

Granddad edges forward to speak. "We don't get to see much of her as her job keeps her quite busy in Jacksonville." His mouth curves into a small smile. "But we're blessed to have this time with her."

Raising his glass of champagne, he addresses everyone. "Here's to many more!"

After everyone toasts, conversations resume, as does the music. I set my glass on a nearby table and hold out a hand to EJ.

"Dance?"

Her eyes widen a fraction before she smiles and sets her own glass on the table beside mine. "I'd love to."

Leading her toward the center of the room, we find an available spot on the dance floor. Taking her in my arms, I can't deny that there's something so easy and natural about this.

This woman has always been the only one who simply *fits*.

"I saw your father take you aside, again."

Her solemn gaze meets mine at my mention of seeing Davis speak to her. He'd excused himself after we'd had our own chat and headed in her direction. I'd kept my distance because it appeared to be a bit cathartic for both. I would've stepped in if I'd noticed her appearing distressed.

"Everything okay?"

She nods, her expression pensive. "It was far better than I expected." Her smile is wistful, tinged with a hint of sadness. "I might finally get a father out of this deal. A little late, but…" She lifts a shoulder in a half shrug. "And my mother and I had a good talk, too. Things are actually"—she twists her lips in a rueful grin—"kind of nice."

"I'm glad." Before I comprehend my actions, my hand cups one side of her face, and my thumb grazes lightly along her cheekbone. Peering down, I find myself mesmerized by the depths of her blue eyes.

"Did you ask them to play this?"

Her question startles me. "Play what?"

She appears to have surprised herself, as well. A faint flush spreads across her cheeks before she ducks her head and mutters, "Nothing."

I now realize that the song has changed over to Max's "Lights Down Low." The lyrics describe how he wishes he could stop time because he wants to bask in their love and sings of how he'd give her everything of himself.

Eyes still averted, she mumbles an apology along with, "Ignore me. I'm delusional from lack of sleep from…yeah. And the crazy development with my father."

But the fact still remains. Something made her wonder if I'd requested this song. If I'd planned for us to dance to it.

"It has been a long day." I decide to grant her a reprieve even though she's piqued my curiosity.

She releases a sigh laced with a touch of melancholy. "And we have to drive back tomorrow morning."

I'm dying to know if she's saddened by the thought of having to leave now that she and her father have made tentative amends or if it's because she doesn't want to leave me and what we've had here.

If I had my way, I would keep her at my house until…

Until she realizes she loves you again, an inner voice finishes.

And it's not entirely wrong, but it's not one hundred percent right either. Because another part of me had answered simultaneously.

Until she tells you why she left.

The problem is, I don't know if I'll be able to face the truth of her reason.

33

Emma Jane

"You know, you could come along with us." Becket offers this with an odd expression. "If you don't feel comfortable staying with your ex-fiancé." He pauses. "In his house."

"I'll be fine. But thank you."

"Meaning," Madison leans toward Becket and says in an exaggeratedly hushed whisper, "she's *fine* getting it on with said ex-fiancé."

I flash her a sharp look of warning. "Madison."

She peers up at Becket, and they exchange a look before declaring in unison, "Totally getting it on."

My eyes close in frustration, and I pinch the bridge of my nose with my thumb and forefinger. "Y'all are killing me right now."

"Is that so?" Becket's voice is dripping with mock surprise, and he adds, with a heavy Southern accent, "Well, you need to get over here and let me give you some sugar."

Madison appears puzzled. "Sugar?" Suddenly, her features brighten. "Oh! That's Southern for kisses, right?"

Dropping my hand, I open my eyes to see Becket softly

pat the top of Madison's head, much like one would do to a small child.

"You are learning, my sweet grasshopper. The ways of the Southern vernacular can be so challenging."

Madison makes a sick face. "The grits, though." She shakes her head emphatically. "I *cannot* get on board with that."

"Preach." Becket holds out a fist, and she taps hers to it. They both break off with a laugh, and I can't help but smile at the two. Stepping forward, I embrace them.

"Thanks for coming. It really means the world to me." Tears prick at my eyes as I look at them.

"We're your friends. That's what we're here for." Becket's voice is softer, tender. Then he winks before leaning in, his tone laden with humor. "Just remember that knee move I taught you comes in handy if you need it." When his eyes lift, focusing over my head, I realize he's mentioning it for someone else's benefit.

"Let's hope I don't get to experience the knee move, then." Knox's voice sounds from behind me, and its huskiness sends a thrill rushing through me.

He sidles up to me and casually places a hand at the base of my spine, but his attention rests on my friends.

"Thanks for coming." Reaching out a hand to Becket, the two shake. When he turns to Madison, she steps up and reaches out to hug him.

Becket pipes up. "Well, we need to catch our flight." He holds his arms out to me. "One more hug for the road?"

I step toward him and allow him to wrap me in his tight embrace. He presses a kiss to the top of my head and whispers, "Be careful. I don't want to have to miss games because I got suspended for breaking some dude's legs for you."

Backing away to peer up at Becket, I laugh. "I love you, you know that?"

His eyes shine with both affection and humor. "I know." He plants a quick kiss to my forehead. "Love you back."

"See you on Monday."

Madison and Becket wave as they exit the near-empty ballroom. Aside from us, only the catering employees remain, cleaning up. We made the most of my father's party, and I'd actually enjoyed myself. My granddad and I danced a few times, and it was wonderful to get to see him again. Knox had even done some "rescuing" when a few not-so-pleasant individuals had cornered me, hungry for details about whether Knox and I were back together, for which I'd been grateful.

"Ready to head back?"

I turn to face Knox with a hopeful look. "Actually, do you mind if we—"

"Head out on the water?" he finishes with a knowing expression. At my nod, he answers, "Not at all."

Extending his palm, those dark green eyes shimmer with a nearly unnerving intensity. "Let's go."

As I place my hand in his and we exit the mansion, it's impossible not to wonder what might have been if things had turned out differently. If he hadn't destroyed my trust in him, hadn't eviscerated my love for him.

This man had long ago etched himself on my soul. Much like an old tree with carved initials in its trunk, the sentimental gesture signifying an undying love, Knox Montgomery had left his mark on me.

For some reason, though, I'm giving in to this chance, allowing myself to get lost in the moment with the one man—the only man—who's ever possessed my heart.

"DO YOU SEE THAT?"

Knox slows the jet ski we're riding and points up at the clear night sky where a shooting star is fizzling out.

"Yes." My answer is breathless, due in part from feeling the hard cut of his abdominals, and I wrap my arms more snugly around his torso. I'm also partially lost to the memories which have been bombarding me since I climbed on the back of the jet ski with him tonight.

We used to go riding; it had been one of those special things we did together. Some Sundays, we'd ride and stop at one of the waterfront restaurants with a dock to have brunch. Other times, we'd head out at night, with the headlight of the jet ski illuminating our way to the uninhabited and secluded Sand Island.

Many times, Knox would lift the seat of the jet ski and withdraw a large, folded beach mat and we'd seek a spot for ourselves on the shoreline, slightly shielded by the large palm trees. We'd lie back and peer up at the stars, sharing hushed conversation about our plans for the future. Then we'd make love in the moonlight with nothing but the melodic sound of water lapping at the shoreline and our staggered breaths lingering in the air.

I realize he's nearing Sand Island now, and his muscles tense beneath my embrace when he slows down, as if preparing to turn around and head back to the house.

Propping my chin on his shoulder, I muse, "Maybe we can stop for a bit."

He turns his head slightly, and his beard brushes against my lips. I can't resist dragging them across his cheek, and his sharp intake of breath sends shimmers of satisfaction rushing through me. Dipping my head, I place a kiss along the side of his throat and dart my tongue out to taste his bare skin, peppered from the slightly briny water of the Bay. I revel in the slight rumble that reverberates through his chest beneath my palms before he increases the speed of the jet ski toward the small island.

Knox kills the engine when we get to the shallow waters, and we hop off. With his hands gripping the handlebars, he guides the jet ski up on the bank a bit more before grabbing the small anchor and securing it. I venture up the shoreline slowly, taking my time to admire my surroundings and reminisce about the times we've been here before.

"Want to bring this along?"

I turn to find him holding the familiar folded beach mat.

Tipping my head to the side flirtatiously, I eye him. "Why, Knox Montgomery. Did you plan on deflowerin' me tonight?"

His grin is mischievous. "Now, Miss Emma Jane. I'm terribly insulted by your insinuation."

"I'm sure." A smile spreads across my face. With a nonchalant shrug, I sigh. "I suppose that beach mat would come in handy for stargazing."

I turn my back to him, continuing along the path leading to our old spot when I hear him mutter, "Stargazin' ain't all it's good for."

"THERE'S CASSIOPEIA, RIGHT THERE."

"Ooh! I just saw another shooting star." I point up at the sky.

We're lying on the beach mat, gazing up at the sky. The unusually warm and slightly humid November night, combined with the soothing sounds of the waves, lulls us into a calmness.

"Make sure you wish on it," Knox tells me, his voice deeper, more intimate.

I fall silent for a moment. Without turning my head, I keep my eyes trained on the sky, my voice barely above a whisper. "Do you ever wonder…" I trail off, afraid to voice the rest of my question.

I detect the movement of him turning his head to look at me before he whispers, "What might have been?"

My eyes drift closed, my chest tightening painfully. It's been eight years, yet I still don't feel like I've ever truly gotten over it—over *him*.

I brave a glance at him, just as he turns his face away, focusing on the sky.

"We're different people now," he murmurs softly.

I know he realizes he hasn't answered my question. Maybe I'm being too pushy, too selfish in bringing up this painful subject. But the truth is, I wonder what might have been. If we'd be doing what we love.

If we'd be *in* love. Still.

"I'd sometimes fantasize about you coming to Jacksonville."

His sharp intake of breath alerts me to the fact that I've voiced my thought, but he still doesn't respond.

I release a sigh laced with a touch of disappointment. "Tomorrow, we head back."

"Yes, ma'am." His voice is subdued, almost thoughtful.

Inhaling a deep, fortifying breath, I decide to be brave and throw caution to the wind once more. Shifting to my side, the breeze tousles a lock of hair that came free from my clip during our ride. Before I can tuck it back, Knox reaches out and tenderly smooths it behind my ear. His eyes search mine, a hint of vulnerability flickering across his features.

"You're breathtaking."

His sentiment urges me on, and I press my lips to his softly. My intentions are for a simple, innocent kiss. To give in to the urge to explore the softness of his lips beneath mine.

That all disintegrates when he makes a harsh sound in the back of his throat and drags my body over the top of his.

My sports bra and thin cotton shorts were all I had since I hadn't packed a swimsuit, and the moment my bare midriff comes into contact with the solid warmth of his muscled torso, my body goes up in flames.

He deepens the kiss, his tongue sweeping inside to toy with mine, and I rock myself over the prodding hardness beneath his board shorts. His hands glide down my back to grip my ass and swiftly pull me down as he rolls his hips upward, pressing into the spot right where I want him—ache for him—most.

He breaks our kiss to shift our bodies, positioning me beneath him, and his thighs straddle my hips. Moonlight casts an ethereal glow around his silhouette and he watches me with an intensity while slowly skimming his palms down over my breasts before he slides his thumbs beneath the bottom elastic band of my sports bra.

"May I?"

My lips quirk slightly. "Knox Montgomery's asking for permission?"

He smirks. "I *am* a gentleman, after all."

My tongue darts out to wet my bottom lip, and his eyes drop, tracking its movement. "Maybe I don't want a gentleman tonight."

His eyes lock with mine, expression turning predatory,

and the scorching heat within the expanse of green causes my nipples to harden instantly.

Knox lifts the sports bra up, helping me get it over my head, and tosses it aside. A sexy smirk plays at his lips when he lowers his head to my breast. "Then you won't get one."

Once he captures a nipple between his lips, laving it with his tongue and suckling it deliciously, a surge of heat shoots straight to my core. Instantly, my hands fly to his head, gripping the short strands between my fingers, and I both hear and feel his groan.

He shifts to the other breast, paying the same homage to that nipple, and the slight breeze that hits my breast, now damp from his mouth, sends a shiver through me at the sensation.

"Knox." I gasp. "I need you."

Releasing the decadent suction of his mouth on my nipple, he protests, "But I'm not done yet."

Without warning, I frame his face with my hands, tugging him closer, and rise up, fusing our mouths together. My lips work over his in a hot, feverishly wet kiss. I draw away and wait for his hooded eyes to lock with mine.

"I need you. Now."

One edge of his lips tilts up. "So demanding."

He shifts to his knees, still straddling me, and shoves my shorts down past my hips and ankles before I gently kick them off. At the sight of my body, now illuminated by the moonlight, his expression gives me pause. There's a trace of reverence in it, mixed with something else I'm unable to decipher.

Calloused fingertips trail down my sides, and his touch elicits shivers throughout me. When he skims over my hipbones and veers to my center, my breath catches in my throat.

Suddenly, he freezes, his eyes flying to mine in alarm.

"What is it?"

He grimaces. "I don't have any condoms."

Warmth unfurls within me at this disclosure, because that means he hadn't planned for this.

"It's okay." I hesitate, my voice becoming more faint. "I'm clean and on the pill."

He searches my features, studying me solemnly before he finally speaks in a tone that's soft and subdued. "Are you sure?"

Running my palm along one firm pectoral before sweeping it down to the center of his abs, I slip two fingertips beneath the waistband of his board shorts. I graze the tip of his cock and gather the moisture seeping from it. Bringing my fingers to my lips, I place them in my mouth and suck his salty essence from them.

He drags in a ragged breath, and his eyes pinch closed in a wince. Then they flare open, flaming with such intense heat it causes my breathing to stutter. Knox rolls off me and onto his back, quickly ridding himself of his shorts before turning his face to mine. Wordlessly, I straddle him, watching him fist his hard cock and guide it to my entrance as I slowly lower myself on him.

Our mingled gasps sound as we savor the way it feels to have no barrier between us. I instinctively roll my hips, and his hands fly to steady me. His hooded gaze holds mine.

"I'm not gonna last long."

I clench my inner muscles and watch his eyes fall closed before they flash open, dangerously.

"You did that on purpose."

"Maybe I like when you lose control." I give him a saucy wink.

His fingers clench my hips tighter. "You think you can handle me?"

"Without a doubt."

With an unyielding grip on my hips, he thrusts deep, simultaneously pulling me down on him, and robs me of breath. He continues this rhythm, and I surrender myself to the intoxicating sensation of him inside me.

"Knox," I moan breathlessly as I grow wetter, nearing the precipice of my orgasm.

His movements become more frantic, frenzied, as he thrusts deeper. "Touch yourself."

His command has my eyes flying open to find his own centered on me. They flicker to where our bodies are joined before he raises them again. "I want to watch you rub your clit and come all over me."

Lord have mercy, this man's the only one who's ever managed to drive me close to orgasm by his words alone. Reaching down, I finger my clit in circles. I'm teetering on the brink and know it won't take long before I find my release.

"Damn." His voice is raspy, hoarse. "So fucking beautiful."

My orgasm crashes over me, and I cry out his name, continuing to circle my clit with one finger and ride out the pleasure as he thrusts frantically, harder, and deeper. His near punishing grip on my hips doesn't register as he pulls me down on him with a force that has me sucking in a sharp breath. My inner muscles clench and release his cock repeatedly, and I feel a surge of wetness just as Knox releases a soft groan, reaching his own climax. His grip loosens slightly, and I slump gracelessly upon his chest, the only sound amidst us is our labored breathing.

He mumbles something against my hair that I can't quite make out, but I don't have the energy to inquire about it. As my breathing slows, I close my eyes and concentrate on the soothing sound of his beating heart beneath my ear. One of his hands grazes my back in a slow, comforting caress, and right now, I'm faced with frightening truths: I never truly fell out of love with Knox Montgomery.

And I have no idea if I'll ever manage to tell him my secret.

Emma Jane

FOUR MONTHS AFTER MOVING TO JACKSONVILLE

"Becket, I'm scared."

I'm trying my best not to burst into tears because I know it won't do me any good. I also know that something isn't right. It feels like my body's attempting to turn itself inside out, revolting, as fierce, shooting pains pierce deep.

"I've got you." He speaks in calm, even tones, in contrast to the vehicle's engine revving as he accelerates, navigating the heavy Saturday night traffic to get me to the hospital. "It's gonna be okay, Blue."

I'm in the passenger seat of his SUV, doubled over, my arms wrapped like a vise around my middle. When the worst of the pain hits, it thankfully doesn't last long because everything grows fuzzy before it fades to black.

A Few Hours Later

"Blue?"

My eyes flutter open weakly at the sound of Becket's

voice. I inspect my surroundings and discover that I'm lying in a hospital bed. He's perched on a chair beside me, holding my hand in his.

"What happened?" I wait for the fog to further recede from my brain to fully awaken. Thankfully, I'm no longer in such excruciating pain. "Was it food poisoning?"

When Becket's dark eyes rise from their concentrated focus on our joined hands, I'm shocked to find them filled with pain.

He shakes his head, averting his gaze again. Leaning closer, he presses his lips to the top of my hand. They linger there, and I feel a drop of moisture immediately follow.

"Becket?" The confusion in my voice is mixed with trepidation. "What's going o—" I break off the moment he raises his head.

His eyes are brimming with tears, and one makes its escape, rapidly descending down his cheek.

His voice is low, subdued, as he gently breaks the news, informing me of the emergency surgery. Then he holds me while we both succumb to our tears.

But even as I give myself over to the grief, a traitorous part of me desperately wishes another man was holding me instead.

34

Knox

PRESENT
SUNDAY

I PEER over at Emma Jane, who's currently asleep in the passenger seat, her head tipped at an odd angle. I told her to recline the seat if she wanted to, but she insisted she was fine and wanted to keep me company on the drive back.

I feel marginally guilty for being the cause of the dark circles beneath her eyes and her lack of sleep. But only marginally, because repeatedly making love to her beneath the stars last night had been nothing short of magical. When it came time to head back to my house, we'd both been reluctant. Our time on the island had felt like we'd been encapsulated in our own world.

"EJ," I utter softly.

I just finished topping off the gas tank, and she still didn't rouse from her nap when I got back in the truck, which is a testament to how exhausted she is.

I lift the center console and lay a small pillow in its

place between us. I'm glad I decided to bring it along for our ride back to Jacksonville.

Reaching over, I try to get slack in her seat belt and guide her to a more comfortable position, to lay her head on the pillow between us. Groggily, her eyes open.

"Just lie here. Then you won't wake up with a kink in your neck."

Without a word, she shifts and lays her head on the pillow, her eyes already closing. Some dark tendrils of her hair spill over my khaki-clad thigh, and I give in to the urge to sift my fingers through it, to smooth it back from her face. The low murmur she emits brings a small smile to my lips.

There were many times when she'd lay her head on my lap while we'd watch TV just so I'd play with her hair. She'd told me it was relaxing, but for me, it was something little, something nonsexual, that only I did for her. The same way she'd been the only one who knew I hated to talk if I'd had a stressful day and just wanted to take the jet ski out on the water. She'd hop on the back, wrap her arms around me, and we'd ride for a while, letting the wind whip at us. We'd ride in silence until I felt calmed by the serenity of both the water and her presence.

As I pull back on the interstate to head toward Jacksonville, my phone, hooked up to my hands-free earbuds, alerts me that I have an incoming call from Wells. Glancing once again at EJ's sleeping form, I quickly fit in the earbuds and press the button to accept the call.

"Hey, man." I still figure I should try to keep my voice lowered for her benefit.

"Are you…busy?" There's avid curiosity lacing his tone.

"I'm driving, and she's asleep."

"Ah."

I wait for him to continue, but when he doesn't, I prod. "Ah, what?"

"Nothing. Just wondering how you and sleeping beauty made out." He chuckles softly. "Pun intended."

"Fine. It seemed like her dad's come around finally."

"That's good, but it's not exactly what I was asking."

"I'm not talking about that, Wells."

"And here I thought best friends were always supposed to kiss and tell," he jokes. There's a beat of silence. "Have y'all talked?"

I know exactly what he's asking. With a sigh, I shake my head even though I know he can't see me. "No." Blowing out another breath, I say, "I just...I'm not sure I want to know."

"You do, but you don't." He releases a sigh of his own. "I get it, man. I do. But there's no way you'll get anywhere pussyfootin' around."

"I know." I recognize how defeated I sound, admitting this. Quickly checking to ensure she's still sound asleep, I return my attention to the road.

"Can I be honest with you?"

Caught off guard by Wells's uncharacteristic question, I can't help but let out a small amused laugh. "Since when have you asked before offering your thoughts?"

His sober tone becomes evident and sets me on edge. "Y'all have changed. Not to the extent that you're unrecognizable but you've both matured and grown into your own persons. I think maybe…" He trails off, and I find myself hanging in limbo, waiting for his next words.

"You think maybe what?"

"Seeing you and Emma Jane together got me thinking that maybe it wasn't meant to be the first time around." He pauses for a beat. "Sometimes love needs a second chance."

As I mull over his words, a part of me realizes how hokey my best friend sounds. In typical Wells fashion, he quickly addresses it.

"I totally saw that on a greeting card when I was picking out a birthday card for Mom. So don't go thinking I'm getting all sappy and suddenly watching Nicolas Sparks movies and shit."

"Noted," I say with a laugh.

"Drive safe and keep me posted."

"Will do. Later."

Once I press the button to end the call and withdraw the earbuds, I turn on the radio to play softly in the background and allow myself to ruminate over everything.

Hoping like hell I'm able to come up with a plan.

The Following Monday

"JUST CANCEL."

"I can't just cancel." She releases an exasperated sigh. "He's my best friend, and this is our designated FWOB night. We plan these ahead of time, especially when it's during the season."

I bristle at the fact that she and Becket actually *have* a designated night.

"Remind me again what that all stands for? The FO—"

"FWOB," she corrects me. "Friends. Without. Benefits."

I narrow my eyes speculatively. "Are you sure about the without part?"

She crosses her arms, her lips pursed. "Knox. He's my best friend. That's it."

I step closer. "I can't help but ask. Because I have a tough time understanding it." I take another step, bringing us closer and leaning in. "How a man like him isn't completely crazy"—I pause and dip my head lower so that, with my next words, my lips drag softly against her own—"for y—"

The knock on the door causes us to jerk apart, and EJ's temporary assistant timidly peeks inside the office.

"I'm so sorry to interrupt, Ms. Haywood, Mr. Montgomery." Keri Mitchell's brown eyes dart to me briefly before returning to address her. "I have the information you requested for the presentation."

EJ flashes the young woman a grateful smile and walks over to accept the file from her. "Thanks so much. This is all we need to finalize things for tomorrow."

Keri dismisses herself, slipping out of the office while EJ walks around her desk to take a seat. Her next words are hushed since her office door is still ajar.

"Is there anything else of importance you need from me?"

Crossing the distance to her desk, I splay my palms flat on the surface across from her and lean in. My voice drops to something low and seductive, hushed and mindful of the open office door. "Be ready for me to come over after your *date*."

I exit, offer a polite greeting to Keri along the way, and return to my own office where I have fewer tasks to reconcile than I'd expected.

My time here is wrapping up, and I know I've done everything in my power to get this business back on its feet. With EJ sealing this deal tomorrow—and I have no doubt she will—*Fit & Fashion* will be back on the most secure footing it's had in a while.

Then I have to figure out where I go from here.

And if it'll be with her by my side.

35

Emma Jane

LAST-MINUTE PREP for the presentation tomorrow for Mr. Feldman is finally complete. Coastal Media is the final box I need checked off the list of requirements Knox originally gave me.

We haven't discussed it, but I'm certain he'll realize I deserve this promotion. Sealing this deal will confirm it.

However, once I dug into this project, I decided to go for the "gold": I'm aiming for a combined deal with Feldman's Coastal Media *and* the magazine he owns, *Elite Fitness*.

With a long, tiresome exhale, I sink back in my seat after saving the completed proposal and the PowerPoint presentation.

"If this doesn't secure my job, not sure what will," I mutter under my breath as I click my mouse and print the necessary number of copies of the PowerPoint. Most clients prefer a hardcopy in front of them, so I normally have that option at the ready.

I must admit, I feel confident about this because I've come to know Mr. Feldman and respect his business practices. We've spoken on several occasions at social engagements, and he always reminds me much of my own granddad.

Fingers crossed, he'll recognize the benefits of my proposal, that *Fit & Fashion* joining Coastal Media, as well as his magazine, *Elite Fitness*, which caters to athletic men and women who are established in their fitness routine, will be mutually beneficial.

Glancing at the time, I realize I'll be late to meet Becket if I don't hurry up and head out now. Hurriedly, I pack up my things, lock up my office and say good night to Keri. I turn in the direction of the bank of elevators when Knox suddenly approaches.

"If you don't mind, Ms. Haywood, I'd like to go over a few quick things regarding tomorrow's presentation on your way out."

I have to bite my lip to try to hide my smile. I'm certain I know what he wants to go over, and it *isn't* tomorrow's presentation. But I know he's trying to maintain professionalism here, so I nod perfunctorily, and just as my lips part to agree, Keri interrupts.

"Ms. Haywood? I know you're on your way out, but if you'd like, I can sort through everything you sent to the printer and staple it for Mr. Feldman and his partners tomorrow."

She's a sweetheart and ever so eager to help. I offer her a grateful smile. "Oh, it's not necessary, Keri. It can be done tomorrow."

Keri frowns slightly, before her expression turns hopeful. "I'd really feel better and not like a slacker if I could just get it done ahead of time."

"Well, then." I toss a look at Knox like, *Wow, she's a go-getter, huh?* before I turn back to her and hand her my keys so she can unlock my office. "Go ahead and get them."

"Thank you, Ms. Haywood." She accepts the keys and darts back to the door, unlocking it and quickly ducking inside.

When I turn back to Knox, his eyes are shining with laughter. He leans in close and whispers in my ear, "Maybe I should call you Ms. Haywood later. You seem much more accommodating."

I swat at him and roll my eyes. Before I can hiss a sharp response, Keri exits the office with the printouts in hand and hands me back my keys.

"I'll have these all set for tomorrow, Ms. Haywood."

"Thanks again, Keri." I flash her an appreciative smile. "Please don't stay too late. Have a good night."

I start walking down the hall after she bids both Knox and me a good night, and he sidles up beside me as we approach the elevators. Once an available car opens, we step inside and wait for the doors to close.

As soon as we begin our descent, Knox moves closer to where I stand on the side near the numbered buttons. Releasing his hold on his briefcase, he lets it drop softly to the floor near our feet, and crowds me in the corner, both hands braced against the wall on either side of my head.

Dipping his head, he skims his lips across my cheek in the softest caress. "I wish you could cancel tonight." His mouth dusts along my jawline as the elevator descends. "And come home with me." He shifts to my earlobe, and his lips latch onto it before he grazes it with his teeth. "So I can show you how much I missed having you in my bed last night."

My breath catches, not only from the magic he's forging with his lips, but because I missed being in bed with him last night, too. He'd asked me to come home with him, but I'd declined, using work as an excuse, telling him that I'd need the proper clothing. I don't like my routine to be thrown off kilter, but it had been so tempting to take Knox up on his offer.

So tempting.

But so much still needs to be addressed. I fully recognize that I—*we* got lost in the moment over the weekend, but it doesn't erase the facts. We still have issues we need to acknowledge.

"Knox, you know I can't." Good grief, even *I* can hear the wavering in my voice.

His mouth descends, trailing delicate kisses along the column of my throat. "You can." One of his hands slips beneath the fabric of my flared skirt and cups me at the apex of my thighs. "You cancel, come home with me, and I can put my mouth all over this sweet pussy." He applies pressure right where I ache for him, sliding a finger beneath my panties and caressing my wet folds. "Right before I sink my cock deep inside you."

My eyes fall closed at his hypnotically arousing words while one of my hands clenches the edge of his suit jacket, and the other holds my briefcase in a white-knuckled death grip.

"Say you'll come home with me, EJ." His words roll over me in a caress, the raspy quality of his voice the only clue he's just as turned on as I am.

My lips part to respond just as the elevator dings. His eyes dart over, noting the floor level, before he ducks and reaches for his briefcase at our feet at the same time the door opens.

Second floor. Another straggler pulling an unusually late Monday steps on board with a tired nod of greeting. We ride the rest of the way to the parking deck in silence, and upon exiting, Knox falls into step beside me.

"You don't have to escort me to my car." My eyes

sparkle in amusement. "I've been seeing myself out for a while now."

"Humor me."

Pressing the key fob to unlock it, I open the door and reach in to settle my briefcase on the passenger seat. I turn to say goodbye to Knox, and I'm startled to find him in close proximity yet again. With a palm resting atop of the car door, he has the other braced on the roof.

"I at least demand a kiss good night." His mouth curves into a sexy smirk.

Uneasy, I survey the near-empty parking deck before I toss out a teasing, "Is that so?"

Wordlessly, he snakes an arm around my waist and yanks me flush against his hard body. His lips crash down on mine in a deep, ravenous kiss before he gentles it to nip at my lips slowly, tenderly.

Once he finally draws away, his eyes lift to mine, and the emotion simmering beneath the surface nearly robs me of breath.

He whispers, "Good night," before dusting one final kiss on my lips.

After I slip inside my car, he closes my door before picking up his briefcase and walking away.

"I CHOSE the worst night for FWOB, didn't I?"

My eyes collide with Becket's in confusion. "Why do you say that?"

He reaches across the small table where we're seated in the corner of the restaurant, away from the bulk of prying eyes. His index finger grazes between my brows as he gives me a soft smile. "That crease right there just won't let up."

My shoulders deflate slightly, and I flash him an apologetic look. "Sorry."

"No worries. There've been many times when I couldn't get my mind to stop replaying an interception I threw." Leaning back in his chair, he removes the cloth napkin from his lap and places it on the table. "So tell me what's on your mind."

With a wry laugh, I shake my head. "Do you have all night?"

"I've got all the time in the world for you." Becket offers this simple response, spoken with pure sincerity.

"Beck." I reach across the table, turn my palm over, and he grasps it. "Do you have any idea how lucky I am that I found you in that bar years ago?"

He flashes me a sweet, boyish grin. "Bet you never thought you'd get scouted in a gay bar to be an NFL quarterback's BFF, huh?"

I shake my head, a soft smile playing on my lips. "Never in a million."

His expression sobers, becoming more thoughtful. "I think it was fate, Blue. We needed each other."

I tip my head to the side with a contemplative expression. "I think so, too." Giving his hand a squeeze, I release it with a sigh. "Ready for what's on my mind?"

"Always." He frowns suddenly. "Wait. As long as it's not something gross with feminine stuff." He makes a sick face.

I raise my eyebrows pointedly. "This coming from the man who volunteered to be a stand-in birthing partner for his friend?" I'm referring to Dr. Presley Hendrixson.

He grins smugly. "I did that mainly to ruffle her husband's feathers."

"The husband who happens to be a former SEAL?" I stare at him incredulously. "The same guy who endured being held captive and tortured for over a year? You want to ruffle *that* guy's feathers?" Shaking my head, I mutter, "Men."

Becket just chuckles. "He loves it. Deep down, he's a big teddy bear like me."

"Now, that much is true."

"So go on." He takes a long drink from his water glass, focusing intently on me. "Tell me everything."

I blow out a slow breath and begin. "I have a lot riding on this proposal tomorrow…"

36

Knox
TUESDAY MORNING

I'm seated at my desk, stunned, while the young, tearful woman sits across from me, on the edge of her seat as if preparing to make a quick escape at any moment.

"To say this is"—I try to form the right words—"disheartening news would be an understatement, Ms. Mitchell."

"I just didn't know what to do," she weeps quietly and dabs her eyes with a tissue, hands trembling.

"Well, you did the right thing by coming to me."

Yet again, I've been misled. By the same damn woman, no less.

Everything at my house, everything that happened the weekend we traveled to Mobile, played into her hands perfectly.

I played into her hands like a fucking jackass.

She'd sunk to an all new low by sleeping with me to try to blind me from her actions here at work. To steal an intern's ideas, one who'd been placed with her while she was short an assistant, no less, is the bottom of the barrel.

I rise from my chair and walk around my desk to

approach Ms. Mitchell. "You'll have to give the presentation today, then."

The frail looking blonde peers up at me with wide eyes. "R-really, Mr. Montgomery?"

"Absolutely." I give a firm nod. "These are your ideas. You should be the person to present them."

She covers her mouth with her hand as if trying to regain composure. Finally, she stands and straightens her shoulders.

"Thank you, sir. I won't let you down."

She exits my office, and I'm left to figure out how to confront Emma Jane.

This time *will* be the final time I have to.

I'VE READ, numerous times, how to generate an air of authority. How to lead. How to run a business and keep it thriving. How to fire employees effectively. How to negotiate.

Nothing I've ever read could prepare me for this moment. The only advantage I have is that I've arrived in Emma Jane's office before her.

I hear her greet Ms. Mitchell, her tone energetic, with an air of excitement. Confident.

What a crock of shit.

Her heels sound lightly on the thin carpeting of her office, and I hear her draw to a surprised stop at the sight of me standing at the bank of windows. My back is to her, but I can see her reflection in the glass. She appears startled.

Good.

I turn slowly, and she raises her eyebrows in question before glancing over at the clock on the wall. "I figured they'd be here early, but I wasn't expecting them this ea—"

"You're going to act innocent?" My voice is deceptively quiet, low, dangerous with steely undertones.

Eyeing me warily, she reaches out to shut her office door behind her with a quiet *click*. She addresses me carefully. "I don't know what you're referring to."

I huff out a humorless laugh, my gaze piercing hers. "You were planning on stealing an intern's ideas and passing them off as your own? And you thought no one would find out? That she wouldn't speak up?"

Emma Jane appears as though she's been sucker punched but quickly composes herself, readjusting the shoulder strap of her briefcase. Pressing her lips thin, her eyes narrow in a frigid stare.

"What exactly are you talking about, Mr. Montgomery?"

My jaw clenches and unclenches tightly before I speak, forcing myself to hold an even, controlled tone. "Ms. Mitchell confided in me. She told me how you took her ideas and planned to pass them off as your own today, with Mr. Feldman and his partners." I fold my arms across my chest and stare back at her. "She was in tears, not wanting to rock the boat since you're her superior. She was worried about being classified as a snitch."

Emma Jane's lips purse as she nods slowly, almost thoughtfully. "And she was terribly upset over this, I'm sure."

I make a derisive sound. "You're not even going to deny it." Shaking my head, I mutter, "I should have known."

Her expression darkens mutinously. "*You* should have known? *You*?" She practically bites out the words. "It's *me* who should have known better."

He Loves Me...Knot

I ignore her outburst. "Ms. Mitchell will be presenting to Mr. Feldman. I'll explain to him that you had an emergency which took you out of the office. We'll hash everything out with HR over your termination once the presentation is completed."

Anger is radiating from Emma Jane—anger at being caught, surely—and she presses her lips thin as though searching for the right response. "I see you've got this all figured out."

With pure disgust rushing through my veins, I nod. "I should've known better, Ms. Haywood. You betrayed me once, and you tried it yet again. But this time, you included Ms. Mitchell in the mix."

"Right." She speaks through clenched teeth.

When she turns to the door, just as her hand touches the handle, I challenge, "That's it?" She freezes without turning back. "That's all you've got to say for yourself?"

Whirling around, she narrows her eyes murderously. "Actually, *no*. That's not all," she practically snarls. "I'd like to say it's mighty telling that you'd toss me under the bus and not even ask for my side of the story." Stepping closer, she fixes a hard glare on me. "You clearly think I lack integrity and morals. Well, not to worry." She lets out a humorless laugh. "I'm taking a personal day, and my resignation will be filed with HR first thing tomorrow."

Emma Jane spins around, laying her hand on the doorknob but doesn't immediately open it. Without looking back, she speaks in a voice devoid of all emotion.

"Oh, and be sure to enjoy slides fifteen, twenty-nine, thirty-three, and forty-six, Mr. Montgomery."

She exits the office, leaving me standing here, perplexed by her cryptic words.

EMMA JANE'S parting words still ricochet within my mind when I stride into the conference room to find Keri straightening up the multiple sets of presentation packets. Her eyes dart up, meeting mine as I draw to a stop at the opposite end of the table from where she stands.

"All set?"

"Yes, sir." She punctuates this with a nod and a tight, nervous smile.

"Have you done a dry run? To prepare?" I ask casually.

"I went through my notes more than anything else. The slides have been all set from the get-go."

"Do you mind if I take a quick look at the presentation?" I advance to where her laptop sits, hooked up to the projector.

"Uh, sure."

There's the slightest hitch of hesitation in her voice, and it prompts a sick churning in the pit of my stomach.

Reaching for the laptop's keyboard, I brace one palm against the flat surface of the conference room table, using my other hand to navigate through the presentation slides on the computer. I scroll through them quickly until I land on slide fifteen.

The queasiness in my stomach escalates into full-blown nausea, and a cold sweat prickles my skin as I stare at the screen. Though I'm certain as to what I'll find on slides twenty-nine, thirty-three, and forty-six, I still click on them, discovering the same small detail. It's so subtle, one could easily miss it if they weren't looking for it.

Quickly, I navigate and access my company email, searching for one in particular where Emma Jane had sent me a past proposal. I open the file attachment which details a proposal from well over two months ago. I scroll down a few pages before I see it yet again. The same detail I've discovered on her PowerPoint.

A goddamn watermark at the very bottom of the slide with the name, Emma Jane Haywood.

I've royally fucked up.

Dragging my eyes from the laptop screen, I regard Keri Mitchell, whose expression is now clouded with uncertainty. But before I can say a word, we're interrupted by my secretary, announcing that Mr. Feldman and his partners have arrived.

Shit.

I rush to greet the three men before I guide Mr. Feldman to the side and lower my voice.

"Mr. Feldman, I apologize but Ms. Haywood's been unexpectedly called away on an emergency."

The older man appears concerned. "Is she all right?" Then he asks the million-dollar question. "Is there a chance she'll be able to do the presentation tomorrow? I can only stay in town until late afternoon due to my schedule."

"Oh, I'm sure her personal emergency will be taken care of, and she'll be able to present tomorrow."

As he and I discuss rescheduling, I internally pray that I can set things right with Emma Jane.

But first, I have to fire an intern.

37

Emma Jane

"He didn't even ask me anything. He just assumed the worst. Like I could be a dirt bag who would steal someone else's ideas!"

I'm whining to both Madison and Becket about what happened this morning. I've already told them the whole story and realize I'm repeating myself, indignant about how Knox treated me. Heck, he probably won't even notice or care about the slides with my watermark. Back at *Southern Charm Lifestyle*, my boss had suggested I include that detail in my presentations as an added safeguard. I just never thought I'd see the day when I had to make mention of it.

Not that it had made any difference, of course.

Madison took a personal day as soon as I'd called her, barely holding in my tears, after I'd left Knox standing in my office. I hadn't even bothered to say a word to Keri who'd been sitting at her desk outside my office door, smiling smugly. I knew it was pointless to waste my breath, to waste one single word on the likes of her. As they'd say back home, she was like a rattlesnake in the tall grasses of the bayou, just lying in wait for the unsuspecting person.

Becket's still in his workout gear since I'd interrupted him from his "light cardio" run on the treadmill.

"So what's your game plan?" Becket asks.

"Well, remember who sought me out at the last gala we attended?"

Becket's eyebrows rise with what looks like surprise. "Elise at *East Coast Couture*?" He mentions the editor-in-chief of the well-known magazine who'd surprised me when she'd easily addressed me by name at the gala.

Elise had taken me aside with her husband and informed me that she'd been following my career and was impressed with my work. She'd mentioned she was starting a new brand of *East Coast Couture* magazine that she wanted to get up and running soon.

As part whim and part job security in case things went south with my position at *F&F* with Knox at the helm, I'd done a live video interview with her. I hadn't heard anything back until she'd contacted me right before I'd left for Mobile with Knox, wanting to schedule a final face-to-face interview. We'd had some issues trying to make our schedules match up, as well as an anticipated start date should they offer me the job.

It's pretty ironic that I should find myself available now for not only the interview, but for the job as well.

"I'm scheduled to fly up late Wednesday and do the interview Thursday morning."

"That's awesome!" Madison gives me an encouraging smile. "So you'll be here still, right?"

I nod and explain that Elise wants to have a southeastern location for their new headquarters and publication, and how she envisions it to be centered around all things known to women in this region. She wants it to be something women can connect with more meaningfully and garner the interest of others who might pick up the magazine.

Madison nudges her shoulder against mine playfully. "This would be a unique opportunity, but I'll definitely miss you at work."

"I still vote for me siccing the guys on him." This comes from Becket who has repeatedly offered to get his linemen to "rough up" Knox.

"You guys don't need any bad press or lawsuits," I say with a weak smile. "But thanks."

Becket's lips part, likely with another maiming suggestion, when his phone rings and plays a song that sounds like…

Madison and I stare at one another incredulously.

"Is that," she asks slowly, "Justin Bieber?"

"Singing 'Baby'?" I echo as Becket frantically answers his phone, darting up from the couch and beginning to pace.

"Are you serious? Holy sh—*er*, I mean, crap!" He runs a hand through his hair, slightly disheveling it, before grabbing his keys from my dining room table. "I'll be right there, Presley. Wait!" His lips curve up at the corners. "Is your Marine husband there?"

I shake my head at Becket's attempt at harassment, but realize there's no need since I soon hear a deep voice boom through his cell phone.

"I'm a SEAL, Jones. Get it right or you'll never get to hold our baby girl."

Becket abruptly stops on his way to the door. "Did you just threaten me?" Then, in a louder voice, "Presley! Did you hear what Hendy said?"

"Get off the damn phone and get your pretty face up here," Hendy growls.

Becket grins mischievously and ends the call before turning to me and Madison. "Do you mind—"

"I've got to head home." She rises from the couch. "I can log in remotely and catch up on some things." Enfolding me in a tight hug, she whispers for me to call her if I need her before pulling the door closed behind her.

Becket tugs on his ball cap and peers down at me. "Presley asked about you, if you might want to come along with me, but I wasn't sure you'd want to…" He trails off, and I know why.

But after the day I've had, I need to witness the love between a husband and wife and the miracle of birth.

"Let's go."

"WHY CAN'T I get a turn already?"

Both Hendy and I stare at Becket in disbelief.

"Becket," I scold, "stop whining."

Presley's husband shoots Becket a glare before responding calmly. "If you want to use that baby carrier you've been trying out, you'll cut down on the whiny shit."

"You should probably watch your language," Becket retorts.

"That's enough," I warn my friend with an exasperated roll of my eyes.

I return my attention to Hendy who's basking in the delight of being a new father. In the rocking chair, he softly murmurs to the tiny newborn lying against his bare chest, and emotion wells up within me at the sight.

This man is such a complex paradox, with his extremely

fit and muscled body in contrast with the horrific scarring on his back as well as one side of his face—a result of what he'd endured while being held captive during his time as a Navy SEAL. His tender expression, filled with love as he talks to his little girl, is something I'll not soon forget.

"You'll be brave and bold, won't you, girl?" he utters quietly, his eyes alight with affection as he peers down at her. "Just like your mom."

Soft footsteps sound down the hallway and one of Presley's four midwives who helped deliver little Emilia emerges with a smile for the new father.

"She's all cleaned up now." The older woman turns to address me and Becket. "Give us a moment and I'll let you know once our new mama's ready to see you."

Hendy carefully rises from the chair, holding Emilia securely as he heads toward the midwife. "Time to go see your mom." He offers his baby a lopsided half-smile, due in part to the scarring on the one side of his face. "You're probably missing her already, aren't you…" His words trail off as he and the midwife disappear down the hallway.

Becket's eyes find mine. "She's beautiful, isn't she?" he whispers with the same awe I feel.

I work hard to swallow past the lump in my throat. "She is."

His gaze is searching. "You okay?"

I nod quickly before forcing a smile. "Just happy for them."

Without a word, Becket rises from the couch and strides over to where I sit in the chair, his outstretched hands beckoning me. I place my hands in his, and he yanks me up from my seat, promptly enfolding me in his strong, comforting embrace.

He presses his lips to the top of my head, and one hand

soothes me in slow strokes over my back as he murmurs softly, "One day, Blue."

I clamp my lips together to withhold the emotion brimming at the surface because this isn't the time or place for my own pity party. Nodding against Becket's chest, I exhale a long breath.

"One day," I echo in a whisper.

BECKET DROPS me off at my apartment, seeing me safely inside even though I've repeatedly assured him I'm fine, just emotionally wrung out after the day's events.

He stands at my door, hesitating, and I know he'll probably offer to stay over just in case I need him. But I also know he has a mandatory workout scheduled early in the morning and needs a good night's rest in his own bed.

"Thanks for everything." I wrap my arms around him in a tight embrace. "You're the best."

"I know." His voice is laced with humor, and he eases away to peer down at me, his face a mask of concern. "I hate that I can't drive you to the airport since I have a team meeting but—"

"Becket." I stop him with a palm against his chest. "I'll be fine. It's really not a big deal."

"And you'll let me know once you land safely? And after the interview?"

"Yes, Mom," I tease softly.

His lips quirk, and he gently cradles my face in his hands before landing a loud, smacking kiss on my forehead. Releasing me, he heads toward the door. "Bye, gorgeous."

"Bye." I close the door after him and lock it. Leaning

my back against it, I release a heavy breath and try to muster up the excitement to pack for my flight tomorrow.

I should feel excited. This is an incredible opportunity. Yet, with everything that's transpired, I'm struggling to generate even a modicum of enthusiasm.

With a sigh, I push away from the door, chalking my mood up to everything that's happened today. Before I can take two steps in the direction of my bedroom, there's a knock on my door.

My brows crease as I wonder what Becket could possibly need. I unlock and tug open my door, all the while trying to think of what he could have left behind…

Only to find myself staring at the last man I want to see.

Abruptly and without a word, I start closing the door. Unfortunately, the force of his strong palm slapping against the hard surface halts the closure.

"Emma Jane, I'm sorry."

My teeth clench in anger. "I. Don't. Care." I lean my weight against the door, to no avail, of course.

"*Please.*" The hoarse desperation in his tone triggers a weakness within me.

Damn him.

My body deflates. "Fine."

What does it even matter? I think to myself.

Spinning on my heels, I leave him to close the door and head into the kitchen. Ignoring him as he approaches me, I feel the full weight of his eyes on me as I pour a healthy amount of cabernet into a wine glass. Lord knows I'm going to need it.

With my back to him, I take a fortifying sip. "What do you want, Knox," I say with weary resignation, not posing it as a question, as I fiddle with the tiny charm encircling the stem of my glass.

"I'm sorry." His apology is spoken softly but with a noticeable firmness, heavy with regret. "I shouldn't have accused you without even speaking to you first. It—everything she told me—fed into past insecurities about you... into my fear of trusting you again. I've never acted that way before with any business decision."

"It doesn't matter." With a weary sigh, I turn, lean back against the kitchen counter, and cross my arms protectively. "It's done. I'm submitting my resignation tomorrow." Just as his lips part, I rush ahead and finish. "I have a final interview with *East Coast Couture* on Thursday."

His jaw tenses, features turning steely, as disappointment cascades over his features. "That's it? Just like that?"

Releasing a humorless laugh, I glare hard at him. "That's rich coming from the man who accused me of stealing intellectual property today."

He throws up his hands in evident frustration. "I came here to apologize!" His voice rises. "Which you never did, by the way."

My own voice increases in volume. "Apologize for what?"

"For leaving me at the fucking altar without a damn word!"

Staring at him incredulously, my jaw slackens. "I can't believe it comes back to that." My tone turns ripe with sarcasm. "You think you were done *so* wrong."

"You left me!" he explodes.

"You betrayed me!" I yell back. "You told my father not to worry," my tone changes, laden with sarcasm, "that you'd give me a little pat on the head and have me forget all about my dreams of having a career I loved."

He falls silent a moment, his brows creasing. "What the hell are you talking about?"

"I heard you, Knox," I snarl. "I heard you and my

father talking right before we were due to walk down the aisle."

He suddenly pales, lips parting in dismay and probably guilt, as well. "Emma Jane…"

I manage to muster a wan smile. "No worries, though. I heard it all, and that's why I didn't stick around. No way was I going to become some Stepford wife with nothing but party planning and gardening to fill my days." I spit the words out with venom. "Hell, even Katherine knew!"

Knox remains silent, standing stock-still, and continues to stare at me. "I don't believe it." He takes a step back, almost clumsily, as if in a daze. "You believed that? That I was telling your father the truth?"

His eyes bore into me as he speaks carefully, his tone even. "I always hated the way your father treated you and your mother. The old-school views he had about women. The opinions he had about you getting your degree and landing that job. I was only," he swallows thickly, "placating him that day. Telling him what he wanted to hear." Pain is etched across his features. "I would never have said you couldn't pursue a career, let alone seek out your dreams."

After a brief pause, he adds vehemently, "And I never told anyone about that conversation with your father, aside from Wells." He shakes his head. "Katherine's always been jealous of you, Emma Jane."

"But," I falter slightly, before regaining steam, "what about the home office you set up for my"—I break off and hook my fingers in air quotes—"'monogramming business'?"

When he answers, his tone hovers between stunned and exasperated. "I thought you might like to do that on the side." A severe crease appears between his brows. "I never meant for it to seem degrading, but for you to have your special place…"

Oh, no. No, no, no. This can't possibly be true.
Can it?

The room feels like it's closing in on me. Like a thousand-pound weight is sitting on my chest.

Is it possible that I'd had it all wrong? Had I wrongly believed what I'd heard? Had I doubted my own fiancé and believed the worst of him?

I'd believed that he was just like my own father.

My hand flies to cover my mouth in horror. "No."

Knox's expression of hurt, the disbelief on his face is like a knife stabbing my chest. "You were only giving him lip service?" I whisper.

He holds my gaze for a beat before his expression hardens. "Of course, I was." Snorting derisively, he adds, "I loved you, Emma Jane."

Oh, God. Clutching desperately at the countertop, my chin drops to my chest as I stare down at the granite, my vision blurring with tears of regret.

Regret for my mistake made in such youthful haste, drenched in utter heartache.

I'd been so adamant about escaping my father's stronghold after fighting him for each and every morsel of independence. No daughter should feel she's incapable of making her own decisions. I hadn't been able to bear the idea of continuing to live like that, with Knox merely taking his place.

"Guess we're even, huh?" he offers with a laugh devoid of humor. "You thought the worst of me back then, and this time 'round, I thought the worst of you. The only thing is, you end up jumping ship each time, right?"

My head whips around as I gape at him. "I'm sorry,

Knox," I offer weakly, my throat painfully tight with emotion.

"Yeah." He runs his hands over his head before slipping them into the pockets of his pants. Staring down at his shoes, he blows out a long, heavy breath. "Mr. Feldman wants you to be the one to present everything to him and his partners. The only time he has in his schedule is for tomorrow morning at nine o'clock."

"I'll be there." My voice is filled with resignation.

He merely nods, his eyes still averted, before turning to exit the kitchen.

I watch him retreat, not knowing exactly what to say or do at this moment. I want so badly to divulge everything, but I'm too shell-shocked at what I've just learned.

Right as he lays his hand on the door handle, the words spill from my lips. "I'm sorry for not believing in you."

He turns his head to the side, eyes downcast, and speaks so softly that I strain to hear him. "You didn't just fail to believe in me, Emma Jane." With a slight shake of his head, he finishes with, "You didn't believe in us." Then, he closes the door quietly behind him.

I promptly crumble to the floor, wrapping my arms around my legs and curl upon myself.

And the tears begin to fall.

Wednesday

I CAN DISTINCTLY RECALL the last time I'd used this much makeup, attempting to conceal the puffiness of my eyes from crying. It seems I've come full circle.

Mr. Feldman made things go much smoother, thankfully, and he immediately insisted that we set the deal into motion as soon as possible. I barely held back a wince when he shook Knox's hand after we'd finished up, telling him how lucky he is to have me on board.

"You'd better do everything in your power to keep her around," he'd boasted while offering me a quick wink.

With a weak smile in return, I'd merely nodded and shook everyone's hands as they'd left with Knox in tow to see them out.

Now, I'm packing up my things, preparing to head out and catch my flight to New York for the interview. I've already submitted my resignation to Human Resources as well as sent a copy to Knox's email.

"I received your email."

My head snaps up at hearing Knox's voice, and I find him standing at my office door. I nod silently and finish packing up my briefcase. Due to my minimalist tendencies, I really didn't have many personal items aside from the few small framed snapshots of me, Madison, and Becket on my desk.

"When does your flight leave?"

I regard him with wary suspicion. "At three."

Glancing up at the time on the clock, I note that it's nearing eleven o'clock. I have to allot the normal two hours to get through the security checkpoints, and it takes about thirty minutes to get to the airport from here.

"Are you driving? Or taking a cab?"

"I'll probably schedule a ride on the Lyft app." I wave a hand toward my cell phone lying on my desk.

"I can drive you." My eyes collide with his in surprise. "So we can talk."

I wonder what else he could possibly want to talk to me about. "If it's to try to get me to stay here—"

"It's not." With the barest smile in place, he shoves his hands in his pockets. "Well, not one hundred percent, anyway." Sobering, he adds, "I really just wanted to discuss some things." There's a brief pause. "And I'd like to show you something before we hit the airport."

I study his features before releasing a sigh. "Fine. I'll be ready to go in a minute."

"I'll get my keys and meet you back here."

38

Knox

I PULL into the driveway and the confusion radiating from her is palpable.

"Who lives here?" There's surprised hesitance in her tone.

"I do." I turn off the ignition of my truck, staring straight ahead at the house. "Well, I have since I've been working here."

Abruptly exiting the vehicle, I round it and open her door, helping her out.

"It's beautiful." She peers up at the two-story home with a porch and balcony on the front.

"Come see the inside." I tip my head in the direction of my house, clenching my fingers to resist reaching for her hand.

She follows me up the sidewalk leading to the front door, and I unlock it and lead her inside.

"Wow," she breathes as she takes in the sight of the open floor plan, the refinished hardwood floors, and the large kitchen. Turning her attention to me, the expression of interest and pride helps to stifle my unease. "Tell me what you did."

I walk her through the house, explaining in detail all the renovations I've done. Once we return to the kitchen, we settle into the chairs at the large island in the kitchen. She runs a hand appreciatively across the sleek granite countertop and heavy silence blankets us.

"I came to Jacksonville to find you."

At my admission, her head snaps up, shock etching her features. "*What?*"

"I came to Jacksonville once I'd found out where you were…a few months after you left. After the first photos showed up with you and Becket together. At the start of the speculation about your relationship."

She's fallen completely silent, but I press on.

"I wondered if you'd had me fooled, if you left me for him, and you'd had some sort of secret affair all along."

"I didn't—"

I hold up a hand to wave off her protest. "I know. I know that *now*. But it was pretty tough to swallow." I break off with a harsh sounding laugh. "That's a lie. It fucking gutted me. Especially when you'd had that, uh," I falter, unsure of how to phrase it, "weight gain at one point."

Her lips part in surprise, but I continue. "I came to see you, to tell you that I still loved you and wanted to know if we could work things out.

"It was the night of some fancy art gallery opening in Midtown." My stomach tightens in remembrance of that night. "Becket kissed you." My jaw clenches and unclenches at the memory. "And that, combined with the speculation about you possibly carrying his baby—that was all I needed to see."

"He didn't really kiss me," she admits in a small voice.

I dart a quick glance her way. "I didn't realize it at the

time, but I know that now. I figured it out later. The one gala where he grabbed you and dipped you dramatically. The moment he kissed you, I thought I saw his hand slide to cover your lips. But I wasn't sure.

"But back then, I'd felt like a fool. Witnessing you both laugh together like a real couple after that kiss, seeing what some were claiming was a baby bump…" I swallow hard, recalling how much it hurt to see her with him. "I left because seeing the two of you confirmed things for me…why you left me."

Her eyes are downcast, and I'm at a loss for what else to say. Cognizant of the time it takes to drive her to the airport and also allotting for how long it'll take her to make it through the often lengthy, congested TSA line for security screening, I guide her out the door and back into the truck in silence.

I STARE STRAIGHT AHEAD, navigating the truck along I-95 amidst the typical thick Jacksonville traffic before exiting the interstate and turning onto Airport Road. The closer we get to the airport itself, the harder it is for me to breathe as the tension increases within the vehicle.

"Knox, part of that was true."

I toss her a quick look and find her wringing her hands in a nervous manner, apprehension lining her features while she stares straight ahead.

After pulling along the curb of the area designated for outgoing flight passengers, I put the truck into park.

Confused, I tilt my head to the side in question. "What was true?"

"I was pregnant."

I rear back as if I've just been slapped.

"But it wasn't Becket's." She turns to look at me, her entire demeanor hesitant. "It was yours."

I'm rendered speechless by her confession and can only manage to stare at her, stunned.

A knock on her window breaks my daze as the curb attendant motions for us to either drop off or continue on our way since we're holding up the flow of arriving passengers.

Glancing at the time, I realize we have five minutes to spare so I quickly pull into the short-term parking lot. Once I find a space, I park the truck and turn to her.

Without pause, she begins, and speaking her words with slow deliberation. "I moved here. Becket got me the interview. After I was hired, everything happened in such a whirlwind that I…" She falters, her focus dropping to the console between us. "I just thought, being so depressed and heartbroken, it was natural to gain a little weight." She pauses briefly. "I didn't even realize… I had no symptoms. I'd only gained about ten pounds. One day, I was cramping badly, and the pain became so unbearable that Becket had to drive me to the hospital. That's when I found out I was pregnant. That I—" She breaks off and tears trickle down her cheeks.

My brain already zeroed in on a key word. "Was?" I question gently. But the moment her gaze raises to mine, my suspicions are confirmed. Agonizing pain clouds her blue eyes, and tears begin rapidly raining down her cheeks.

"I miscarried at about four and a half months."

She covers her mouth, attempting to stifle a sob, as her shoulders quake. Quickly releasing both of our seat belts, I flip up the center console and take her in my arms as best I can. Her face is pressed against my collarbone, and she weeps while I attempt to soothe her, running my hand up and down her back.

"I was so scared, and my parents weren't speaking to me—no one was speaking to me—and I couldn't tell Granddad. The only person I had was Becket." Her words cut deep as sobs wrack her body. "I lost her."

Her. A girl. Jesus, we had a baby girl.

She raises her head, pain etched across her features. "I didn't know how much you could want something—someone—until you lose it." Her face crumples. "I loved her."

"I know you did." I gently frame her face with my hands, my thumbs tenderly smoothing away tears. "I know you did." As much as it pains me to say it, I have to voice it. "I'm glad you had Becket."

She inhales deeply, as if to regain composure. "I was going to tell you, but I just wasn't sure how…"

Numbly, I nod, trying to fully grasp what she's just revealed. My eyes flick over to the clock, and I realize time is not on my side.

"It's time to go," I tell her gently. She nods and we both fasten our seat belts as I quickly maneuver the vehicle out of the lot and drive to the drop-off area once again.

Putting the truck in park, I exit and rush around to help her out. I grab her small rolling suitcase from the back and set it on the sidewalk beside her before I pluck what I'd quickly picked up from the house.

Offering the daisy to her, she accepts it with a weak smile, seemingly entranced by the flower. At a sudden loss for what to do with my hands, I slide them into my pockets.

"Good luck with the interview. I hope, if it's really what you want, you end up happy there." I curl my lips inward, trying to choose my words carefully. "But, I want you to know what's waiting for you back here."

She scans my features, as if trying to gauge the truth to my words. "Are you saying I can keep my job here?"

"Your job is here if you want it." I lift one shoulder in a half shrug. "If that's what you decide." Again, I shrug. "Take a few days off to think about it."

Her lips part, but I interrupt quickly. "But I'll be here, too. If you decide that you"—I clear my throat nervously—"want me." While holding her gaze steadily, I add, "Again."

A car horn honks in the distance, breaking our moment, and I muster up a weak smile. I reach out to caress her cheek with my thumb. "Be safe."

When I walk around to get in my truck and drive away, there's no mistaking the fact that I just left my heart back there at the airport.

With the one woman—the only woman—who's possessed it.

39

Emma Jane
THURSDAY

This interview's gone extremely well considering I felt emotionally wrung out by the time I'd checked in to my hotel last night.

Elise is finishing up the full tour she's been giving me of their location, informing me that the Jacksonville offices are nearly finished—they're in the final stages of installing basic décor—and will look much like these.

"You'll be one of my first picks to come aboard." She gives me a sly smile. "So that means you'll get your choice of which office you'd prefer there."

"Wow," I breathe out in surprise. Their building is located in one of the best, most scenic spots overlooking the St. Johns River, so it's practically guaranteed to have gorgeous views.

"However," she adds, "part of your job requirement will necessitate you to fly up here for three weeks every quarter within the first two years, in order to facilitate things more smoothly and ensure everyone's on the same page."

Oh, wow. I'd be required to fly to New York for nearly a month four times each year.

"Do you think you could give me a firm answer by Monday?"

Nodding slowly, I smile. "I definitely will."

"Great." Elise beams at me. "I look forward to hearing from you on Monday with the news that you'll be joining the *ECC* family."

I leave *ECC* intent on returning to the hotel to grab my luggage and catch a cab to the airport for my flight back to Jacksonville. Yet somehow, I find myself taking a slight detour and entering a nearby florist. When I exit the shop with a single daisy in hand, I amble along the bustling sidewalk and give in to the urge.

Releasing a sigh, I begin plucking petal by petal, muttering to myself, "Take the job. Stay. Take the job. Stay..."

I'M FINISHING PACKING up my suitcase when I finally notice the voicemail notification on my phone. I'm surprised at the sound of the voice that greets me.

"Hey, it's me, Knox. I, uh, wanted to call because I just...shit." He breaks off and I imagine him dragging a hand through his short hair and slightly ruffling it. *"Hell, EJ,"* his voice deepens with emotion, *"I just keep replaying our conversation at the airport, and I know it means nothing, but I wish I could've been there for you back then. When you were in the hospital and—"* He clears his throat abruptly. *"I just know that I never want you to have to go through anything like that without me again. And if you ever want to talk about it, I'm always here."* There's a brief pause before he speaks again, and his voice is husky, intimate sounding. *"I'm sorry, Emma Jane."*

"SWEET PEA, I was hoping you'd call."

Normally, the sound of Granddad's voice lifts my spirits, but it's not working its usual magic today.

"I don't know what to do." I slump into a seat in the far corner of the gate area for my flight, away from the majority of the other passengers. Everything pours out of me, and I find myself divulging what happened between Knox and me years ago, why I left, the miscarriage, and the job dilemma.

"Do you know why I never pushed you to tell me why you left?" he asks, gently.

"I always wondered."

And I had. Even now, I can recall his voicemail message with the simple request.

"Please call me when you've made it safely to wherever your destination might be. Love you, Sweet Pea."

He'd never asked for more information. Months passed and he still never pushed me for an explanation. He'd simply accepted my decision to leave everything behind.

"Your grandmother taught me to never mess with fate." Before I can manage a response, he continues. "Did I ever tell you about how your grandmother was engaged to someone else?"

This stops me in my tracks. Leaning back in my seat, the din of the airport disappears. "I never knew she was engaged to someone else."

"She was engaged to Mathias Bentford. His family was wealthy, and she loved him…or so she thought. But when we met while I was delivering milk for my family's farm, it changed things. I knew she was the one the moment I laid eyes on her." The wistfulness in his voice amidst the layers of emotion is a testament to how much he adored my grandmother.

"She saw me set down one of the milk bottles to help Old Lady Huntly when she'd tripped and twisted her ankle. Your grandmother came rushing over to help, and the moment our eyes met, there was something there. Something I can't describe. After we made sure Old Lady Huntly was safely inside her house, your grandmother insisted on accompanying me to deliver the milk, and then I escorted her home.

"We talked about everything under the sun. She told me about her engagement, about the man she planned to marry. And once we arrived at her door, I knew what I had to do." He releases a soft chuckle. "I kissed her and told her that she belonged with me. That I would make her happier than he could." Another chuckle slips from him. "And then I turned around and left."

"What happened then?" I'm fascinated by this tale I've never heard before.

"I didn't hear from her for two whole weeks."

"*What?*"

He laughs. "I thought for sure she figured I was a few sandwiches short of a picnic. But two weeks passed and then one Saturday, when I was delivering milk on the same route we met on, she was waiting for me.

"She said that fate should never be ignored or tampered with, that something told her to come back to me."

"What happened next?" I ask, hanging on his every word.

"She called off her engagement, and I courted her for the next four months before I asked for her hand. I knew then, just like I know now, that fate intervened that day.

Fate brought us together. But you don't mess with fate. You let it operate on its own timeline, Sweet Pea."

Faintly, I register the announcement that my zone is boarding for my flight. Granddad finishes with words which resonate with me.

"Emma Jane, always respect fate. It knows best. It always had a plan for you and Knox."

Minutes later, when I'm buckled into my seat on the airplane, I'm curious about fate's plan.

I wonder what it has up its sleeve next.

40

Emma Jane

Welcome home from prison, Blue!

This is the sign that greets me at the Jacksonville airport.

Of course, the tall, muscular man holding it is wearing a ball cap pulled down low along with a pair of dark sunglasses to disguise his identity.

As I approach him, his lips curve up into a wide grin. He drops the sign to his side and opens his arms, allowing me to step into his embrace and relish in the tight, comforting hug.

"Like the sign?" he murmurs against the top of my head.

"Best one yet."

"Ready to head out?"

Backing away, I release a tired sigh. "Am I ever."

He walks me out the automatic double doors of the airport, and I realize his SUV is parked, unattended, right at the curb.

Giving him the side eye, I tease, "Using your celebrity status to get away with parking here?"

He winks smugly. "I'm carrying precious cargo."

Confused, I start to ask, but as soon as Becket opens the passenger door for me and I slide in, I see exactly what he means.

Presley, Hendy, and baby Emilia are in the back seat.

"Hi, guys," I greet them curiously, as I buckle my seat belt. "Dare I ask how you got lassoed into this?"

"Becket wanted to practice buckling Emilia into her car seat and drive her around." Presley announces this with amusement lining her features.

"And to see if she preferred the lullabies of Jack Johnson or Dave Matthews." Hendy offers this up before deadpanning, "Because you know. Newborns are so particular about music."

Suddenly my phone rings, alerting me that Madison is requesting a FaceTime chat. I'd forgotten that we'd agreed to catch up after my flight landed.

Turning to the back seat, I address Presley and Hendy. "Uh, do you guys mind if I FaceTime my friend Madison really quick?"

"Of course not," Presley says.

Quickly, I accept Madison's call and give her the rundown on everything that happened in New York, to catch her up since she's out of town at a conference in Orlando.

"I've got to be honest, Emma Jane. I feel like your heart's not in it."

"Probably because she knows *ECC* readers don't appreciate me as much as *F&F* readers do. Snooty women don't like real men who sweat." Becket shakes his head as he navigates his way through the airport traffic.

Madison and I both roll our eyes at him. "Becket," I warn.

His expression sobers. "Honestly, I think your mind's already made up."

"But when will a job offer like this come around again?" I ask, anxiety weaving its way into my tone. "Maybe never, right?"

Madison shrugs. "Maybe. Maybe not. But the point is, if you turn it down, will you be able to live with that decision?"

"Or if you turn Knox down, can you live with that?" Becket lowers his voice. "Can you imagine spending three solid weeks away from him every three months? Is that what you want?"

I don't answer; instead, I internally muse at how I've never made decisions pertaining to my career with anyone else in mind. I've been too driven and intent on achieving my goals.

"Is that what you want?"

I allow this question to roll around in my mind. I mulled it over repeatedly on the plane ride back, and each time, I came up with the same answer.

"I think you know what decision you have to make."

Madison nods to affirm Becket's declaration, and I have to agree. I know what I need to do on Monday morning.

I'm just not entirely sure I have the guts to do it.

"THANKS FOR BEING cool with us making a quick stop to drop them off."

I flash Becket an amused look, gesturing to the soft baby carrier he has strapped to his front with Emilia inside, happily snuggling his chest. "Are you kidding me? This is a side of Becket Jones I never thought I'd get to see."

He slings an arm around my shoulders as we follow Presley and Hendy up the steps to their home. "Uncle Becket has to prove his baby prowess somehow."

Once Hendy unlocks the door, we all head down the hall to the living room and take a seat. All of us except for Becket, of course.

His enormous palm cups the back of the baby's head, and he gazes down at her small face.

"What was that I just heard? Do you have gas? Say *no*, Uncle Becket. *No*, ladies don't have gas," he coos. "You just snuggle me, and everything will be A-okay."

We all watch in disbelief as Becket continues talking to her. Emilia appears to be listening, completely enthralled as he goes on about how "Uncle Becket snuggle time is the cure for everything" before he walks over to the large sliding glass door facing the Atlantic Ocean. Opening it and the sliding screen door, he slips outside and slides the screen door closed, still chattering away. He heads farther onto the deck where the sun is quickly disappearing beneath the horizon.

"He'll make a great dad someday."

Hendy's quietly spoken remark garners my attention, and I turn my eyes away from the scene outside. He winks at me, his eyes sparkling with humor. "But don't tell him I said that."

"So you have to fill me in on everything." Presley takes a seat on one end of the couch and curls her legs beneath her. Her eyes rest on me. "Becket mentioned that things went sour with your job before you left for the *ECC* interview."

I decide to get comfortable in the oversized leather chair across from her. Hendy takes a seat beside her, resting an arm along the back of the couch behind her head. Automatically, she leans into him and rests her head against his shoulder, listening as I give her a quick recap.

"Wow," Presley muses, appearing a bit stunned. "I can't imag—"

"Yeah, that's right. Real men snuggle babies."

Becket's booming voice interrupts, traveling through the screen door, and we turn our attention to the sight outside on the deck. His back is turned to us, but it's clear in his posture that he's preening while standing by the railing. One hip is propped against the wood, and he waves at a few women strolling along the beach a few yards away from the end of the deck.

"He's pimping himself out with our baby." Hendy's tone is a mixture of disbelief and amusement.

Presley laughs and shakes her head. "You can't possibly be surprised."

"He's been waiting for this moment." I smile and watch him through the sliding screen door as he mumbles something to Emilia with a sly smile before continuing to walk around and point out certain sights in the distance. Turning to the couple, I tip my head to the side as I regard them. "He really is a proud"—I break off to make finger quotes—"'uncle.'"

Presley's expression softens. "He is, isn't he?" She peers up at Hendy. "See? I told you he wasn't so bad."

Her husband looks like he's on the verge of a begrudging agreement when we hear more commotion from outside.

"Uncle Beck is your favorite guy, right? That's right. Way cooler than your daddy. I mean, geez. A former Navy SEAL pales in comparison to a quarterback who's won the Heisman and…"

Hendy raises an eyebrow pointedly at his wife who just laughs, and I can't help but join in.

41

Knox
FRIDAY

I haven't heard from Emma Jane since I dropped her off at the airport days ago. She hasn't called or sent a text message. She's officially gone radio silent.

And it's killing me.

I left the ball in her court. Guess she doesn't want me, after all. A small part of me thinks I should just move forward and hire a replacement to fill her position.

If only I could find a way to fill this gaping hole she's left in my heart.

"You on the way back?"

"Yep," I answer Wells while I drive the boring stretch of interstate along I-10 leading back to Mobile, talking to him via Bluetooth.

He sighs loudly, the exasperation practically radiating through my vehicle's speakers. "You need to delegate a bit better if you have to rush back to Mobile for something like this," he remarks, referring to the minor issue I'd mentioned one of my local businesses is experiencing.

"Wells," I warn tiredly.

"Just didn't take you for tucking tail and running

away."

Gritting my teeth, my hands clench the steering wheel in a painfully tight grip.

"Jesus, Wells." My tone is wrought with irritation. "Give it a rest, would you?" My voice rises with frustration and anger. "She's gone completely silent, and I need to…regroup."

"She was pregnant with your baby, Knox."

I wince at the reminder of the devastating loss of our baby.

"I know," I utter quietly. "But she also skipped out on our wedding, believing I'd been just like her damn father." I drag a hand down my face wearily. "We both have things to work out."

"Well, Christmas is barely a week away. At least there's that."

I make a face at his oddly abrupt subject change. "What the hell does that have to do with anything?"

"Santa always brings presents for good boys and girls." Wells releases a long, exasperated sigh. "You know this."

Leaning my head back against the headrest, I roll my eyes. "That cheers me right up."

"Figured so."

I pull off at an exit to fill up with gas. "Gotta run, man. I'll touch base with you once I get in."

"Later."

THE CALL COMES ON SATURDAY, just as I'm stepping out of the office here in Mobile and heading back to my truck. Wells was one hundred percent right when he'd said I didn't have to come back here and ensure things would smooth out.

I'd come back here to lick my wounds. Yet I feel like it's made things worse, being back in Mobile, since this is where it all began.

Where it all went wrong.

"Hello?"

"Mr. Montgomery, this is Sheila with St. Johns Realty. I wanted to let you know that we've received an offer on your home..."

Sheila's voice fades out as shock takes over. I'd never expected the house I'd renovated to catch interest so fast in such a competitive housing market.

But this is great news. I'd gone into it with the intention of flipping the Jacksonville house.

Liar, a voice echoes within my mind. *You hoped for a home—a home with EJ.*

"Mr. Montgomery?" Sheila's voice jars me from my inner turmoil.

"I apologize, Sheila. Can you email me the information since I'm driving right now?" She readily agrees, and we end the call.

Once I'm back at the house, I rush inside and toss my keys on the kitchen counter, setting my briefcase on one of the barstools. Loosening my tie, I tug it off before tackling the buttons of my shirtsleeves and quickly cuffing them at my elbows as I head down the hallway. I draw to a halt before I approach my bedroom and abruptly turn toward the closed door to the left. The door that's remained closed for a little over eight years, aside from the monthly cleaning service that comes in when I'm at work on Monday mornings.

Twisting the doorknob, I open it and inhale a sharp breath at the sight of the bed we'd chosen together, the armoires, the comforter, the color of paint we'd used on the walls. Everything about this room reminds me of her.

Slowly, I walk over and settle myself on the edge of the bed. I sit, staring at the top dresser drawer. The drawer that contains the gift I'd been planning to give her after we'd returned from our honeymoon.

I'd searched high and low for the perfect necklace for Emma Jane that would tie in our nuptials and her tendency to use daisies as a fortune-telling device, with *He loves me; He loves me not.* I'd finally discovered a gorgeous necklace with a diamond encased in a love knot and instantly knew I had to get it for her.

Sitting here, memories begin flooding me full force.

I recall how proud I was of her for scoring the job at *Southern Charm Lifestyle*. I knew she'd landed the job on her own merit and not her father's name. She was a whiz at marketing and advertising, had that talent of thinking outside the box and finding unique ways to market ideas.

I lean back to lie on the bed and swear I can still detect the scent of her even after all these years. God, how many times we'd made love in this bedroom, how many times we'd lain here talking about the future.

When she'd left, I'd immediately gone to work on adding the en suite bathroom to what's now my master bedroom. It was far too painful to stay in here, to sleep in here without her. The number of times I'd reached out for her, only to come up empty, had been too much for me to handle.

Now, I'd done the unthinkable and let her back in my life, invited her into my home and into my bedroom.

With a humorless laugh, I think about the fact she's left her mark on every part of this house now and mutter to myself, "What are you gonna do, now? Demo and then rebuild?"

Heaving an arm over my eyes, I can't help but admit the idea has its merit.

42

Emma Jane
SUNDAY

I TOOK a few days after I returned from New York to really mull things over. Days dedicated to thinking, to soul-searching.

"You think way too much."

Madison informs me of this while we're out at dinner.

I wave a hand as I protest. "How is that even possible? Especially in this case, with everything that's gone on?"

She lets out a sigh of pure exasperation and sets her fork down on the table. Forearms braced on the table, she holds my gaze steadily. "You're using your brain."

I can't help but stare at her. "As opposed to what?"

Her head drops, and she shakes it in exaggerated disappointment. "Oh, Emma Jane. You should be thinking with your *heart*."

I roll my eyes. "That's what got me into this mess in the first place."

She holds up her index finger. "No, it's not. What got you into this mess was a misunderstanding along with a large dose of immaturity and insecurity."

I visibly tense as her words hit their mark, and Madison's expression softens. "Look at it this way. If I were still carrying around a handkerchief in my purse that had the initials of some guy from my past, what would you think?"

I exhale slowly. "I'd think you were still hung up on him."

Her pointed look grates on my nerves slightly, but I have to admit she has a valid point. "So you're saying I should give it another shot?"

"No." Madison offers an encouraging smile. "Giving something a shot has a connotation that's half-hearted. Like you're expecting to fail." She raises her eyebrows meaningfully. "I'm saying you give Knox and Emma Jane —EJ—all you've got. That you put your one hundred and ten percent into it."

After taking a quick sip of her drink, she tacks on, "Because you have, as Becket calls it, unfinished business."

Monday Morning

"IT'S great to have you back, Ms. Haywood."

I flash an amused look at Tim, after he's assisted in wrapping up a few loose ends with the legal aspects of Mr. Feldman's contract. "Were you worried?"

"You have no idea." He shakes his head as he taps a few keys on his computer. "No one could replace you." A few more keystrokes. "And if you don't get that promotion, I'm certain everyone will hold a protest in your honor."

I tip my head to the side with a smile. "Well, let's hope it doesn't come to that."

After I leave Tim, I head straight over to Knox's office, slowly drawing to a stop in front of his secretary's desk. My eyes take in his closed door curiously.

"Karen, is he in?"

"No, ma'am. He had to leave unexpectedly."

My body jolts in silent alarm. "Do you know where he went?" I ask slowly.

Karen eyes me oddly, and I realize how intrusive my question is, so I attempt to cover my gaffe.

"I'm asking because of this contract with Feldman and…"

"Well, if it's urgent, that's a different story, but"—she breaks off to flip through a small notepad on the side of her desk—"he specifically requested to not be contacted on December sixteenth unless, and I quote, 'the building has been damaged by a natural disaster or arson.'"

December *sixteenth*.

"Oh, no." I can't resist a slight wince.

My traveling and distraction with everything going on completely threw me off. Hurriedly, I back up from Karen's desk. "Thank you!"

December sixteenth.

There's a completely valid reason he doesn't want to be interrupted on this date.

"I MANAGED to get everything in order, thanks to both Tim and Madison helping me."

I turn the wheel of my car, navigating down the streets alight with antique-style lanterns.

"I'm proud of you, Blue." Becket's voice rumbles through the hands-free earbuds I have in. "Not only did you sign a massive deal with Feldman, but you're kicking ass in your personal life, too."

I laugh nervously. "Let's not get ahead of ourselves."

"Hey." His voice deepens with affection. "I know it's in the bag."

I pull in and park my car a few feet away from the entrance of Granddad's home, The Haywood Mansion, before turning off the ignition. Thank heavens Granddad had alerted me to the personal request he'd received earlier today. Heaving out a long breath suffused with nervousness, my hands begin to tremble slightly.

"Becket," I start.

"Blue," he counters calmly. "You've got this."

I nod, and it's more for my own benefit, an attempt to psych myself up. "Right."

"Love you. Now, go do your thing."

"Love you, too. Bye."

"Bye."

Disconnecting the call, I dislodge the earbuds and toss them and my phone onto the passenger seat. Then I emerge from my car and close the door, clenching my keys anxiously.

As I approach the entrance, my heart races wildly and my mind starts a high-speed reel encompassing all my memories of this place.

The first floor is beaming with lights, and I quietly enter and make my way to the ballroom.

My breath hitches at the sight of him, standing right in the center, much like he was that very day. Except now, he's facing away, allowing me a view of his partial profile. Knox appears lost in thought, eyes downcast, one hand in the pocket of his khaki shorts while his other dangles at his side in a fist. He's wearing a worn T-shirt that stretches across his firm, broad shoulders and his feet are encased in a pair of leather flip-flops.

Slowly, I step forward, and he's held so captive by his

own thoughts that my quiet footsteps don't register my presence.

"If you had to do it all over again, would you?"

His head whips around at my question, clearly surprised to see me, but intertwined with his expression is anguish. When he doesn't immediately answer, my entire body tenses, going rigid in fear.

Maybe I was wrong. Maybe I'm too late. Maybe I—

"Yes."

I didn't realize I was holding my breath until a whoosh of air rushes past my lips.

Turning to fully face me, he doesn't approach, but instead regards me carefully. "I'd do it all over again."

"Even though things turned out the way they did?" I probe.

He nods slowly, his eyes never leaving mine.

I take a step toward him and stop as I inhale a fortifying breath. "I realized something recently."

"What's that?" His voice is subdued, guarded.

"Becket told me that we have unfinished business that needs to be settled. And I realize Becket was right."

His jaw works, and his expression becomes shuttered. I know what he's thinking though, which is why I rush on.

"There's only one problem with what he said."

Knox's throat works, and he swallows hard before prompting, "Which is?"

"We do have unfinished business, but I'm okay with that. Because, if I had my way, I'd always have unfinished business with you." I swallow past the nervous lump in my throat. "Forever."

I wait for him to understand what I'm trying to say. That I don't want us to ever be finished.

That I want *us*.

My words pour out. "I'm sorry, Knox. I'm sorry for not believing in you, for not believing in us, for thinking the worst. I'm sorry for"—I pause, pressing my lips thin in an attempt to gain composure as the tears threaten to spill over—"hurting you. I thought…you didn't really love me." I shake my head at myself, at my overreaction, and stare down at my toes. "I'm so sorry," I whisper and watch my tears give way, dropping down to plop right upon the skin of my feet bared by my flip-flops.

The silence is deafening, and without any response from him, I realize it's a sign that I'm too late. He's obviously come here for closure. I'm just mucking things up, all over again.

As surreptitiously as possible, I swipe at my cheeks before I withdraw the object I'd tucked into the pocket of my pants. I unfold it carefully, reverently, and peer down at it with vision that's cloudy from my tears.

"This is what I came to give to you when I overheard you and my father talking. I'd made it especially for you." My lips tremble, and I work hard to withhold an impending sob.

I step forward and hold the monogrammed handkerchief with downcast eyes. I can't look—don't want to—because I don't want to look back on this day and recall the pity in his eyes.

"Just take it." My hand wavers as I hold it out for him. "Throw it away. Burn it. Whatever."

"Only if you'll eventually consider taking this."

His softly spoken words cause me to raise my eyes and I blink, trying to see through the sheen of tears.

Then I blink again. Because I can't possibly be seeing what I think I'm seeing.

He holds the small box containing the ring I'd left behind years ago.

"Emma Jane Haywood, I've loved you from the

moment our lockers were side by side in the tenth grade. And I never"—his throat works as he goes on—"gave my heart to anyone else.

"Since it's the anniversary of the day I asked you to marry me, I came here to reflect on everything." His eyes shimmer with emotion, his features taking on a sudden intensity. "But, I was coming back for you. The only difference is, this time I was going to stay as long as it took to prove to you that we're meant to be together."

My lips part in disbelief, only to immediately snap shut when his thumb flips the lid closed on the ring box, and he slides it in his pocket.

43

Knox

Her surprise is tangible.

I think she expected me to drop down on one knee right here, but I need to do this right.

"I'm going to prove that I'm the one you're meant to be with." I take a step toward her. "To prove my love for you." I advance another step. "To prove that I won't let anything ever come between us again." I close the distance, the tips of my flip-flops touching hers. "I'm going to make sure I erase any doubts that we're meant to be together.

"Even after all this time, I still can't—don't *want* to—imagine growing old with anyone else. And it seems fitting that we've both come back to the same place where I first asked you to be my wife." I hold out a hand, and she places her trembling one in mine. "Will you give me another chance?"

Nodding, she swallows thickly and smiles through a sheen of tears. "Yes."

Relief surges through me, and my eyes fall closed as I send up a silent prayer of thanks that I'm getting a second chance with her.

A second chance to make things right.

I gently take the handkerchief from her grasp and carefully use the soft fabric to rid her of the stray tears which escaped. My voice grows thick with emotion as I peer into her cerulean eyes and raise my other hand to show her what it holds.

A daisy with only one petal remaining.

"I love you, Emma Jane Hay—"

My words are swallowed when she lifts up on her toes and wraps her arms around my neck, lips colliding with mine in a fierce and passionate kiss. Her fingers sift through the hair at my nape, and my breath catches in my throat as I'm bombarded by the emotion-laden kiss. It's one that contains so much more than love.

She's telling me she's on board, that she wants to bet on us, that she's giving it her all.

Her kiss tells me that even though we've hurt one another, we're not a lost cause.

When I deepen it, my tongue sweeping inside to toy with hers, I'm assaulted by a multitude of emotions.

I draw my lips from hers and wait for her eyes to flutter open and meet my own which burn with a sheen of tears I don't bother hiding.

All I care about is the woman standing before me.

The only woman who's ever owned my heart.

"This time will be different, EJ," I vow, holding her blue gaze with mine. "I promise you."

Her mouth curves into a smile I know I'll never forget; the way it brightens her features, radiating with a hint of amazement.

When she plucks the white petal from the daisy, my heart skips a beat, my eyes falling closed to savor this moment. Because it's the combination of her words and the wonder in them that steals my breath.

She wraps her arms around me tightly, burying her face in my neck and faintly whispers, "He loves me."

And as I hold her, I can't help but smile and whisper back a simple response.

"He loves you." My voice is guttural. I ignore the stray tear that escapes, trickling down my cheek and landing in the long, thick tresses of her hair. "God, does he love you."

44

Emma Jane
SIX MONTHS LATER

I meet her eyes triumphantly, and there's no way to restrain my wide smile.

"Yes?" Alissa's eyes are wide, brimming with excitement.

"*Yes.*" I can't possibly smile any bigger.

After discussing every contractual point in depth—and practically talking it to death—I've managed to finalize a deal with Eastern Sports, a company based in the northeast which began small but quickly gained traction, expanding rapidly. This partnership will take *F&F* to the next level.

I check the time and notice it's fast approaching five o'clock, which means I need to hurry and get on the road. As it is, I won't get into Mobile until after ten o'clock tonight.

I direct my attention back to my assistant. "Go home and get some rest and enjoy that sweet baby. On Monday, we'll do a long lunch to celebrate."

At the prospect of seeing her young daughter, Alissa's

expression brightens even more. "That sounds great. Have a wonderful weekend, Ms. Haywood."

My expression gentles when I think about who I'll get to see this weekend. "Oh, I will."

Stepping inside my office, I hear my cell phone ring as I'm approaching my desk. I already have a good idea of who might be calling, but when I note the name on the caller ID, it's clear that I'm mistaken.

It's my *other* favorite guy.

"Hey, handsome."

"Hey, Blue. You miss me?"

"Like a toothache," I tease.

"That wounds me." He falls silent for a beat. "So are you planning to make an honest man out of Knox anytime soon?"

I reach out to the vase sitting on my table and toy with the delicate, soft white petals of the daisy contemplatively.

"Honestly?"

"Honestly…" Becket prompts.

"I'll still be happy even if we don't get married." My voice wavers with emotion. "As long as I have him in my life."

"Good answer."

My head snaps up in surprise at the sound of the familiar male voice behind me. Whirling around, I find Knox standing in the doorway of my office, and my breath catches at the sight of him.

"I'll let you go." Becket's voice rumbles, heavy with affection, clearly overhearing Knox's voice. "Talk to you later. Love you."

"Love you," comes my soft reply before I end the call, my hand dropping to my side to take in the man standing before me.

Still dressed in his perfectly tailored dark gray slacks

and a white button-down shirt with gray pinstripes, he's rolled up the sleeves and cuffed them at his elbows, displaying his strong, tanned forearms.

His mossy-green eyes sparkle as he approaches me. "So you'd be fine if we never got married? As long as you have me in your life?"

I attempt to school my expression to be one of sternness when I tease him. "Don't let it go to your head."

Suddenly, he slips an arm around my waist and tugs me flush against him. With his other hand, he cups the side of my face and his thumb skims across my cheekbone. Knox regards me with a reverence that causes my heart to skip a beat, my pulse to become erratic.

"God, I've missed you." He dips his head and dusts his lips across mine tenderly.

"It's only been a few days," I whisper back.

"Two days too many." He wraps both arms around me, tucking me against the broad wall of his chest, burying his face in my hair. "I'm ready to spend this weekend with you."

"I was supposed to drive to you." I smile, eyes closed, with my cheek pressed against him. "My bags are in my car."

"I couldn't wait."

Something in his tone makes my eyes flash open. Backing away slightly, I meet his gaze, and a mixture of affection and happiness shimmers within the depths. But there's something else, almost a faint hint of…nervousness?

"Ready to go?"

I reach up and cup his face in my hands, relishing in the sensation of the soft, short hair of his beard against my palms. "Ready."

His mouth curves up, and there's a mischievous glint in his eyes. "Let's go, then. I've got plans for you."

45

Knox

Later That Night
MOBILE, ALABAMA

"I HAVE A SURPRISE FOR YOU."

I hope like hell she can't tell how damn nervous I am. Although, with her body pressed flush against mine as I maneuver the jet ski along the smooth waters of Mobile Bay, I'm certain she can feel the stiffness of my spine.

"Is that what you're calling it now?" Her teasing remark, spoken against the side of my throat before she places a soft kiss there, sends shivers ricocheting throughout my body.

Turning off the engine as we approach the shallow shoreline of Sand Island, I slip off the jet ski and assist EJ down. After securing the anchor, I withdraw the beach mat from the storage compartment along with the waterproof dry bag where I normally keep my cell phone in case of emergencies.

This time, though, the bag contains more than my phone.

And one more item, albeit a bit crushed and wilted from transport.

Once I unfold the beach mat and lay it carefully on the sand, I covertly withdraw the ring box from the bag as she peers up at the night sky, relishing in the peaceful beauty that surrounds us. The summer air is still heavy with humidity, and sporadic clouds cover the moon.

When I step closer, and she turns to peer up at me, the love shining in the depths of her gaze alleviates a fraction of my nervousness.

I gently skim my knuckles along her cheekbone and drag in a deep, fortifying breath.

"Emma Jane Haywood, I need you to do something for me."

She searches my features curiously. "Okay."

I hold out the daisy for her. Her eyes dart between me and the flower before she accepts it.

"Go ahead."

Blue eyes regard me with a hint of confusion. Her finger and thumb pluck the first petal. "He loves me." The next petal follows with, "He loves me not." She continues, and when all but two petals remain, I drop to one knee.

There's a reason I chose this particular flower. Because I know how it ends.

"He loves me." Emma Jane's voice comes out wispy, slightly breathless as she plucks the final petal and allows it to drift to the sand soundlessly.

I withdraw the ring from the box and swallow past the tight lump in my throat. "It's the truth." I press my lips thin, attempting to fight the nerves trying to get the best of me. "I love you, Emma Jane Haywood. I never stopped." Holding out my other hand, palm upturned, I wait until she places hers in it to continue. "Marry me. Let's have our own happily ever after." I pause when my voice cracks with emotion. "God knows we deserve it."

Her blue eyes fill with tears. "Yes."

Relief surges through me. "Yes?" I can't help but question her, needing to hear it again for affirmation.

She tugs on our joined hands. "Yes. Now get up here and kiss me."

I slide the diamond engagement ring on her fourth finger, and I can't help but repeat myself as I hold her gaze, my words chock-full of emotion. "I love you so damn much."

As soon as I rise to a standing position, she hurls herself into my arms with such force that I nearly lose my balance. Quickly righting myself, I hold her tight as she presses a string of kisses along the cords of my neck. "I love you." Her whispered words are punctuated with the wet tears dampening my skin. "So much."

With her in my arms, I let my eyes drift closed, relishing this moment.

Because I'm getting a second chance with the woman who's always held my heart.

46

Emma Jane
TWO YEARS LATER

Standing at the end of the pier overlooking Mobile Bay, I close my eyes and allow the breeze to wash over me. It's good to be home, even if it's only for a few more days before I'm due to head back to Jacksonville for meetings.

Exhaling a long, slow breath, I look down at the flower in my hand, slowly plucking off the delicate white petals of the daisy. A few get carried away by the slight gust of wind, and I watch as they float for a bit before gracefully drifting and soundlessly landing on the surface of the dark water below.

"He loves me, he loves me not, he loves me, he loves m—" Just as my fingers move to pluck the last remaining petal, strong arms slide around my waist, and one large palm covers the gentle swell of my belly.

"Woman, you'd better not be getting superstitious."

My lips curve into an easy smile, and I relax against him, feeling the security his embrace offers. "Maybe a little," I tease softly.

His lips graze against my temple when he speaks. "Emma Jane Montgomery." My breath hitches at the way he murmurs my name—I still love the way it sounds coming from his lips. "Maybe I need to show you just how much I love you?" he taunts huskily, skimming one palm up along the thin fabric of my sundress to gently cup my breast. I can't withhold a tiny gasp when the pad of his thumb grazes over my sensitive nipple, causing it to harden instantly beneath his touch.

This man is my everything, and I know without any doubt that I'm his. Our rocky past is firmly behind us, and each day, I fall more in love with him.

Turning within the circle of Knox's arms, we lock eyes, and I can't resist teasing him. With a mischievous smirk, my thumb and forefinger pinch the flower petal between them and tug. "He loves me n—"

His lips cover mine, the now petal-less flower slipping from my fingers as he deepens the kiss. My hands clutch at his broad shoulders, and as I kiss my husband on the pier of our second home in Mobile, I realize something.

Sometimes love just needs a second chance, when it wasn't quite ready the first time around.

THE END

He Loves Me…KNOT Playlist

IF YOU'RE a music lover like me, you might enjoy checking out the playlist for Emma Jane and Knox's story!

https://open.spotify.com/user/rcboldtbooks/playlist/4IpzlZlkNnBguqGIy94CFR

Dear Reader

If you would be so kind as to leave a review on the site where you purchased the book, it would be appreciated beyond words.

If you send me an email at rcboldtbooks@gmail.com with the link to your review, I'll send you a personal 'thank you'!

Please know I truly appreciate you taking time from your busy schedule to read this book! If you'd like to stay up to date on my future releases, you can sign up for my mailing list (I'm the most anti-SPAMMY person ever—promise!) via this link: http://eepurl.com/cgftw5.

If you enjoyed Emma Jane and Knox's story in **He Loves Me…KNOT**, be sure to check out my other books:

Standalones
DITCHED (Becket Jones' story)
Out of Love
CLAM JAM
Out of the Ashes
BLUE BALLS

Dear Reader

Tap That (with Jennifer Blackwood)
The Good Samaritan
The Teach Me Series
Wildest Dream (Book 1)
Hard To Handle (Book 2)
Remember When (Book 3)
Laws of Attraction (Book 4)

Stay Connected to RC Boldt

Facebook: https://goo.gl/iy2YzG
Website: http://www.rcboldtbooks.com
Twitter: https://goo.gl/cOs4hK
Instagram: https://goo.gl/TdDrBb
Facebook Readers Group:
https://www.facebook.com/groups/BBBReaders

Out of the Ashes

Intrigued by Becket's friends, Hendy and Presley? Keep reading for an excerpt from *Out of the Ashes*.

Out of the Ashes
PROLOGUE

Walter Reed National Military Medical Center
Bethesda, Maryland
Hendy

I COULD HEAR the voices at the doorway of my hospital room, and while I recognized both, one of them stood out.

One of them caught me off guard.

That same voice elicited anticipation from within me. I'd never gotten serious about any woman, but she was one I thought might have potential, the only one I could see myself getting serious with.

Katie was a nurse I'd met while visiting another SEAL in the hospital, and we had hooked up anytime I returned stateside. For whatever reason, she hadn't been a hit-it-and-quit-it for me, and we'd kept in touch via email and sometimes Skype—whenever I was graced with a decent internet signal on my deployment.

"How is he?"

"He's...doing better." The hesitation was clear from Nurse Ratched's tone. That woman earned her nickname. Her bedside manner was non-existent—not to mention, she could give the Navy medics a run for their money when it came to the "I start an IV by shoving a needle in your arm and then dig around to find a vein" thing.

"They've been working me nonstop, and I just now got a chance to come see him." Katie sounds nervous.

I'd be lying through my teeth if I said I wasn't nervous as shit for her to see me.

"He's been awake for a short time, but he might still be a bit groggy," Nurse Ratched warns. What she doesn't realize—or doesn't care to notice—is the fact I rarely press the button that automatically dispenses pain medication via my PCA pump. After hearing "Pain is just weakness leaving the body" over and over from the start of BUD/S training—Basic Underwater Demolition/SEAL training—and throughout my career as a SEAL, it's engrained in me.

Not to mention, feeling pain means I'm not dead, and I have to admit I'm still shocked I made it out alive.

The tentative footsteps entering the hospital room draw my attention from where a muted *Jeopardy* plays on the television. Katie comes into view; her blond hair pulled back in a clip, she's clad in plain scrubs. Luckily for her, the door to the room is to my right, so she's greeted by the unmarred side of my face.

Unlike the left side. *Much* unlike the left.

Drawing to a stop at the foot of my bed, she offers a gentle smile. "Hey, handsome."

I attempt a slight smile—at least as much of one as I can offer. The scarring and muscle damage in my left cheek creates more of a lopsided grin now. When I turn toward her—allowing her a full view—I see it.

The revulsion.

The horror.

The disappointment.

It's all written there on her face. It's in those widened, hazel eyes.

"So, uh…" she falters, stammering as if we're acquaintances and not two people who've gotten to know one another—intimately, if nothing else. "How are you feeling?" She winces as she realizes how lame her question is.

But I answer just the same. "I've had better days."

Her laughter sounds stilted. "I can imagine." Her eyes dart to the left side of my face before jerking away, as if she's looked directly at the midday sun. Wincing. Painfully.

"It's good to see you, Katie." My tone is far too polite.

She needs to go. I know this, and so does she. Obviously, she was only into me for my looks, and I should've known better. After all, I *was* the manwhore who slept my way through quite a few single women before all this happened.

I never had any complaints—all of them knew the score. A SEAL. A guy who'd deploy to some random part of the world no sane person wants to visit. A guy who chose his country over himself. A guy who killed sometimes as much as he saved.

For those reasons, I was also a guy who didn't do attachments—a fun guy. I'd never slept with a woman who turned into a "bunny boiler" or flipped out on me in some equally psychotic way. We always parted on good terms, amicably, thanks to the charm instilled in me long ago, courtesy of my mother.

But it isn't until this moment that I realize how vain and callous I'd been. Shallow. Because at times like this, people need support—need to be appreciated and loved for more than their looks.

Life is totally giving me a big fat *fuck you* right now. That much is certain.

"Yeah, it's…great to see you home." She clasps her

hands together; her expression so overly bright it's painful. "And doing so well, too." Her energetic tone grates on me.

"Well"—I blow out an exaggerated breath—"I'm actually pretty beat, so I think I'm going to rest."

It's an easy out. I know it, and she knows it. I'm giving her the reprieve she's searching for, so she doesn't have to look at the damage. More specifically, she doesn't have to look at the left side of my face.

Relief washes over her features before she stifles it. She might have been quick but not quick enough.

"Oh, of course." Her words come hastily, almost frantic. "I'll let you rest."

I close my eyes, partly to shut her out. "Take care, Katie." *Goodbye, Katie. Have a nice life.*

"Bye, Hendy," she says softly before her footsteps fade away.

Only then do I open my eyes. Training my gaze on the television, I press the button to increase the volume slightly.

"Who is Rembrandt?" I murmur.

And I continue doing so—rambling off answers and answer attempts—until exhaustion finally overtakes me. All the while, in the back of my mind, it's confirmed; it's a done deal. The damage to my face is far too extensive for anyone to see past it. I was right—I wasn't completely off-base when I first caught sight of my reflection in the mirror.

My face is the sight of horrors, and no one will be able to see past it.

Not even me.

Acknowledgments

This book was tremendously fun to write and none of it would have been possible without a team helping me each step of the way (and listed in no particular order):

My readers—The fact that I actually have readers is just…incredible!! Thank you for choosing to read these books. Without your support, your sweet emails and reviews, and you sharing my books with others, none of this would be possible. I am forever grateful.

My husband and my daughter—For being freaking awesome beyond words.

My parents—For their continued support. Also, FOR THE LOVE OF EVERYTHING THAT'S HOLY, just admit that I'm your favorite child, already. Geez.

Sarah, my Australian BFF—There's no way I could have made it this far without you or our WhatsApp texting, voice messages or phone dates. Rome is going to be epic simply because I'll finally get to hug the crap out of you!!! #LYLT

Amber G.—I adore you and your gracious generosity! I'm so incredibly grateful for all of your help!!

Heather R.—Thank you could never suffice. But I have a trillion and one of them for you, for taking me under your wing, being the best publicist I could ask for, and helping me navigate this crazy career of mine. I adore you!!

The ladies at Give Me Books—For putting up with every single time I ask for your help with a cover reveal or release. You ladies are the best!!!

Jill at Love Affair with Fiction—For being so sweet and gracious and helping me out with this release!!

Lana at Dirty Girl Romance—You always make the best teasers in the world. Thank you so much for making that process go smoothly and end up with such stellar results!!

Dani and Lauren at Barclay PR—You ladies helped me tremendously and I am so grateful for it!! Massive thanks!

Marisa—For knocking this cover out of the ballpark!! You took my vision for the book and absolutely made it come to life!

My readers group—You guys are the most stellar individuals! I am beyond grateful for your support, excitement, and feedback when I share my ideas with you. I'm clearly biased but I think I have the best readers group!! Love you all!!

All the book bloggers & reviewers—I could never manage to truly show my gratitude for all of your support. Please know that the time you take to read and review my books and/or do promo posts is appreciated beyond words.

My beta readers—For being so awesome and willing to read through my amalgamation of nonsense and help me make it better!!! I'm so grateful for your help!!

Hazel—Where would I be without you? You helped me transform this dumpster fire of a book into something I can be proud of. And you should take pride in knowing you played a HUGE role in this!! I love the hell out of you. <3

Mel—For supporting me throughout the crap that went along with this book and combing through it for me!! I freaking love you, mi playa.

Wine and coffee (don't judge me, people)—For being there when I'm under duress because of deadlines. Without you both, this book wouldn't be possible.

About the Author

RC Boldt currently lives on the southeastern coast of the U.S., enjoys long walks on the beach, running, reading, people watching, and singing karaoke. If you're in the mood for some killer homemade mojitos, can't recall the lyrics to a particular 80's song, or just need to hang around a nonconformist who will do almost anything for a laugh, she's your girl.

RC loves hearing from her readers at rcboldtbooks@gmail.com. You can also check out her website at http://www.rcboldtbooks.com or her Facebook page https://www.facebook.com/rcboldtauthor for the latest updates on upcoming book releases.

Manufactured by Amazon.ca
Bolton, ON